Lady of the
NORTH

Lady of the NORTH

TOMMY GEYER

Lady of the North
Copyright © 2020 by Tommy Geyer. All rights reserved.

No part of this publication may be reproduced, stored in a retrieval system or transmitted in any way by any means, electronic, mechanical, photocopy, recording or otherwise without the prior permission of the author except as provided by USA copyright law.

The opinions expressed by the author are not necessarily those of URLink Print and Media.

1603 Capitol Ave., Suite 310 Cheyenne, Wyoming USA 82001
1-888-980-6523 | admin@urlinkpublishing.com

URLink Print and Media is committed to excellence in the publishing industry.

Book design copyright © 2020 by URLink Print and Media. All rights reserved.

Published in the United States of America
Library of Congress Control Number: 2020912005
ISBN 978-1-64753-421-9 (Paperback)
ISBN 978-1-64753-422-6 (Digital)

06.07.20

INTRODUCTION

On August 17th, 1896, a historic discovery was made on a little creek in Yukon Territory. George Carmack and his wife, Kate, were fishing for salmon along the Throndiuck River, which later for ease of pronunciation came to be called the Klondike. Kate's brother, Skookum Jim Mason had come to help, along with their cousin, Tagish Charlie.

On Rabbit Creek, which Carmack later renamed Bonanza, gold was discovered by one of the party, and there are conflicting reports as to whom.

The men staked claims, and Carmack headed downriver to record them in Fortymile, a boomtown at the mouth of the Fortymile River.

Rumors of the strike spread quickly downriver into Alaska Territory. Miners from Circle City and other outposts along the Yukon quickly rushed upriver to the Klondike, and staked claims along Bonanza, Eldorado and Hunker Creeks. Here where the Klondike River flows into the Yukon, Dawson City was born.

It became evident as prospectors worked their claims that winter of 1896 and 1897, that these creeks and surrounding hills did indeed hold the mother lode. Throughout that brutal first winter, the miners burned down through the permafrost, accumulating heaps of gravel laden with course gold. In the spring, after washing the rich paydirt in their sluices and rocker boxes, they suddenly found themselves very wealthy men.

News of the discovery didn't reach the outside world until July of 1897, when steamers docked in San Francisco and Seattle, bearing prospectors from Dawson and their fabulous treasure.

The nation went wild for gold. Newspapers spread reports of the incredible discovery, both legitimate and erroneous. Shipping companies and outfitters persuaded hordes of people to risk all for the gold of the Klondike, with their exaggerated and unrealistic promises. People sold their homes, farms and businesses to outfit themselves for the journey north, in hopes of striking it rich. Tens of thousands flocked to the port cities on the west coast to embark on this perilous adventure.

Only a small percentage of the forty thousand who stampeded to the Klondike in the late 1800s became wealthy. Most went broke, and many lost their lives in pursuit of the precious yellow metal. Some drowned along dangerous stretches of the Yukon River, such as White Horse Rapids and treacherous Miles Canyon. An avalanche along the Chilcoot trail in April of 1898 claimed 53 lives. Some died of disease in Dawson City those first two winters, brought on by malnutrition due to a lack of provisions.

Of those few who found themselves suddenly wealthy, only a small fraction invested wisely. Many drank and gambled their fortunes away or squandered their newly found wealth on lavish parties and foolish business ventures.

In the fall of 1898, gold was discovered on Anvil creek on the bleak west coast of Alaska. Nome sprang up, and thousands evacuated Dawson and headed downriver toward the next big strike. In 1902, a prospector named Felix Pedro discovered good color in the creeks along the Chena River, initiating yet another stampede. The city of Fairbanks grew up around these claims. By this time, Dawson City and the

Klondike had seen its peak and in the few years that followed would begin to languish.

Those brave men and the handful of women who left that which was familiar to seek their fortunes in this strange, cold land were a breed apart. Their journals and biographies leave us an obscure picture of their lives on the last frontier. Many of the characters and accounts from this era are long forgotten, and many of their stories were never told.

CHAPTER

1

Southeast Alaska Territory, September 1897

A pod of killer whales swam along the starboard side of the sternwheeler, drawing the attention of the beleaguered passengers on deck. The whales plunged and surfaced, bobbing in a graceful water ballet as they played alongside. The great forests in the distance stretched down from the mountains to touch the water, the dark green color of the mighty Sitka spruce contrasting vividly with the golden birch. Eagles soared in the cloudless heavens, leaving the rocky beaches and lesser altitudes to the lowly seagulls.

The deck of the steamboat was crowded with hopeful, jubilant adventurers, for their long journey up Alaska's Inside Passage was coming to a close. Huge piles of provisions were stacked haphazardly across the deck of the steamer, provender and implements destined for the gold fields of the far north. Resourceful prospectors and industrious miners loitered among the great stacks of supplies, along with merchants, peddlers, gamblers and confidence men. There were women on board as well, several of whom were wives of the gold seekers.

The rest of the feminine class were society's rejects, misfits caught up in the great race north. There was one exception among the single women, a high-spirited twenty-year-old who had stolen the hearts of the bachelors on board.

Miss Lindsey Graham stood on the bow of the steamship, absorbing the warm rays of the fleeting September sunshine. Her father and brother stood at the rail beside her, lost in their thoughts and dreams of the Yukon gold fields.

The girl's eyes were wide with wonder as she beheld Alaska Territory at its finest. The high rugged mountains that rose up out of the emerald sea stretched as far as she could see in every direction. The glaciers thrilled her, these enormous rivers of ice which flowed from the highest peaks down to the water's edge.

"Oh Papa!" she exclaimed. "Isn't Alaska just glorious?"

"I must say, Lindsey, it's not bad a'tall when the sun's shining. Of course, we've had little enough of that on this trip. This is the first decent day we've had."

"If you ask me Sis, this rugged land is just a stopover where a man can get rich and then get out," said Horace. "It's a desolate, godforsaken country that no man would care to settle in permanently. You just take the riches it has to offer and run."

"That's about it Horace," agreed their father. "There's gold here, and silver, and probably minerals of lesser value that would be worth mining. There is fur for the taking as well. A man could make a fortune here trading fur, but you could never farm this land. Farming is essential to settle a country and no man in his right mind would want to settle here."

"Me, I'll be coming out about this time next fall," declared Horace. "That'll be plenty of time to stake a claim, work it for a few months and be done. We'll all be rich by this time next year, if it's as good as they say. Why, on some of those creeks up north you can't even walk without stepping on a nugget."

"I'd say you've got a severe case of gold fever, Horace," suggested Lindsey.

"You're probably right Sis. You'll get the fever too when you start sacking up your first nuggets."

"I'm afraid I already have it, to an extent at least. It seems to be a contagious disease in Seattle, and certainly on this ship."

"We must all have it bad to have endured what we have on this ship and still be excited," added Mr. Graham.

"I can't bear the thought of going back down below decks tonight," said Lindsey. "It smells so awful down there."

"Well Sis, if you can tough it out tonight we can probably get a room in Skagway tomorrow evening. I hear we're getting close."

"Oh! I can't wait. Just a bit of privacy would be nice, and a long, hot bath. Surely they have such comforts in Skagway, Papa?"

"Of course they do Lindsey dear. In a town the size of Skagway, there's not much that money can't buy."

The Grahams remained on the deck until the sun disappeared. The little steamer progressed steadily up the Taiya Inlet through the night, bearing its cargo of grasping, hopeful gold hunters and their belongings.

It was late the next morning when they reached Skagway. A bank of clouds rolled in during the night and a steady rain began to fall. This rain was much colder than the passengers were accustomed to. It was a numbing, bone-chilling downpour that made one long for the comfort of a warm fire.

Despite the pouring rain, the streets of Skagway were choked with people, goods and animals. The beaches and docks were littered with shipping crates, stacks of flour, tools and equipment. A sea of white canvas tents stretched for a mile in no apparent order. The continuous din of barking dogs and shouting, angry men reached the ears of those on the steamboat. Men everywhere were struggling with heavy canvas tarps to cover their goods. The streets were chaotic quagmires of mud and horse manure. Skagway wasn't quite what Miss Graham had pictured.

A strange sense of foreboding settled on Lindsey Graham. A feeling of uneasiness and uncertainty seemed to drift down from the shrouded mountains and roll out of the distant canyons to come and abide in her soul. It was a premonition of disgrace, misfortune, heartache and difficulty. But as the line of people began to move down the gangplank, she took a deep breath and stepped out into the unknown.

The rain continued unabated throughout the day. The ship's cargo was dumped recklessly on the beach by the crew, as they were in a frenzy to reach Dyea that evening. The men sorted and rooted through the enormous pile of goods, endeavoring to give each his own.

While Horace located their trunks and supplies, Lindsey and her father looked for a room. After an exhaustive search they located a vacant room for the outrageous price of fifteen dollars. It seemed to be the only room available and the Grahams considered themselves fortunate to have a place out of the rain.

The Grahams were immediately accepted into Skagway's upper society, as women of Lindsey's caliber were a rarity this far north. She was polite and gracious, and in one of her fine evening gowns could be called ravishing. It was imperative that their stay in Skagway must be brief, as winter was coming on quickly. Already there was a chill in the air. For a few short days and nights however, they were treated like royalty.

There was much to do yet and young Horace applied himself to practical matters. There were still more supplies to purchase and crates to pack, along with other small items of preparation. It was crucial that the Grahams find a competent packer with some horses, as it would be impossible to carry all of their gear and provisions on their backs. Horace was able-bodied with an indomitable spirit, but the elder Graham was pudgy and soft and Lindsey could hardly be expected to carry a pack up a steep mountainside.

As luck would have it, there was a packer in town by the name of Big Mike Teague. He had drifted into town that summer and acquired a few worn-out horses. He was a mountain of a man who weighed more than 350 pounds and stood more than six and a half feet tall. His arms were like fence posts and his chest was as big as a barrel.

Horace was taken with Big Mike immediately. He was thirsty for the stories and bits of knowledge about the Klondike, and Teague loved to talk. He told endless tales about his exploits in the north. He spoke of the gold fields and the wealth and riches to be obtained there. He bragged of navigating dangerous rivers, fighting off grizzlies and wolves and told other incredible stories. Yet Teague was unknown in Skagway.

Rumors were rampant in this gold camp, and news came with every ship from Seattle and every pack train that returned from the headwaters of the Yukon. There were reports of the rich pay dirt dug from the claims on Bonanza and El Dorado creeks. There were tales of fortunes won and lost over a game of cards. And there were other incredible stories about the courageous men who prospected the lonely canyons and crossed the perilous rivers.

The winds that swept down from the high mountains brought rumors of an explorer named Pierce. He was trusted and revered by the Athabaskans and the Eskimos, and it was said he moved freely among their tribes. Pierce traded in fur, trapped, and occasionally packed supplies to the native villages far above the Arctic Circle. One man said that Caleb Pierce was born in the Brooks Range, up near the headwaters of the Chandalar River. Rumor was that he knew the north like no other, from the Kuskokwim and the Koyokuk Rivers in the west to as far east as the Mackenzie.

Pierce was a strange and intriguing man, a loner who preferred the warmth of his own campfire over a room in Skagway or Dawson. He did not frequent the saloons and gambling dens when he passed through Circle and Coldfoot, and this bothered the miners. It was believed that Pierce had rich claims somewhere in this wilderness because he traded for his goods in gold. This was a common practice among the miners and prospectors, but Pierce's gold was of very high quality and unlike that found in Dawson or the Circle mining district. This chafed at the gold seekers and prospectors in the Interior region, as it was understood by all that if a prospector made a promising discovery, he staked his claim and then called for his comrades. Out of jealousy rumors sprouted up, and the deep, dark legend of Caleb Pierce was born.

It was over dinner at the Emporium that the subject of Pierce was brought up, and the Grahams listened attentively to the reports. A quartet of Skagway's most prominent men were at a table with the Grahams, dining on fresh halibut and crab from the bounty of the sea. Outside, the rain began to pour down in earnest. There was talk of the trip up from

Seattle and of the difficult journey ahead to Dawson. Others drifted into the dining room to eat their evening meal and sat at small tables around the perimeter.

A young man in buckskin and knee-high moccasins stalked in and seated himself in the corner. His clothes were those of an Athabaskan and he wore both a knife and a pistol on his belt. He was seated not far from Lindsey and on occasion she would feel his eyes upon her. By this time she had become accustomed to the miners looking at her, but for some reason she resented this man's bold stare.

The men, oblivious to the stranger, prattled on and on about the gold fields and the rich pay dirt to be found on El Dorado and Bonanza creeks. They spoke of nuggets the size of a man's fist, and of a pan of gravel, dust and nuggets worth a thousand dollars. These rumor sessions, which were so prevalent in Skagway, incubated that perilous and nearly incurable disease known as gold fever.

"I've heard Caleb Pierce is in Skagway," observed Mr. Hawthorn, proprietor of the Emporium. "I wouldn't know him if I saw him, but it might be worth your time to look him up."

"Well now, I've heard mixed reports about Pierce," suggested a tall man with a handlebar moustache. "They say he's a squaw man, with a different woman in every Indian village along the Yukon."

"George, do you have any facts to back that up?" asked Hawthorne. The man said nothing. "There's a lot of rumors floating around this country about Pierce and Dave Henderson and everybody else that's panned along the Yukon."

"He's not a packer as I understand it," said an older, balding man. "Nor is he a guide; more of an explorer and a prospector. I don't know him myself, but I hear he's a man to ride the river with."

"We've already hired a packer," related Horace. "A man by the name of Mike Teague."

"I've never heard of Teague," said Hawthorne, "and I know all the packers that are working the White Pass. I suppose he's been working over on the Chilkoot and I've just never run into him. There's a lot of men and goods going up over Chilkoot Pass right now."

"Teague just blew into town recently," the thin man said. "Bought a few sored-up horses from Alex James and hired a couple of Tlingits and their squaws to do his work."

"I'd be really careful here Graham," said the balding man. "When you're asking a man to take you to Dawson this time of year, you're trusting your lives into his hands." He paused. "For all we know, this Mike Teague could be one of Soapy Smith's hooligans."

"Well, Pierce is definitely capable," said Hawthorne. "That much we do know. If Caleb Pierce is in town, it would be worth it to ask him."

The young man in buckskin rose and approached their table. His skin was tanned by the long hours of summer daylight. His eyes were clear blue and penetrating, honest eyes, but now contemptuous. "You could ask Caleb Pierce to take you to Dawson," he said, "but the answer would be no. I can tell you that because I am Pierce." There was a look of astonishment on the men's faces.

"I just came from Dawson," continued Pierce. "I mean you no disrespect," he said, looking first at Thomas Graham and then at his daughter, "but I would discourage anybody from going up there this fall." Something akin to defiance began to rise up in Lindsey. "There's not a decent claim that hasn't been staked within ten miles of Dawson City," Pierce continued. The men were flabbergasted.

"There are at least three thousand people there already, and they've cut down every tree for miles and killed every moose and caribou in the district. They're depending on steamers coming up the Yukon for supplies, but the two that are on the river now won't make it as far as Circle before she freezes up. Mark my words, come early spring men'll be boiling their boots to eat. There's not enough food in Dawson to feed a thousand people until next spring."

These men of Skagway were stunned. They made a good living by outfitting the prospectors who ventured to the Klondike. "Every day," continued Pierce, "a hundred more miners head up the Chilkoot Trail. I'd wager that one in a hundred will strike it rich. Ten or less will break even. And as for the young lady here, you men know that North Country is no place for a tenderfoot."

Lindsey was stung by Pierce's hard words. How did this uncouth backwoodsman know her limitations and capabilities? Surely these men would not take this prophet of misfortune seriously!

"Hogwash Pierce!" declared the balding man. "You want all that gold for yourself, don't you?"

"I've got all the gold I need, old man. Just trying to save these nice folks some heartache." With that, he pulled a small pouch from his pocket and placed a small gold nugget on the table. "That's for my supper," he said. He turned and looked at Lindsey once more. "Don't say I didn't warn you." Then he was gone.

CHAPTER 2

While the Grahams were a bit worried now and in a hurry to get on the trail, Mike Teague showed no such urgency. He piddled at this and that, drinking and talking the precious hours away. Thomas Graham had given him a healthy sum to secure his services, and Teague seemed intent on squandering it all before they left Skagway.

The horses, an unfortunate string of seven, had fallen into incompetent hands. They were not old, but the few short years in southeast Alaska had been hard. They were covered with sores and were poorly shod, certainly in no condition for another pack trip over the pass.

When at last the Graham party prepared to leave Skagway, Big Mike chose the stoutest of the horses for himself. The others were loaded down heavily with supplies essential for survival in the north and many unnecessary items as well. Miss Graham's belongings consisted of two large trunks packed with evening gowns, slippers, petticoats, books, silverware, an assortment of parasols and a setting of fine china. Thomas Graham's personal items, while fewer, were nearly as impractical and extravagant.

Big Mike loaded down his native packers almost as heavily as the horses. The men were required to carry ninety-pound packs, while the women shouldered nearly seventy pounds. Horace, the only able-bodied Graham, prepared a heavy pack for himself and a light one for his sister. Teague carried nothing on his horse except a bedroll, a bottle of whiskey and a box of foul-smelling black cigars.

The Graham party was late in leaving for Dawson. Already the leaves were beginning to fall from the birch and the cottonwood trees, the aspen and the alder. Droves of gold seekers were leaving Skagway every day in hopes of getting to Dawson by fall. Lindsey could not erase Pierce's warning from her mind. It seemed to haunt her soul as a word of truth sometimes troubles the deceived.

Nothing could have prepared Lindsey Graham for the horrors she would encounter on the trail across the White Pass. It had been dubbed 'The Dead Horse' Trail' and Lindsey soon discovered the reason for this. Words are inadequate to describe the difficulty, brutality and inhumanity she witnessed as she walked those forty-six miles to Lake Bennet.

The trip began pleasantly enough as the rains ceased for a day. The first few miles were not difficult, except for an occasional swamp to cross. Yet, as the terrain began to steepen, they found themselves on the tail end of a giant, human centipede that stretched from Skagway to the headwaters of the Yukon.

Along the mountains, the trail became so narrow in places that one could not pass. In the canyons huge boulders and uprooted spruce trees created a deadly obstacle course. When a horse stumbled or was swallowed up in a bog, which happened often, all those on the trail behind were forced to stop. The horses were made to stand fully loaded, because the procession could resume at any time.

Big Mike's horse was clearly struggling from the outset, as the man was huge and seldom dismounted. Lindsey pitied the poor creature, all seven of the horses in fact. She was compelled to turn her eyes away when the packs were stripped from the animals each night. Big Mike did nothing for their sores and there was no feed for them. They were hobbled and turned loose to forage on the steep mountainside until morning.

Teague seemed to grow more angry as the difficult journey unfolded. He cursed and complained, smoked his foul black cigars and drank from the bottle. When his horse stopped to try to catch its breath, he beat it unmercifully. Lindsey could feel his eyes upon her and his bold glances sent chills down her spine. Her father and brother were obviously afraid of him. There was no word of rebuke from them regarding his behavior.

Lindsey soon developed a habit of falling behind the pack string, in part because of the blisters on her feet and partly to get away from Big Mike Teague. There were others in line behind her; hopeful prospectors and businessmen, merchants and dance hall girls. She preferred the company of these strangers now to the obnoxious Teague and her silent father and brother.

On the third day as Miss Graham struggled up a hill called "Summit," she paused to catch her breath. There were springs on the trail here, if one could call it a trail at all. It was really a continuous stream of mud and horse manure that wound its way down the mountain. She heard footsteps coming up quickly behind her, and then a man seized her arm and turned her around.

If there was one man in the world she did not want to see at that moment, it was Caleb Pierce. He stood there in his leather clothing, a look of disdain on his solemn face. His clear eyes seemed to look right through her, and for some reason she felt ashamed. "Missy, I thought I told you not to come up here this fall," he scolded.

"Whoever you are," she retorted, "I don't recall asking your permission. And please let go of my arm!"

"Please listen to me. "There's no food in Dawson," he told her, shaking his head. "And the winters here are long and cold. If you don't turn back now, you're putting your own life in jeopardy."

"As I understand the situation sir, there are several steamboats on the water even now, en route to Dawson."

"Don't count on those steamers ever reaching Dawson. I know the Yukon River ma'am, and she can freeze up in the middle of October."

"Why should you care?" she asked haughtily.

He hesitated to answer. "I just care," he said finally. "I don't say a lot of words, but I'll warn anybody that will listen. I've seen starvation and I've seen scurvy and it's not pretty. I'd hate to see a girl like you wasting away up there in Dawson this winter."

"Well for my sake, I hope you're wrong. Now Mister, if you don't let me go, I will scream."

Pierce dropped her arm and looked down the hill at the long line of people. "You're all a bunch of fools," he told her.

His words stung like a knife, wounding her delicate pride. "We'll see about that!" she snapped. "We'll see who the fool is." She could see the frustration then written on his face and the hurt in his eyes. He slowly turned away and left the trail, walking up the side of the mountain into the trees. The pack he wore on his back was huge, but he carried it with ease.

Where was he going? She wondered. Was there another trail to the Klondike known only to himself? This man Pierce was a mystery, she decided. He had warned her twice now of the eminent famine in Dawson. He might be a squaw man, but she knew he was no liar. His words were the truth and they were all so deceived in their gold-hunting fantasy that they would never heed his warning. As she continued to struggle up the mountain, a dull, sick feeling began to wash over her, the same sense of impending doom she had experienced before she stepped off the boat in Skagway.

The horrors of the Klondike trail had barely begun for Thomas Graham and his two beloved children. The long line of prospectors and their pack animals often came to a halt. Horses struggled and disappeared in bogs and drowned in the river. They slipped from the narrow trail on the side of the mountain and fell to their death hundreds of feet below.

The trail was littered with dead horses, abused and abandoned by the greedy hordes of people heading north. Along the most difficult stretches such as Dead Horse Gulch, their carcasses were strewn haphazardly along the trail, creating a horrible stench. Multitudes of ravens and numerous eagles patrolled the length of the Dead Horse Trail, flocking from one equine graveyard to another. Those horses that died quickly on the trail across the White Pass were the fortunate ones. Death was a godsend, a sweet release from pain and misery. Those who endured would continue to suffer until they too, dropped in their tracks.

A handful of disillusioned travelers turned and headed back toward Skagway, knowing full well they would not reach

Dawson that fall. Lindsey too wanted to turn back, but didn't have the nerve to mention it to Horace. He was a determined young man and wouldn't know the meaning of the word quit. This venture meant everything to him. If anyone could find gold in the Klondike, she knew, Horace could.

Mike Teague's brute strength and nasty disposition served the party well on the White Pass Trail. He bullied his way on toward Dawson, dragging his pack train of exhausted horses and terrified natives. He passed anyone he pleased, and picked a fight with anyone who protested.

Teague wasn't the only brute on the Dead Horse Trail that fall, by any means. The situation, with winter coming on and hundreds of miles yet to go seemed to bring out the worst in everyone. Angry, desperate men goaded and tortured their pack animals and fought with one another. They cursed the trail, cursed their horses, cursed Alaska and cursed God.

On the fifth day, as they struggled up the side of still another mountain, Teague's saddle horse collapsed on the trail and died. It was fortunate that the horse died immediately, because Teague became so angry he would have certainly beaten it to death. In a swearing, fuming rage, he jerked the pack saddle from the next horse in line and threw it down beside the trail. The panniers were filled with sacks of flour and beans, tins of fruit and cans of coffee. Lindsey shuddered when she saw the badly infected sores on the horse's back. Teague paid no attention to the condition of the animal, but angrily threw on his own saddle and adjusted the cinch. Horace and the Tlingits took the food from the discarded panniers and secured it on the remainder of the already overloaded horses.

The travelers who braved the White Pass Trail that fall were greeted at the Canadian border by the Mounted Police. While lawlessness reigned in Alaska Territory, the Mounted

Police ruled the Yukon with an iron hand. A small regiment of Mounties had been deployed to bring some order to this invasion of people, which had become known as the Klondike gold rush. They too were concerned about a potential famine in Dawson and insisted that every group of travelers have adequate provisions for the winter.

The Graham's food supply was skimpy at best, as they were counting on purchasing some supplies in Dawson. It was obvious to the Mounties that the horses were in bad condition and covered with sores. They had already turned many travelers around for these reasons, but one look at Big Mike Teague and his sour countenance convinced the police to let them cross the border. They had seen Teague before and knew he was not a man to be trifled with. Almost all of the horses on the White Pass Trail were in poor condition by this time, and many were sored up like these. Many of the stampeders had gone on to Dawson with little or no grub. Reluctantly, the Mounties allowed the Graham party to pass on.

A heavy weather system rolled up into the mountains from the coast, bringing heavy rains and snow with it. The continuous precipitation eventually permeated all things which were dry. After several hours in the downpour, everyone was soaked to the skin and the supplies and food were wet. But Big Mike Teague led them on through the pouring rain, stopping only when the trail became too dark to see.

Horace took an inventory that evening of their dwindling food supply and discarded that which had been ruined. The next morning one of the horses could not stand, but lay on its side, breathing heavily. Teague and the packers tried to get him on his feet but his strength was gone. The giant flew into a terrible rage. Lindsey could not bear to watch him beat and kick the poor animal and ran back along the trail. The remainder of the Graham family and the natives watched in horror, but they dared not interfere. A gunshot rang out at last, and Lindsey knew that the horse had been killed.

The natives loaded the supplies on the four remaining pack horses and the Graham party started off once again for Lake Bennet. Lindsey fell quickly behind the packers, as was her habit. She began to cry softly to herself as she slogged along in the rain and ankle-deep mud.

Throughout the day they passed hundreds of travelers going back to Skagway. "You'll never make Dawson this winter!" they declared. "The Mounties are holding everybody back at Lake Bennet." This was not welcome news for the Graham party, but they pressed on into Yukon Territory. Teague was determined to lead them to Dawson, or so it seemed.

Lindsey was exhausted that night as they made their camp. She was so tired that even the bold glances of Mike Teague failed to annoy her. Her legs and back ached, but she said nothing. If anyone had a right to complain it was the Tlinglit packers. Their burdens were extremely heavy. They hustled around camp however, unloading the horses and preparing supper. They were obviously in high spirits. Tomorrow they would reach their destination.

Lindsey's own heart was heavy. Something was wrong and she knew it. Mike Teague was an evil man and her family was now at his mercy. If only she had listened to the frontiersman, the explorer who dressed in Athebaskan clothing. The girl lay in her bedroll for a time, crying silently in the darkness. "Horace, I think we should go back," she said quietly to her brother.

"What, Lindsey!" Her brother was astonished. "After we've come so far?"

"It's so awful here Horace. This incessant rain, the never-ending mud and this horrible trail are a nightmare. And Mike Teague scares me, Horace. He looks me over like I'm a piece of livestock."

"I've been carrying a pistol Lindsey. If he ever lays a hand on you, I swear I'll shoot him." He put a hand on her shoulder. "Don't worry Sis. I'm looking out for you. We're so close now Lindsey. It's all an easy boat-ride down the Yukon from Lake Bennet. You'll be the queen of Dawson. You're the prettiest thing that ever floated down the Yukon River. You'll probably marry one of the Bonanza Creek gold barons."

She considered that for a while, but somehow the thought was not pleasant. She would never marry a man for his money.

Lake Bennet was a large body of water surrounded by an even larger sea of white canvas tents. Thousands of people, mostly men, lined the shores of the lake. Building boats was the objective for the stampeders now, and hundreds of craft could be seen around the shoreline. There were rafts and keelboats of every shape and size, from large, sturdy, well designed vessels to tiny jon boats and canoes. The boats were in various stages of completion; some stood ready to sail, but most were just piles of boards.

A continuous din of hammers, saws and loud voices filled the valley. Horses, oxen and dogs added their voices to the chaos. Bennet, once a quiet lake tucked away in the mountains, was now a small city.

The newcomers unloaded the exhausted horses for the final time and then turned them loose to drink and graze. These poor animals, along with many others that had served so faithfully on the Dead Horse Trail that summer would soon encounter the angry Yukon winter and starvation.

When Teague paid the Tlinglit packers, it was obvious to all that he cheated them. The leader of the group tried to explain their situation in broken English, appealing to the benevolent Mr. Graham. Mike Teague grabbed the native by the arm and hurled him to the ground. The Tlingits had no choice but to take what he had given them and turn back toward Skagway.

"You ungrateful rogues!" boomed Teague as the natives retreated. "Git outta' here!"

"You cheated them!" accused Lindsey, turning to face Big Mike. "After all they did for us, you cheated them out of half their wages."

"They don't need very much to get along," answered Teague.

"Father, this isn't right," contended the young lady. "Can't you do something?" But the elder Graham just sat quietly, looking at the ground. Big Mike laughed mockingly. Horace too, stood dumbfounded. Lindsey went to her small pack, which she had carried over the White Pass. She pulled out a small handbag and from it drew some paper bills. Without another word, she left to find the Tlingits.

The packers had disappeared into the horde of humanity that was now Lake Bennet. Lindsey wove her way among the tents and the boats that were in progress. Hundreds of pairs of admiring eyes followed her and dozens of men cheerfully greeted her. Eventually she caught up with the packers, who accepted her money with big smiles and expressions of gratitude. But her mission had taken her far away from her father and brother. She was returning to her camp when she saw him for the third time.

It was Caleb Pierce, and he was standing in the midst of half a dozen men. He appeared to be explaining something to them and they were taking in every word like small schoolchildren. She hoped he would not see her, but he looked up to catch her eyes. She returned his glance briefly and then sauntered off toward her father's camp. Pierce made no move to speak with her this time, but his steady gaze followed her as she made her way along the shoreline.

"What's a good girl like that one doing up here in this north country?" asked one of the men in the group. "What a pretty little bolt of lightning she is!"

"Well, we're gettin' all kinds in here now Joe," replied another. "Could be a dance hall girl."

"She ain't dressed like one."

"She's traveling with her pa and brother," Pierce explained. "Real cheechakos too, it seems. Fell in with a bad hombre down in Skagway. Big man by the name of Teague."

"I've heard of him. He's a freight packer, ain't he?"

"He's no packer," answered Caleb. "He's a hooch runner from down on the lower Yukon. Trades the natives whiskey for their furs. I've had a few run-ins with him and none of them pleasant." He paused, trying to catch another glimpse of Lindsey. "I hate to see a decent family get mixed up with filth like him."

CHAPTER

3

The Northwest Mounted Police had deemed it necessary to hold the thousands of potential prospectors at Lake Bennet and Lake Lindeman for the winter. Dawson was not prepared for this multitude of invaders, nor were there facilities or provisions to accommodate them. The journey from the headwaters of the Yukon to Dawson was nearly five hundred miles, and certainly not an undertaking for a tenderfoot.

It was nearly the first of October. Already the leaves of the aspen and birch had fallen in the high country and the water was freezing along the shoreline of the alpine lakes. The cold winds swept down from the high mountain passes, whispering a warning of a long, cold winter.

Mike Teague had no intention of spending the winter at Lake Bennet, no matter what the Mounties said. The big man immediately began searching for a boat to buy, or possibly two. There was neither the time nor the wherewithal to build one. Thomas Graham had money, Teague knew, and the Grahams were as eager to get to Dawson as he was. Mining claims were staked on a first-come, first-served basis and it was critical that the Graham's reach Dawson before this horde of people.

Lindsey Graham quickly became the chief topic of conversation along the shores of Lake Bennet. She was refined and sophisticated, a real lady it was said, and beautiful as well. The boldest inhabitants of this tent city came to call on the Grahams, as had been the custom in Skagway.

The men talked of Dawson and the Yukon River. They spoke of hazardous Miles Canyon and the White Horse Rapids. They prattled on and on about that of which they yet knew nothing. And always, there were rumors of Pierce. Lindsey listened attentively to the rumors about the frontiersman, as he had spoken to her on two occasions.

It was confirmed by a dozen or more sources that Caleb Pierce knew the Yukon and its tributaries. He had explored the Porcupine River country and the Fortymile region. He had ventured far above the Arctic Circle to Wiseman and Coldfoot and to the many native villages beyond. It was rumored that his sled dogs were the fastest on the Yukon, and each carried at least a trace of timber wolf in its blood. His gold was different from that which had been mined in Dawson or Circle, and he had never disclosed the location of his claim. This confounded the gold hunters. It was customary to record a claim of any value. He was hiding a significant discovery, the next big strike.

In the early morning hours of the second day in October, two small boats entered the outlet of Lake Bennet. Long before dawn they slipped quietly into the source of the Yukon and began moving steadily northward toward Dawson.

Mr. Graham had purchased the boats at an outrageous price from a disillusioned gold seeker. The man managed to build the boats before winter set in but exhausted his resources in the process. Without enough provisions to endure the winter, he turned a tidy profit in the sale of his boats.

Those who witnessed the departure of the Graham party did not inform the Mounties. They were satisfied to be rid of the likes of Mike Teague, for rumors of the big man's dishonesty were in full circulation. The girl was another story, however, and they all hoped to see her in Dawson the following spring.

It was cold on the water that early morning as the two craft slipped along in the slow current. The boats were heavy and cumbersome, having been fashioned with green lumber, and sat low in the water. Lindsey was in one boat with her brother, having made it clear that under no circumstances would she ride with Mike Teague. The guide and their father manned the other boat and it too, had little freeboard. Most of the food had been loaded into Horace's boat, while Teague and Mr. Graham carried clothing and some tools.

The outlet from Lake Bennet led to Tagish Lake, and after Tagish was yet another, called Marsh Lake. Heavy winds blew down from the mountains here, kicking up substantial whitecaps on the water. Teague rigged a makeshift sail from a blanket in his boat, the winds being in their favor. Horace did likewise, and the two boats moved along steadily throughout the day. They camped on the lower end of Tagish Lake that night, and by the following afternoon the Graham party had entered the very headwaters of the Yukon River.

What began as a tranquil ride down a gentle stream soon became a terrifying nightmare for the Graham party. As tributaries flowing out of the high country joined the Yukon, it became swifter and deeper. The water hurtled down out of the mountains, adding both volume and momentum as it came.

Both Horace and Lindsey quickly realized that they were at the river's mercy. Horace struggled with the rudder, endeavoring to keep the boat straight in the current, while Lindsay just sat paralyzed, her hands glued to the gunnels. Mr. Graham sat likewise, while Teague manned the rudder at the stern of the second boat.

High stone cliffs rose up from the banks of the Yukon to flank the river on each side. The water continued to gain velocity as the Yukon narrowed between the high walls of the canyon. Horace managed to overcome his fear and right the boat as they entered the treacherous gorge. They seemed suspended momentarily, being hurled along by the angry river. Massive bodies of rock rose up here and there, creating deadly, giant whirlpools. The deafening roar of this turbulent serpent echoed off the towering walls.

Running the gauntlet of Miles Canyon without a mishap might be considered providence. After the travelers were spewed out of the mouth of the violent gorge, they immediately found themselves in the midst of Squaw Rapids. It was a treacherous, chaotic stretch of fast-moving water. Spires of sharp rock protruded from the river here, each capable of ripping the hull out of a passing boat.

Horace followed the lead of Teague and Mr. Graham, who were weaving their way through the deadly obstacle course. Waves of ice-cold water accosted the wooden craft, soaking the passengers and their goods. Water spilled over the gunnels, threatening to swamp them.

That sick, helpless feeling haunted Lindsey Graham. This was what she had dreaded, what she had sensed on the boat in Skagway. That which she had feared had now come upon them. And yet she did not despair.

With an inner strength born of desperation, she took her oar in hand and began to paddle. Together she and Horace carefully guided the heavily-laden boat through the maze of whirlpools and boulders. After a few tense moments the river deepened and settled. The members of the Graham party slowly made their way over to a sandbar on the west side of the river.

"We made it!" exclaimed Horace jubilantly as they pulled the boats up out of the water. He hugged his sister and swung her around. "You're the greatest, Lindsey. We'll make a squaw out of you yet."

"I was scared to death back there," Lindsey confessed. "I've never experienced anything quite that dangerous."

"I was born for this," said her brother as he looked out across the river. "I just believe this is my destiny."

Lindsey was seeing her brother in a new light these days. Since their arrival in Alaska Territory, he had grown immensely in her eyes. This wild place and its hardships were transforming him into a man she did not recognize. He was bold and courageous now, like the explorers of the north. It was Horace who was in charge of their expedition, she realized, and not her father or Mike Teague. It was not wealth that he craved, she knew, but adventure. He belonged here among the strong and valiant, among famous men like Bob Henderson, Al Mayo, George Carmack and others who were legends in the North. She neglected to add that impertinent frontiersman, Caleb Pierce, to the list of heroes.

"Well, that's about the worst the river has to offer," said Teague. "We'll have the Whitehorse Rapids yet, and the Five Finger Rapids farther down, but we're over the worst."

"There's no turning back now," observed Thomas Graham. "We would never be able to get back up to Lake Bennet, even if we wanted to."

"We're committed, all right," agreed Horace.

They camped on the river that night. "It's much quieter here than at Lake Bennet," observed Lindsey as she lay down to sleep. The only sound was the lazy melody of the mighty Yukon as her waters drifted past. Something changed that day for Lindsey Graham. She had braved the waters of Miles Canyon and Squaw Rapids. In those critical moments she had faced her fears and prevailed in spite of them.

The Five Fingers was a modest rapid in comparison to what the Graham party endured at Miles Canyon. Another terrifying stretch of water, the Whitehorse Rapids, was now a mere memory. The most difficult of the upper Yukon's turbulent waters lay behind them and they were progressing steadily toward Dawson.

High on a bluff above the river was a tiny cabin. A canoe rested on a gravel bar on the east side of the river. Here the Yukon divided into five fingers, each hazardous and choked with boulders. The best route here was the finger on the far east side. The Graham party approached cautiously, with Thomas and Teague in the lead boat.

There was a large whirlpool here where the river split, and the first boat hit it perfectly. Teague's boat was hurled out of the whirlpool and into the fifth finger of the Rapids.

Lindsey remembered very little about what happened next. When their skiff encountered the whirlpool, it was hurled violently against the rock wall. The last thing she remembered was the loud crack of splintering boards as the boat was torn apart. Then she and Horace were both swallowed by the frigid Yukon.

The siblings could swim reasonably well, but they were no match for the waters of Five Finger Rapids. Heavily clothed and helpless against the chaotic, mind-numbing current, they were quickly sucked down into the belly of the Yukon.

What Lindsey had sensed and feared had come upon them. Misfortune was theirs.

Lindsey felt the rocky bottom of the river, and yet she was powerless against the torrent. She was drifting in the icy abyss, drowning and dying. All became dark around her.

Something bumped her in the water, and then she was suddenly engulfed by powerful arms. She wanted to reach out, but could not bring herself to move. Then she heard once more the roar of the rapids and a distant, frantic voice. It was her father calling, yet she could not answer him.

Lindsey was locked in an embrace of iron and was being towed through the water. After a tremendous struggle against the unholy rapids, a man emerged from the river and carried the girl's limp body up onto the bank. He laid her down gently upon the gravel. Thomas Graham came from downriver, gasping to catch his breath, leaving Teague to tie up the boat.

Lindsey began to show some signs of life. She commenced coughing up the water she had swallowed and inhaled. Her father knelt beside her, mumbling to himself.

"Look's like she's gonna be all right," said Caleb Pierce. "I'll go look for the boy." With that he strode back upriver for his canoe. In a moment he shot past, guiding the canoe deftly through the water.

Mr. Graham turned on Mike Teague. "Why didn't you go after Horace?" he demanded. "He shot right past us and you didn't lift a finger to help him!"

"In a situation like this," Teague retorted, "it's every man for himself. That kid would have drowned me too."

"Some guide you are, Teague! You've ruined us."

"Don't get lippy with me old man. I'll take you by the seat of the pants and toss you right in along with him!" There was anger in Teague's eyes and contempt in his voice. There was something sinister inside Teague, something evil. Thomas Graham had overlooked it thus far, but now could see it clearly. He must be careful with Mike Teague. If the giant killed him, who would look out for Lindsey?

After Lindsey regained her senses and was breathing comfortably again, the threesome walked up to the little cabin on the bluff above the river.

"Horace probably just got washed down the river a'ways," suggested Graham hopefully.

"Oh Papa, I do pray that you're right," replied Lindsey. "I would just die if we lost him." She paused, and then asked quietly, "Papa, who was that man who pulled me out of the river?"

"It was Caleb Pierce, Lindsey, the same man who warned us in Skagway. Must have seen us coming down the river. I'm just thankful he was here."

Teague left them alone in the little cabin and wandered back down to the river. As the afternoon lengthened, the wind picked up, blowing steadily from the north. By nightfall it was snowing heavily. The raw wind was howling, driving the snow horizontally up the Yukon before it.

Teague did not return to the cabin, and there had been no sign of Pierce. The Grahams made light conversation, each trying to encourage the other. The ferocious wind accosted the tiny cabin on the bluff above the Yukon. Visibility outside the confines of their shelter was nonexistent. Mr. Graham lit a coal oil lamp and stoked the little shepherd's stove in the corner.

It was long after dark when Caleb Pierce entered the cabin. He was alone. He moved immediately to the stove and began to thaw his hands and feet while Thomas and Lindsey stood silently, dreading the news he might bring.

"I followed the river downstream for several miles," he said softly. "No sign of the boy. When the storm blew in I couldn't see a lick, so I had to pull out."

"This can't be happening!" Lindsey exclaimed. It was as if trying to awaken from a nightmare.

"Do you think there's a chance he might be alive downriver somewhere?" pressed Graham.

"Not likely," answered Pierce soberly. "Even if he made it out of the river alive, this storm would have done him in." He paused. "I shore hope I'm wrong."

"Perhaps Mr. Teague has found Horace," suggested Lindsey hopefully.

"Mike Teague skedaddled," said Pierce. "He unloaded what was left of your belongings and dumped them down on the river bank."

Thomas Graham cursed Teague, but Lindsey was too concerned about her brother to worry about their outfit.

"I think I must have passed Teague somewhere on the river," continued Pierce. "I couldn't see much after that norther started up. He could have slipped by me easily enough." Pierce hesitated. "Did you have any valuables amongst your things?"

Thomas Graham's face became ashen. "I had a sizable amount of money in my satchel," he answered.

Pierce and Graham went down to the river to check on things. The gear was scattered along the river bank and covered now by several inches of snow. Mr. Graham looked through his bags, and as he had feared, the money was gone. He sat down in the snow muttering angrily to himself.

Caleb quickly shook the snow from the remainder of the Graham outfit. He came upon a pile of women's clothing, and these things he carefully placed in an empty burlap sack. *No point in causing the girl any more heartache*, he thought. There was little of value in the Graham's belongings, Caleb decided. There were no tools, no food and no heavy clothing for their expedition farther north. Teague had taken everything of value. The wind continued to drive the falling snow up the river. Caleb left Graham alone there and walked wearily back up to the cabin.

Lindsey sat on the bunk with her head in her hands. She was sobbing. "I'm sorry," she said after a moment. "I lost control of myself."

Caleb was at a loss for words. He had told the girl and her family not to come, but they had disregarded his warning. Now they were in a difficult predicament, with no food and no boat. He studied the girl for a moment. He had been born and raised near the headwaters of the Chandalar and had seen few white women in his lifetime. Now, with Dawson City booming, they were coming into the Interior in droves. First there were a few in Circle City, but the discovery in Dawson had created a stampede of humanity heading north. They were men mostly, young and in their prime, but a good number of women had followed.

"I'm sorry about your brother," offered Caleb at length.

"It's no fault of yours, Mr. Pierce," whispered Lindsey. "Heaven knows you tried to warn us. From the moment I stepped off the ship at Skagway, I have had a terrible feeling about this venture. Now it seems that misfortune has found us."

As she continued speaking, she seemed to cast a temporary spell over Pierce. Her voice was music to the lonely wanderer, this king of the wilderness. Her well-chosen words were guileless, her speech flawless. Her eyes were dark green and lovely, commanding the undivided attention of his own. Her dark hair had not been brushed and yet was remarkable. It was full and long, fitly framing her beautiful face. Sorrow and heartache were etched in her countenance, but never had sadness appeared so becoming.

Thomas Graham returned to the little cabin on the bluff above the Yukon River. Lindsey tossed and turned on the bunk that night, while the two men occupied the floor. The little shepherd's stove popped and crackled throughout the night, while the wind outside shrieked and moaned. Far into the night, Caleb awoke and listened to the sounds in the darkness. The girl was crying again, ever so softly, and somehow he seemed to feel her pain.

Pierce had never been blessed with a brother or sister and knew he could not identify with her great loss, yet his own heart ached for her sake. Had he ever cried? Strangely, he couldn't recall a time when he had shed tears. Like the natives here in the far North, he had been taught to control his emotions, to bury them really. Tears were not considered manly. He had buried a great heartache of his own once, or desperately tried, but it still haunted him. The hurt he had buried several years before was still eating away at him, ever molding him into a hard man and a loner.

CHAPTER 4

A frigid October morning on the upper Yukon only added to the magnitude of the Grahams' predicament. They were stranded out in the middle of nowhere without food, adequate clothing or transportation. Not only were they ill-equipped, but they were cheechakos, tenderfeet as it were. They had no grasp of the perils of winter; the scurvy, frostbite, the privations of life that this inhospitable wilderness could hold. They lacked even the fundamental skills and knowledge to survive for a week.

Pierce had his own agenda for the winter, which would take him north and east from here into the Mackenzie Mountains. There was prime fur there, pelts of marten, lynx and wolverine. His pack was heavily laden with items to trade; knives and hatchets, salt and sulphur matches. For these necessities the Natives would be willing to trade their fur pelts. When Pierce made up his mind to do something, it was difficult to stop him.

Thomas Graham pleaded with Pierce to escort them on to Dawson, but the young man was set on going east, then farther north. There was a good chance that a party of disillusioned stampeders would be coming upriver, retreating from Dawson City. If not, the freighters would be on the river by November with their dog teams. The Grahams would be able to get a ride back to Skagway, but it would be very costly.

Caleb divided the food that was in his pack with the Grahams. As he was preparing to leave, he was approached by Lindsey. "Mr. Pierce, I want to thank you for all you've done for us, for me especially. You tried to warn us, but in our stubborn pride we came anyway. Then you risked your own life to save mine, a tremendous act of kindness that I didn't deserve. I'm afraid that I have misjudged you. We owe you more than we can ever hope to repay," she finished with large tears in her eyes.

"I wish I could take you back to Skagway Miss Graham," Caleb told her.

"We'll be fine," she assured him. Someone will be by here in a day or so."

Pierce turned away and hoisted his heavy pack onto his shoulders. He grabbed his rifle and walked down to the river. The Grahams followed him down and watched as he shot the rapids and disappeared around a distant bend.

A strange feeling began to gnaw at Caleb. The more distance he put between himself and the Grahams, the more intense the eerie feeling became. The girl and her father would not be fine, and there was a chance that no one would be by here for weeks. One of the family had already drowned, and he had been the strongest. The freighters who would eventually come up the Yukon… would they be honest men, or would they be predators like Mike Teague and the other riffraff who that were infiltrating the country?

The Grahams were astounded, but relieved to see Caleb back at the cabin. "I just couldn't, in good conscience, leave you stranded here," he explained. "There's no guarantee that anyone will come by here before freeze-up. It's pretty dead on the river right now, with the police holding everyone up at Lake Bennet."

"So you'll take us to Dawson then?" asked Mr. Graham hopefully.

"We don't have any choice really," answered Caleb. "But let me tell you what we're up against." He paused. "The river'll be freezing up soon. When that happens, we'll be walking. The snow could get deep and it might turn cold."

"Colder than this?" asked Lindsey.

"Miss Graham, I consider this warm," he grinned.

While Caleb negotiated the rapids with the loaded canoe, Lindsey and Mr. Graham walked along the bank of the river. Already, shelf ice was forming along the banks of the Yukon. Below the rapids, the Grahams were loaded into the canoe and they launched out together into the current. The canoe sat very low in the water, but from here the Yukon was mostly gentle.

As they floated on toward Dawson, Lindsey diligently searched along the shoreline for her lost brother. This evil river had taken her brother from her, and now she hated it. This eternal waterway, this vital artery that brought life to the Interior also brought tragedy and death. For Lindsey, the day seemed to float by as if it were a dream. She could simply not accept the fact that her brother was dead.

The river was rugged and beautiful, the landscape picturesque. Flocks of ducks and geese stopped occasionally to rest on the river before continuing their migration. Small bands of trumpeter swans hurried south amid enormous flocks of sand hill cranes. There were dog salmon in the river now, pushing on to the Yukon's uppermost tributaries to spawn.

As they drifted down the river, Lindsey considered this man, Caleb Pierce. He was of medium stature, lean and muscular like so many of the young men who were venturing north. He seemed to be in his element on the river, at one with the trees, the mountains, the wildlife... and she and her father were the intruders here. He must surely despise her, she reasoned. The old sourdoughs and prospectors who haunted the upper Yukon all resented the cheechakos, the newcomers who were flocking into the country by the thousands. The Grahams had been both arrogant and foolish in their blatant disregard for Pierce's warnings, yet he had not abandoned them. He had plunged into the icy Yukon to save her life and yet she would have preferred death to being in his debt. If only he had rescued Horace instead of her!

The shadows were beginning to fall that evening when they approached an Indian village on the east side of the river. These were the Stick Indians, and they were accustomed to bartering with the freighters who ran the Yukon. They traded smoked salmon and furs, and garments fashioned by their women for those necessities which could not be found in their native homeland.

Two young boys were at play by the river and quickly scurried up the bank to announce the canoe's arrival. The entire village soon swarmed around them, articulating in a language foreign to Lindsey. One man in particular seemed to have a story to tell and conversed with Caleb in serious tones for several minutes. Turning to the Grahams, Pierce explained.

"Says he caught a man's body in one of his gill nets this morning. I expect it might be that of your brother."

Pierce and the Grahams moved somberly up a low hill to the village. As they followed the procession of curious natives, a small girl reached up and took Lindsey's hand. She was a beautiful child with smooth dark skin, innocent eyes, and long black hair. Lindsey clutched the little hand tightly, as if to draw strength and courage from the child.

The body recovered that morning belonged to Horace Graham. The sand and rocks of the river had taken a hard toll on the corpse and left it barely recognizable. Caleb wrapped the body in an old tarp and, with the assistance of one of the young men, carried it several hundred yards from the encampment. The Grahams sat in stunned silence as Pierce and a young native dug a shallow grave. After the body was covered, the elder Graham stumbled back toward the village and the young man disappeared. Lindsey observed stoically as Caleb fashioned a crude cross at the head of the grave.

Pierce glanced occasionally at Lindsey, wondering how she was holding up. He could see the immense hurt in her eyes and hear the pain of her heart when she spoke.

"Mr. Pierce," the girl began, "it would have been far better if you had saved my brother rather than I."

"How do you figure that, Miss Graham?" he asked.

"I don't belong here. I've had a terrible feeling about this country since the moment I set foot in it. I won't be any good to you on this trip either. I'm a tenderfoot of the worst sort, Mr. Pierce." Lindsey paused. "This entire adventure was Horace's brainchild. I know he would have done well here." She began to cry then, and Caleb did nothing to stop her.

The threesome camped on the river that night, not far from the Indian village. It was a clear night, and cold. The Aurora Borealis danced in the heavens, its magnificent colors shimmering across the sky.

They were on the river again by daybreak. There was no time to make breakfast. They were racing against time. The large chunks of ice floating in the Yukon were a stark reminder that she would soon freeze solid. A frigid gale from the north met them head-on and fought their progress toward Dawson. The biting wind whipped over the Yukon's silt laden waters to chill Pierce and his companions. As they flowed along in the swirling current, the girl sat in the middle of the canoe, fighting off blocks of ice with a short pole. The old man did likewise at the bow, while Pierce skillfully guided the canoe through the waters.

To be fair, the young man's eyes were not entirely on the river. He glanced occasionally at the young lady. She was a woman with some fine qualities, he decided. She seemed fit now, strengthened by her first few weeks in the Yukon. He knew she was cold. Her store-bought mackinaw could hardly repel the icy October winds that whipped along the river. She never complained, however, unlike the few white women who now inhabited Dawson City. She seemed determined to pull her load and this pleased Pierce.

The gold barons of Dawson would love her, he knew. Big Alex McDonald and Antoine Stander, Joe Ladue and the Lucky Swede would surely charm her and lure her away with their fat pokes of gold dust and nuggets.

They pulled out of the river around noon, as Lindsey became hypothermic. She had eaten little that morning and her light clothing could not protect her from the elements. Her body began to shake uncontrollably and she became disoriented. Caleb put her bedroll inside his and the two men wrestled her into it. Mr. Graham held the girl close to him while Pierce scrounged through his outfit for some food. After she had eaten, she slowly began to warm up. The precious hours of the afternoon slipped slowly by as she recovered. Darkness came early in October in the far north, and they were unable to make any further progress toward Dawson City that day.

The following day was even more hazardous for the travelers. The river was choked with great slabs of ice, which could easily slice through their canoe. They fought off the ice throughout the day as they drifted slowly on toward Dawson. Lindsey, dressed warmly now in borrowed men's clothing, toiled bravely.

Their canoe was punctured just before dark and had to be abandoned. Caleb was worried now, being caught so far from Dawson with a pair of greenhorns. Even for the hardiest of souls, the Alaska and Yukon natives and those few white men who roamed the mighty Interior, winter could be deadly. The temperature plummeted to twenty below zero as they slept. While Caleb rested soundly, the Grahams tossed and turned in their bedrolls in an effort to stay warm.

When they awoke, the river was completely covered by a thin layer of ice. There would be no further navigation on the Yukon until the following spring. Dog teams would test this river in a month when the ice was nearly a foot thick.

Pierce was resolute, knowing full well the ordeal that was before them and what would be required if they were to reach Dawson. Another two hundred miles lay between them and their destination. The days were growing progressively shorter. The Grahams' clothing and boots were hardly adequate, and if the temperature were to bottom out at forty or fifty below they would be in a precarious position. Caleb had seen firsthand the effects of the brutal northern winters. Temperatures dove into the abyss and hovered there for weeks and relentless winds rolled down out of the mountain ranges and howled along the river bottoms, continuing for days on end. Heavy, deep snow made traveling nearly impossible at times and hung in the air, soaking everything it touched.

Thomas Graham was despondent. In two short months he had lost not only his son, but also squandered a small fortune. His lust for gold had lured him to the Yukon where foolish men took great risks and often lost everything. He had nothing left except a small satchel, a change of clothes and a few personal items. The burning desire to strike it rich was gone now. There remained in its place only a deep sense of shame and regret. He was a fool like the thousands of others who had sold out and headed for the Klondike.

The girl was quiet, her heart hanging in the balance between courage and despair. She watched Pierce carefully, as if waiting for a hint of what might come next. He had every reason to abandon them, as Teague had done and she feared he might. She handed the frontiersman a cup of coffee and he sat down beside her.

"A penny for your thoughts, Mr. Pierce," she offered.

He sipped the strong coffee and smiled. "Well, we've got some obstacles to overcome," he began. "We're about two hundred miles from Dawson City. We're short on grub and if it turns really cold, we may be in real trouble. I've got a cache and a little cabin at the mouth of the Stewart River, if the bears haven't torn it to pieces. The good news is that you're with me and not with Mike Teague," he continued.

"I felt bad about that evil man from the very beginning," she confessed. "I'm glad he abandoned us. He's probably sitting in a saloon in Dawson City right now, drinking our money away. Will you stay the winter in Dawson, Mr. Pierce?" she asked.

"I expect not," he answered.

"Where will you go then?"

"I try not to plan too far ahead," he answered. "When I get restless in a place, I just go. One of the benefits of being a loner is there's no one to worry about, and no one to worry about you."

CHAPTER

5

The city of Dawson lay under a choking blanket of wood smoke so thick that it obscured the last rays of the fleeting November sun. The smoke billowed from the mining shafts on Bonanza and El Dorado creeks, where determined miners worked to thaw the frozen gravel. Down through the layers of permafrost they excavated until they touched bedrock. The gravel grew richer in gold dust and nuggets as they descended, until at last they reached the richest pay dirt ever discovered.

A mile from bustling Dawson, three souls traveled along the river. In the lead was a man in a harness of sorts pulling an older man on a makeshift sled. The first man, Caleb Pierce, was exhausted. Many days on the trail had robbed him of his strength. The heavy pack on his shoulders bore down upon him, the hard muscles in his legs cramping constantly. But he was close now. He could smell the smoke of the city and hear the eerie howling of Dawson's countless sled dogs. This had been a close one, but the weary man's determination had served him well.

The older man on the sled, Thomas Graham, was conscious but very weak. He was a heavy man and not in good physical condition. After several days on the trail he had collapsed and had been suffering since from severe chest pains.

Behind them trudged a beautiful young woman, thoughtful now that Dawson lay so close. What would she do? She had no money and her father needed a doctor badly. Lindsey considered the man who walked before her, this Caleb Pierce. His strength was enormous, his determination incredible. In this North Country, so full of greedy, grasping prospectors all seeking their own, he alone had reached out to help her. He had watched over her from the beginning and she had resented it. But now as they were approaching Dawson City, Lindsey was beginning to realize the magnitude of her debt.

The river was frozen two feet thick now. There would be no escape from Dawson until next spring. Somehow, she must earn enough money this winter in this boomtown to buy passage home for her father and herself. To strike it rich here had been her brother's dream, a vision which she no longer shared. She did not belong here in this cold, desolate wilderness. Her heart yearned for the city, the security of her childhood home.

News spread rapidly of the Graham's arrival in Dawson City. Miners flocked in from their claims to see the young beauty who had arrived with Caleb Pierce. They were not disappointed. Never had such a fair jewel graced the tent city's dismal streets.

The young frontiersman pulled a small pouch from his pack and laid it on the counter at the hotel. Its contents amounted to a handful of gold nuggets and a cup of dust, but it was a bit different from the gold found in Dawson. The color was somewhat lighter, but it was rich and pure, and it was a substance some men would risk even death to obtain.

Caleb purchased a hotel room for the Grahams and then called upon the town's only physician, William Judge, who was also a Jesuit priest. The doctor was a personal friend of Pierce and he came at once to tend to Mr. Graham. Meanwhile, Caleb faded back away from the town and set up a lonely camp.

Lindsey caused an immediate stir in Dawson the next day. Even the wealthiest of the gold barons descended from their claims on Bonanza and El Dorado to behold the girl who had arrived with Caleb Pierce. They lavished their attention on her and her father, and the conquest for the prettiest girl in Dawson City began.

Lindsey and her father quickly became preoccupied with Dawson society. When Thomas Graham began to recover, he was invited to the card tables and there he established himself. Lindsey reveled in her new environment. The music and the dancing were a welcome contrast to the weeks of quiet and solitude with Pierce.

Dance hall girls from the Nugget and Monte Carlo cast jealous glances as they observed Lindsey dining and waltzing with the wealthy miners. She enjoyed the attention, as any young lady would, and gradually the glamour of Dawson cast a spell upon her.

There was something not quite right about the materialism, the excessive drinking and gambling that enamored Dawson's night life. The miners were honest and rugged, yet were consumed with the lust for gold and the wealth it brought. They knew minerals and mechanics, freighting and dog-mushing, but they were like lost children searching for something to satisfy and entertain them for a while.

Two weeks passed. Lindsey fully intended to see Caleb Pierce again but Dawson City was a bustling community, even in winter. Pierce proved difficult to locate in this city of three thousand and there was always something to distract her from finding him. She wanted to see him again, to talk with him and thank him. In a sea of chaos and uncertainty, she knew Caleb Pierce was a rock that could not be moved.

Her search for Caleb ended abruptly when Lindsey approached Father Judge, the priest. "Where is Mr. Pierce?" she asked anxiously.

"Pierce is gone," answered the old man wistfully, fumbling for something in his pocket.

Lindsey was stunned. "Where did he go?" she managed at last.

"Downriver. He pulled out with his team last night." He drew a leather pouch from his pocket and placed it in Lindsey's hand. "He wanted me to give you this," explained the priest. "He said it should buy you enough grub to make it through the winter. I'm not a betting man, but if I were, I'd wager that's all he had to give. That's the kind of man he is."

Indefinable emotions suddenly overwhelmed Lindsey and she began to cry softly. Feelings, mysterious and unexplained, were playing like music on the strings of her soul.

"There, there child," comforted the priest. "Things will work out fine for you if you will put your trust in God." He put a hand on her shoulder and the two began walking slowly back toward the river front.

"Pierce asked me to find you a place to stay," Father Judge offered. "There's a little cabin on the outskirts of town that may be suitable. A few cabins opened up when that last bunch fled Dawson," he explained. "Word is that they only made it to Fort Yukon before the river froze up."

"Why did they leave?" she inquired.

"There's no grub here," replied the priest, "at least not enough to feed so many. You'd be wise to purchase a grubstake while there's still time."

Caleb Pierce was not altogether the rock that Lindsey supposed. He was a conqueror to be sure, a nomad who ruled the endless northern wilderness. He had known trial and hardship and had been molded by them, shaped into a living legend. He had braved the high mountain passes and crossed the frigid, swollen rivers. He was respected by men, both white and native, and his name was whispered around a thousand campfires. But Caleb Pierce was no rock, because a wisp of a girl, a dark-haired, dark-eyed beauty had deeply shaken him.

Pierce picked up his team and sled over on Hunker Creek, where a friend had been boarding them. They were wolf-dog hybrids, each carrying a percentage of wild stock in his lineage. They were large animals and fast, and no finer team ever ran the Yukon. When he left Dawson, the temperature plummeted to fifty below zero. The Interior region was captive once again, held prisoner by the iron grip of deadly cold.

Pierce moved carefully along the Yukon, stopping every few hours to rest his dogs. When the temperature fell to fifty or sixty below zero, an error in judgment could cost a man his life. Such a cold snap could last for a day or two, or settle in for three or four weeks.

Hardship was a way of life for Pierce and for those who lived on the frontier. While the newcomers to this land huddled around their wood stoves and shivered in their bunks, the frontiersmen freighted supplies and trapped for furs in the loneliest outreaches of the north.

Circle City, or what was left of it, lay quiet now under the clear arctic sky. The northern lights shimmered brilliantly across the heavens, but the inhabitants of Circle did not look up. There was trouble brewing here, and Big Mike Teague was at the heart of it.

The little boomtown was all but abandoned when the first rumors of a new strike drifted down from Dawson. A few hearty souls with good prospects stayed on, but the discontent and restless headed upriver. There had been a mad scramble to evacuate Dawson City before freeze-up because of the lack of provisions. Some sixty people headed downriver toward St. Michael on a steamship, hoping to get out of Alaska that fall. They had run out of money, provisions and the will to continue, and their hardships had only begun. After a torturous ordeal down the ice-choked Yukon, they were forced to put in for the winter at Circle City.

It was late evening when Caleb Pierce reached Circle. He made camp on the north side of the river and then approached the little boomtown cautiously. He was respected here but certainly not appreciated. The frontiersman had found gold somewhere in this wilderness, but would not disclose its whereabouts. Some admired him and some resented him, but nobody dared to cross Caleb Pierce.

Another man heavily resented here in Circle City was Big Mike Teague. He was a liar and a braggart, but none dared to tell him so. He was built like a mountain, huge and heavy, and the miners walked softly around him. To the lawless town of Circle City he had come, bringing with him guile and hatred, cruelty and fear.

Teague sat at a bar in a nameless saloon in town with his back to the door. A pistol on his belt and a knife in his boot made the giant even more formidable. Every man in the tavern would have liked to whip Mike Teague, for they all despised him. Some knew him as a thief, a scoundrel and a hooch runner on the lower Yukon, but everyone knew that he had robbed the poor Grahams.

Teague was beginning his evening ritual of intoxicating himself when a strong hand seized him and jerked him backward off the stool. The huge man landed flat on his back on the sawdust-covered floor. The little saloon was suddenly as silent as a tomb. Teague reached for his gun, but Pierce's was already in his hand.

"I should do Alaska a favor Teague, and shoot you right now," growled Pierce. "Pull that shootin' iron out real slow now, and toss it over by the piano." The big man complied. Pierce slid his own gun down the counter to the barkeep.

"Where's the money, Teague?" Pierce demanded.

Mike Teague cursed the frontiersman bitterly as he struggled to his feet. He had boasted freely amongst the lower element in Circle City of robbing the Grahams. Now his time of reckoning had come.

Fights were a common occurrence in the boomtowns along the Yukon, from Dawson City to Fortymile, and from Fort Yukon to Circle City. This however, would be no ordinary scrap. Two of the territory's toughest fighters were locking horns in a saloon just south of the Arctic Circle, and it promised to be a bloody, ferocious battle.

Word spread like wildfire to the other saloons in town, and soon most of Circle City was watching. Mike Teague was powerful and heavy, but the man in buckskin was quick and cunning. The giant rained heavy, reckless blows in Pierce's direction, but seldom connected. Caleb's punches, on the other hand, were well-timed and accurate. Except for the four log walls and the heavy bar, the saloon soon became a shambles. The owner however, was not disturbed, as he had a front row seat and was enjoying the fracas.

After a while, Teague became desperate. He was gasping for breath, his face and eyes red and swollen. The crowd suddenly grew silent when a knife glittered in his huge hand. "I'm gonna kill you Pierce!" he growled. Somebody swore. Teague charged at Caleb with the blade, but the nimble frontiersman eluded him. Teague slashed and hacked and lunged at Caleb, who managed to stay just out of reach. Other miners offered their knives to Pierce, but he dared not pull his eyes away from Teague. The big man worked Caleb into a corner and went in for the kill. He stabbed wildly at Pierce, who just managed to sidestep and catch Big Mike's wrist.

Suddenly there was a loud snap, and the big man bellowed like a bull. The knife dropped into the sawdust and Teague's wrist dangled limply at a queer angle. Caleb swung with all his might, and the giant staggered back and fell. The miners roared. Quick as a cat, the frontiersman was on top of Teague with the knife, bringing it to bear on the big man's throat. This was the moment of truth.

"Don't kill me," begged Teague.

"Where's the money you took off the Graham's?" demanded Caleb.

"I don't have it," Teague wheezed.

"Where is it then?"

"I drank it away," Teague confessed.

Caleb pressed the cold blade down to show he meant business.

"Please don't kill me," whimpered Big Mike.

Pierce considered his options for a moment. Finally, he took the knife and flung it toward the log wall, where it stuck tightly. The miners roared again and applauded as Pierce rose, retrieved his pistol from the bar and left the establishment.

CHAPTER

6

News spread quickly up and down the river that Caleb Pierce had whipped Big Mike Teague. The next freighter to come up the river carried the important news on to Fortymile and Dawson City. Pierce had licked Teague in a fair fight it was said and had broken his arm to boot.

While the citizens of Circle City now boasted of his exploits, Pierce slipped quietly away into the frigid lonely Arctic. He headed for the Chandalar River country, where the fur was prime and the game plentiful. Teague on the other hand, holed up in Circle City, licking his wounds. Unfortunately, his recent thrashing only served to nurture the hate and evil within him. Already he was planning to retaliate, and when he did, Pierce would pay with his life.

In Dawson City, Lindsey Graham had ravished the hearts of a thousand miners. Months and years in the forbidding north had bred a legion of lonely men. She was lovely, young and innocent, an elegant rose in a desolate wasteland. The men flocked around Lindsey, lavishing gifts and praise upon her.

She was now receiving marriage proposals daily, both oral and written, from wealthy gold kings and hopeless ne'er-do-wells.

In all her glory and popularity now as the Queen of Dawson City, a small inner voice cautioned her to beware. The same eerie foreboding she had first experienced in Skagway haunted her. It was odd that in the midst of all this masculine attention, she felt strangely insecure and alone. Her brother was gone. His body now lay under the caribou moss near an Indian village far up the Yukon. Her father's health was failing. He seemed consumed by gambling now, having been spoiled by an early run of good luck. He moved back and forth among the gambling dens and casinos in Dawson, and she seldom saw him.

Caleb Pierce had walked right out of her life without a word. He was somewhere in the territory of Alaska, alone and wandering. She had been so preoccupied here in Dawson that she neglected the one man to whom she owed her life. Now he was gone and she would probably never see him again.

There was a rumor floating around Dawson now of a tremendous fight over in Circle City. It was said that Caleb Pierce had whipped Big Mike Teague soundly and broken the big man's arm. Just the thought of Mike Teague sent a shiver down Lindsey's spine. She could scarcely imagine the two powerful men fighting. Teague was a huge man, but Caleb was as strong as an ox. Hadn't he dragged her father nearly a hundred miles on a sled? Hadn't she seen him shoulder a huge pack and walk up the side of a steep mountain in Skagway? And it was Caleb who had pulled her out of the roiling Yukon current at Five Finger Rapids.

Weeks passed, and things began to grow desperate in Dawson City. Food became extremely expensive in town and prices rose higher daily. Days grew shorter and the temperature plummeted ever lower. The sun made a brief appearance on the distant horizon each day, but by mid afternoon it grew dark.

By the time Miss Graham bought her supplies for the winter, there was very little left in town to be had. Two sacks of flour and a bag of beans, a tin of lard and a sack of dried apples were all she could afford. The gold Caleb left for her was gone now. Her father had been borrowing from the poke of dust and nuggets to support his gambling addiction. The gold barons were generous however, and gladly paid for her meals just to be in her presence.

The Grahams' tiny cabin was drafty at best, but the miners kept it well stocked with firewood. They were fortunate to have a cabin at all, for many in Dawson were still sleeping in canvas tents and on benches in the saloons and hotels.

One by one, the cafes closed their doors because they had run out of food to serve. Some unscrupulous citizens in Dawson hoarded stashes of flour and bacon in hopes of reselling their goods later in the winter at exorbitant prices. There were those in Dawson who had little or no food left by midwinter, but there were no beggars on the streets. Those who had none quietly starved, or succumbed to disease in their weakened condition. Typhoid fever and scurvy, brought on by malnutrition, claimed once-hardy bodies and ravaged them.

In the midst of starvation and despair, the parties never ceased along Front Street. There was still plenty of whiskey, and an abundance of gold to buy it. Pianos played and the dance hall girls swayed far into the night, every night.

They say that jealousy is as cruel as the grave and it was jealousy that ended Lindsey Graham's brief reign as the Queen of Dawson City. There was a certain young lady in town named Susan Bennett, who danced at the Monte Carlo. She was a pretty girl, but devious, and she had eyes for a frontiersman named Caleb Pierce. She had spoken with him on occasion and they had danced once at a dance hall in Circle City. Miss Bennett was smitten with him and deeply resented Lindsey Graham's rapid rise to prominence among the belles of Dawson. She knew Miss Graham had been with Caleb for weeks on the trail, a predicament many women would have appreciated. And now, it seemed that every man in Dawson was taken with her. They flocked around her like vultures.

Miss Bennett had approached Caleb when he brought the Grahams into Dawson. He was cordial but distant, and instinctively she knew that he had strong feelings for Lindsey. Frustrated now and heartbroken, Miss Bennett began to spread rumors about the Grahams. Ugly, vicious rumors spread down Front Street and throughout Dawson about Lindsey Graham and Caleb Pierce. Another rumor labeled her father as a card cheat and a thief. No one confronted him on either issue, but his associates were suddenly suspicious of him.

Joe Hanson, a miner who had a promising claim on Bonanza Creek, had recently been quite successful. He was fond of the dance hall girls who worked at the Monte Carlo and especially enamored with this new girl in town, Lindsey Graham. When his men hit bedrock with an exploratory shaft, it quickly became evident that Joe was now a very wealthy man. Gold nuggets gleamed in the pans he was washing out, and in the heaps of gravel that had accumulated on his claim. As was customary when a miner struck it rich, Joe Hanson went on a spree.

Down Front Street Joe and his trio of jubilant laborers marched, shouting and hooraying the town. They turned in at the Northern Saloon and bought drinks for everyone in the house. Then it was on to the Pioneer, where drinks and cigars were purchased for all. From saloon to saloon they went, gathering friends along the way to share in the spree. The celebration came to crescendo at the glorious Monte Carlo, where three rounds of drinks were offered, all courtesy of Joe Hanson. There was lively music, and the miners danced until they were exhausted.

Again and again, Joe Hanson danced with Lindsey, who had come to the Monte Carlo for dinner with the Lucky Swede. Susan Bennett, who also danced at the Monte Carlo, became infuriated as she watched Lindsey dance with this new king of the Klondike. When the hour grew late and some of the miners began to filter out, Joe Hanson called all the girls together.

"How would you gals like to go up to my claim tonight and get some nuggets?" he offered. A chorus of squeals and cries of delight were his answer. The Monte Carlo was quickly deserted as the ladies scattered to find warmer clothing and the men went to harness the dog teams.

It was a grand procession that made its way up the river toward the claims. Half a dozen screaming girls and eleven drunken miners broke the silence of the cold arctic night. Laughing and shouting, they mushed up Bonanza Creek under a brilliant full moon.

The party unloaded at Hanson's shanty and began to examine the piles of gravel. One by one, Joe took the girls and dug for nuggets in the rich gravel, making an elaborate show of the whole affair. In the middle of this ceremony, Hanson strode into his dark hovel of a cabin and emerged with a can. It was a tobacco tin, and he proudly displayed it for each of the ladies to see. It contained seven pounds of gold nuggets.

After a time, he returned it to the cabin and continued with the next girl, looking for gold nuggets. He gave each of the girls three nuggets but had something else in mind for Lindsey. With a lantern, he descended down into his exploration shaft. After several minutes he emerged with a mining pan filled with gravel, which he gave to Lindsey. Everyone crowded into the dimly-lit shanty to observe as Joe carefully washed out the gravel. When he was finished, the girls gasped at what they beheld in the bottom of the pan. There were several nuggets of various sizes glistening in the light of the coal oil lantern, and a handful of gold dust.

"That's for you Miss Lindsey," Hanson beamed. "All of it. There's about a hundred dollars worth, I reckon." He poured the precious metal into a small leather pouch and handed it to her. There was a big cheer for Lindsey, and then one for Joe Hanson.

"Thank you! Thank you Joe," said Lindsey as she came near. She kissed him on the cheek, and there was another cheer as his faced blushed a deep red.

"That made it all worthwhile," Joe declared.

It was a wonderful grand finale to a spectacular evening, the night of Joe Hanson's spree.

The next day was a dark one in Dawson, and it wasn't for lack of sunlight. It was dark because of a robbery, the robbery of a good man. Joe Hanson's tobacco tin had been stolen, the can that contained seven pounds of gold nuggets.

Robbery was a common occurrence in the lawless towns of Skagway and Dyea and was not unheard of in the Alaska boomtowns along the Yukon. In Canada however, it was a rare thing. The Northwest Mounted Police ruled Dawson City with an iron hand, as well as the upper Yukon and the Chilkoot Trail. There were trivial misdemeanors which one could expect in a hard-drinking town of thirty-five hundred, but robbery was a rare occurrence and a serious offense.

To rob a miner of his gold was to rob a man of his dream, his very life. Weeks, months and even years in the cold, dark North Country took a steep toll on a man. Years of hard work, loneliness and privation were represented in Joe Hanson's can of nuggets. The miners around Dawson were appalled at the news of the stolen gold, and each could identify with Hanson's great loss. There was a thief walking among them. It was declared by one and confirmed by all that the robber should be hanged when apprehended.

Inspector Jonathon Conway and his troop of Canadian Police were on the case immediately. The premises around Hanson's claim were thoroughly combed for clues, but miners were moving up and down Bonanza constantly. All of those involved in the foray to Bonanza Creek the previous night were questioned extensively. It certainly must have been one of them, the police were convinced, but the thief had been careful. There was absolutely no evidence that would indict anyone.

Two days passed and it became increasingly evident that Hanson would never recover his gold. He posted a hundred dollar reward for information, but none was forthcoming. Joe had nearly given up hope when an envelope was found in the Monte Carlo with Jonathan Conway's name on it.

The envelope was taken to the police barracks where it was opened and the note read by Inspector Conway. It was an anonymous note in fine handwriting, and it identified who had taken the gold.

Lindsey Graham was handsomely dressed and preparing to go out for a night on the town when the visitors came.

"Ma'am, may we have a word with you?" asked Inspector Conway.

"Certainly. Come in," she invited, supposing the police had come for more routine questioning.

"I have a search warrant for your cabin, Miss Graham," Conway declared. "Would you mind if we look around a bit?"

"Certainly, you may. I have nothing to hide," she answered.

The Mounties began to search the little cabin. Inspector Conway watched the girl carefully as the others searched. *She seemed so calm*, he reasoned. She was either a brilliant actress... or she was innocent.

"Look here Sir!" said a young officer as he pulled something from under the bed. It was Joe Hanson's tobacco tin and in it were the stolen nuggets. The men talked excitedly, but Lindsey could scarcely hear them. It seemed as if she were in a dream, a nightmare, and could not awaken. Where was her father now when she needed him?

The Northwest Mounted Police placed Lindsey Graham under arrest and escorted her to their headquarters. She was placed in a solitary cell away from the other prisoners, for they were all men. She could hear the shouts of the miners as they gathered outside to observe. They were astonished that the Queen of Dawson, the most beautiful girl in all the North Country, was a thief.

Lindsey's father was also brought to police headquarters and thrown in a cell with three ruffians. They batted him around for a few minutes until he collapsed in a corner. Outside, a mob of angry miners was gathering. It was fortunate for Miss Graham that there was a strong military presence in Dawson. In other mining camps, she was likely to have been hanged, woman or not.

Joe Hanson came down from his work on Bonanza Creek to retrieve his stolen gold. Together with Conway, he confronted Lindsey. The hour was growing late by this time and the girl was exhausted.

"I never dreamed in a million years you was a thief, Miss Graham," began Hanson. "I would have given you all the gold you wanted girl, if you'd just asked."

"I'm no thief, Joe," she answered. "I've never stolen anything in my life."

"Then how come my gold was under your bed?" he countered.

"I don't know," she sobbed.

"It was your pa then, I reckon. They say he's a card cheat anyhow."

Lindsey became suddenly defiant. "My father has never cheated anyone, anywhere!" she exclaimed. "Nor would he stoop so low as to steal."

A question about the robbery was playing on Inspector Conway's mind, and it involved the anonymous note he had been given. Why had the writer of the note chosen to remain anonymous? The lawman inspected the message again carefully, noticing again the elegant penmanship. For some reason it reminded him of a woman's handwriting. The informant could have claimed a hundred dollar reward if he, or she, had come to the police, but for some reason had chosen not to do so. This didn't make sense.

Conway took Mr. Hanson aside and explained his concerns. An inner instinct told the inspector that the writer of the note might be the guilty party and that Miss Graham may have been framed. After a few minutes the interrogation was over and Lindsey was left alone in her cell. She was extremely worried about her father, but she couldn't see him and could not hear his voice.

Lindsey lay shivering in the cold cell considering her predicament. Just a few months earlier the Grahams had been on top of the world before setting out on this nightmare of an adventure. This terrible, unforgiving North Country had taken her brother from them. They had left Skagway with money and enough provisions, but now they were destitute. Their good name had been desecrated by an enemy they didn't even know. Now they were being held as criminals. How she hated this treacherous, inhospitable land!

CHAPTER 7

Toward midmorning the following day, Lindsey and her father were set free by the Northwest Mounted Police. Miss Graham was formally charged by Conway, but because the gold had been recovered and because of Mr. Graham's poor health, they were released. Where could they flee? They had no money to hire a freighter to take them outside Dawson.

The girl helped her father down Front Street. Most of the miners were out on the creeks working their claims, but those who weren't heckled the Grahams. Some laughed and joked as father and daughter passed by; others hurled obscenities at them. No word of kindness greeted them now, only words of rejection and disdain. It was apparent that all of Dawson had suddenly turned on them.

Thomas Graham was a very sick man. He had developed a deep cough and was running a high fever. They walked over to the hospital, where Father Judge examined him.

"Miss Graham, I'm afraid your father has consumption," sighed the priest. "There's a lot of it here in Dawson. Many of the men out on the claims won't see another spring. We've seen a lot of typhoid as well, but I'm praying your father doesn't have that too. This fever may be the early stages of pneumonia. I'll need to keep him here so I can care for him."

Lindsey was bewildered. "Father Judge," she said, "I have no money to pay for medical expenses."

"Don't fret, Miss Graham. God will meet our needs," assured the priest.

Lindsey stayed with her father for a time and then hurried back to her cabin. The log shanty was cold and dark and miserable. She tried to build a fire, but could not get the stove to draw. She succeeded only in filling the room with smoke. The miners had been so kind and helpful before, but now there was no one.

A policeman who was on his way out to Bonanza Creek happened by and was kind enough to help Lindsey. He started the fire, but said very little. "I wouldn't plan on going anywhere if I were you," he managed at last. "Inspector Conway says that as soon as your pa's better, we'll have your trial."

"There shouldn't even be a trial" she responded. "I didn't take Joe Hanson's gold."

"Well, you'll have to prove that to a jury." The policeman excused himself and went on about his business.

The weeks that followed were dreadful for Lindsey. While her father suffered in William Judge's makeshift hospital, she struggled for survival in the miserable cabin. It was more like a dungeon really. It was dark and lonely. She existed on beans and bannock bread and was grateful to have that. There were some out on the claims who had nothing. Her provisions were meager and certainly would not last the winter.

Thomas Graham grew worse as the days and weeks crawled by. Lindsey and Father Judge tended to him, but could only watch helplessly as he continued to weaken. Lindsey too, began to grow frail on the poor diet of bannock bread. Endless hours spent caring for her dying father was taking a toll on her own body.

Miss Graham's firewood pile diminished as the relentless cold continued. The miners, who once had fought for the privilege of cutting her firewood, were now negligent. No one spoke to her except the priest, and her father who would occasionally whisper to her. She was an outcast now, branded a thief by those who had once honored her. She had done nothing, but now all of Dawson treated her as if she had leprosy.

Out on the claims, the work continued quietly. Up on Bonanza and El Dorado Creeks, the miners were thawing and digging their way down through the permafrost. When the wind shifted, the eerie creaking of the windlasses could be heard in the town if one listened.

News of Lindsey Graham's crime traveled along the river as fast as the freighters could carry it, west from Dawson City along the winding Yukon and all the way to Saint Michael. In the opposite direction, word of her great transgression spread south from Dawson, toward the upper Yukon and over the Chilkoot Pass.

At Lake Bennet and Lake Lindeman, a multitude of potential prospectors huddled in the cold, waiting to besiege Dawson when the river broke up. A steady stream of humanity and goods trickled up and over the mountain passes all winter.

The trails to the Yukon were now littered with discarded possessions. Furniture, tools, broken sleds, and empty shipping crates now marred this once pristine wilderness. Tents and shanties along the trail provided shelter for those who had lost hope and could go no farther. A small, but steady stream of those who had gone broke trickled back to Skagway and Dyea.

Lindsey Graham was at her father's bedside when he passed from this life. This vicious, dreadful North Country and this wild rampage for gold had now claimed the lives of both her father and brother. A river of tears had fallen for Horace, but there were few left for their father. It seemed as if she were in a terrible nightmare and it would never end. From one tragedy to the next, she walked. Where was Father Judge's God now? She wondered.

Inspector Conway wasted no time in setting up a trial for Miss Graham. He was a practical man, and this trial was long overdue. At an impromptu hearing, he pulled Lindsey aside. "Miss Graham, it would simplify things considerably if you would just plead guilty. As a judge, I would certainly be more lenient if you told the truth."

"Inspector Conway," she answered, "if I were guilty, I would plead guilty. But I am not!"

"Oh, I'll bet not," he said disdainfully. "You Americans are nothing but a bunch of troublemakers."

The inspector had become convinced of the girl's guilt due to the following: If she had been framed as he had first thought possible, why had the informant, probably one of the dance hall girls, given her all of the gold? It would stand to reason that if the accuser had ever had the gold in her possession, she would have kept at least a fraction of it. It seemed more likely that the informant had witnessed the theft and merely chose to keep her identity hidden.

Lindsey Graham's trial was a grand occasion in Dawson City. The Monte Carlo Saloon and Dance Hall was the only building in town large enough to accommodate a reasonable crowd. Seats were given on a first come, first served basis, and the place was packed. Hundreds of miners stood outside the saloon, having come down from their claims to see that justice prevailed. The temperature hovered at twenty degrees below zero, and a chilling wind blew out on the river.

Inspector Conway and his band of Northwest Mounted Police were the law in Dawson City. He considered himself commander in chief, chief magistrate and foreign secretary in this frontier boomtown. Conway was a fair, no-nonsense officer who went by the book.

From the claims registration office he chose a jury of seven, all men and all of whom were miners. They were grave and serious men, speaking to no one, nor acknowledging the welcome of the crowd as they took their seats. The gravity of their appointment as jurors seemed to weigh heavily upon them all.

Inspector Conway entered and moved through the crowd and up onto the stage. The terrified defendant then entered the Monte Carlo, escorted by two Mounties. The crowd whispered to one another and some even taunted Lindsey verbally.

"Silence!" shouted Conway and those gathered grew quiet. "Anyone in the crowd who speaks out will be shown the door!"

"Miss Graham, you have been formally charged with stealing Joe Hanson's seven pounds of gold. May I remind you again that if you will confess to this mischief, the court will certainly be more lenient. How do you plead now?"

"Not guilty, sir," the girl answered bravely. There was a long, pregnant silence.

"Evidence," began Inspector Conway. "We do have a bit of evidence." He pulled the incriminating note from his pocket and read it aloud. "Heretofore," he continued, "the writer of this note has chosen to remain anonymous, but just this morning, the informant contacted me and has agreed to testify before us here today."

"Quiet!" warned Conway again as the room exploded with chatter. "I would like to call Miss Susan Bennett forward please."

All eyes turned toward the back of the Monte Carlo, where Miss Bennett rose to her feet. Lindsey turned as well, curious as to whom her accuser might be. But as she searched the crowd, she caught sight of a familiar face. It was the frontiersman, out in the midst of the crowd, smiling at her.

Caleb Pierce was conspicuous in the crowd of miners, most of whom had worn their best doodads for the special occasion. They were dressed in white shirts and bowler hats, with polished shoes and colorful vests. Pierce was dressed like a wild creature, wearing his buckskins, a fur parka and a fur hat. His easy smile mocked and shamed her. She now cared nothing for the miners, nor what they thought of her. However, to have Caleb Pierce see her in this predicament, penniless, starving and branded a thief was a bitter pill to swallow.

Susan Bennett made her way slowly through the crowd and up onto the stage to stand before almighty Conway. She glanced at the handpicked jury, a jury of Joe Hanson's peers. The crowd grew still.

"Miss Bennett, please explain in detail to the jury what you saw and what you know about Joe Hanson's stolen gold," guided Conway.

The witness pulled a handkerchief from her pocket and began to wipe her eyes. When she had gained her composure, she began. "It happened the night of Joe Hanson's spree," she said. "A bunch of us girls from the Monte Carlo went up to Bonanza with Joe and his men to pick up a few nuggets. Joe showed us his tobacco tin with the gold in it. We all passed it around and took a look, never dreaming that one of us was a thief." She turned her dark, mocking eyes on Lindsey.

"Well, the fellows were busy looking for nuggets," she continued, "and we were all about half drunk, but I saw Lindsey Graham slip out of Joe's shanty with that can of nuggets. She put them under some things of hers on the sled, and I never saw it again."

Lindsey was stunned by Susan Bennet's lies but could not find words to defend herself. What spirit possessed this woman to bring these false accusations against her?

"Miss Bennett," questioned Conway, "why haven't you come forward until now with this evidence?"

"I didn't want Lindsey..." she hesitated, "Miss Graham, to know that it was I who ratted on her. We've been very close friends since she came into Dawson, but I felt it would be the right thing for everybody if I came forward and told the truth."

Lindsey was dumbfounded. Never in her life had she felt so betrayed. She sat shaking her head, astonished by the lies she had just heard. She thought of the premonition, the forboding she had experienced when she first set foot on Alaska soil. Misfortune and disgrace were hers at last.

"Miss Graham, do you have anything to say for yourself?" asked Conway.

"I didn't take Joe Hanson's nuggets," she said softly.

"Miss Graham, you're going to have to speak up," chided Conway.

The crowd grew silent, anticipating the girls testimony.

"I said, I didn't take Joe Hanson's gold nuggets." The young woman was on the verge of tears. "I've never stolen anything in my life," she continued, but she was speaking only to Caleb

Pierce. She cared nothing for Conway or his self-righteous Mounted Police, or this Dawson City rabble.

Someone in the back of the Monte Carlo snickered and then the place erupted with a discourteous outburst of laughter.

"Silence!" demanded Conway, and the crowd quieted. "I believe the evidence is clear," said the lawman, satisfied now with the way things were shaping up. "But we'll let the jury deliberate and give us their decision in this matter."

The men of the jury circled their chairs on the stage and talked in hushed tones for no more than five minutes. Lindsey was forced to stand on the stage of the Monte Carlo with Conway, an object of ridicule and humiliation for all to see. When the jury had concluded their reasoning, a representative approached and conferred with Inspector Conway. The boisterous Monte Carlo was graveyard silent, as each observer listened intently for the verdict.

Inspector Conway stood to his feet and addressed all present. "This court finds Lindsey Graham, of Seattle, Washington, guilty of stealing Joe Hanson's gold." He hesitated to finish until the crowd had quieted.

"It is with great difficulty that I now pass judgement on this young woman. But the law must be upheld, and there will be no exceptions." He paused. "This court sentences Miss Lindsey Graham to seven years in the Vancouver women's reformatory. One year for each pound of gold that was stolen. She will be escorted to Skagway by my men, and then on to Vancouver. Let this be a lesson and a warning to all citizens of Dawson City. Behavior of this sort will not be tolerated in the Canadian Territories."

Lindsey was shocked. Had he actually sentenced her to prison? Was this whole thing Conway's big joke? But the crowd began to file out of the building, and a Mountie came and took her by the arm. She searched the crowd for Caleb Pierce, but the frontiersman had vanished.

CHAPTER

8

Lindsey was ushered back to police headquarters and placed in a cell. The Mounties only laughed when she asked to go to her cabin for a few things. "Ma'am, I don't know if you noticed," explained one young man, "but you're a prisoner now. You don't just come and go as you please."

"Where will they take me now?" she asked. "What are they going to do with me?"

"Well, I heard Inspector Conway say that we're to take you up the Yukon to the Chilkoot Pass," he answered. "We'll take a dog team out of here in a few days and then turn you over to the authorities at the Chilkoot border station. I guess from there you'll be escorted to Skagway, get on a steamer and then head south to Vancouver."

"To prison," Lindsey breathed.

"Yes ma'am, that's right. Just because you're a girl doesn't mean you can break the law and get away with it. There are consequences for your actions. Of course there are women breaking the law around Canada all the time. They send most of the bad ones to Vancouver, the killers, cutthroats and such.

Some thieves get thrown in there too, I reckon. Like yourself. Probably ain't one of them prettier than you though, I'd bet."

The young man was in a mood to talk, and she did nothing to stop him.

"It's a women's prison Missy, or reformatory as they call it, but don't let that fool you. They've had riots in there, and murders and such, but at least you won't starve. Some say it's worse than the fella's prison, but I can't believe it." He was quiet for a moment. "They say Caleb Pierce was at the trial today," he continued.

"Yes. I saw him," she said.

"I hear he whipped the devil out of Big Mike Teague down in Circle City. Had a knife on Teague's throat, they say, and wasn't man enough to finish the job. I'd have given my right arm to see that fight. Teague's gonna kill him though. I know he will. He won't do it over here in Canada because he's scared to death of us Mounties. He'll bushwhack him over in Alaska one of these days. Anything goes over there, and Teague don't fight fair."

"A lot of these miners despise Caleb Pierce," he continued. "He's got a good placer mine somewhere in these mountains and won't tell a soul about it. Just disappears into the wilderness now and then and shows up later with a poke of that queer gold. That bothers a lot of people. Some say he's a squaw man, but everybody's afraid to ask him about it. Of course, there's a lot of rumors flying all around this country about a lot of folks. Conway says Pierce is a fine man though, and he's a good judge of character."

"Oh my. He certainly is," she retorted.

"They say Pierce is a tough customer and I know it's true, but I wouldn't mind going a couple of rounds with him myself. You see, I used to be quite a boxer before I came up here to Dawson." He proceeded to give her a brief history of his boxing career.

They talked for a while longer and then the Mountie wandered off to talk to someone else.

The afternoon and evening passed slowly. The other prisoners came in from cutting and splitting firewood just after dark. They mocked and taunted the beautiful new prisoner as they filed past to their cells. Lindsey lay down on her bunk and covered her head with a blanket, succumbing to the weariness of the day.

When she awoke, all was quiet. It was dark in the jail, but a faint light glimmered around a corner. Something had awakened her, a noise she could not identify. Strange noises came from the room with the light. Something big and heavy slammed against the wall. A man groaned and she heard something hit the floor. There was a long, awkward silence. Then she saw a man walking toward her with a lantern. Her heart was racing and she was trembling uncontrollably. He came to the door of her cell, and she recognized the frontiersman.

"Caleb!" she gasped.

"Let's go Lindsey, Now! No time to talk."

"Hey! What's going on down there?" shouted one of the prisoners. The other prisoners awoke and began shouting as Caleb unlocked the door. He took Lindsey by the hand and led her down the hall and past the lighted room. In it were two Northwest Mounted Policemen, tied and gagged. When they reached the front door, a full blast of an angry arctic winter hit her. She was not prepared for the cold. Behind them they heard shouting and cursing. She pulled away from him.

"Caleb, I can't do this!" she cried. "I can't run from the law!"

"Halt!" shouted a Mountie who appeared in the doorway with a pistol. The frontiersman dropped the lantern and swept the girl up into his arms, and then he was running. There were gunshots behind them as the policemen scrambled from their barracks. Caleb felt a searing pain in his left arm, and knew that he'd been hit. Amid the chaos and confusion, a mountie's bullet had sliced his arm from shoulder to elbow. This gunplay was more than Pierce had bargained for. His original thought was that busting the girl out of the Dawson City jail might be a bit of fun. But the Mounties didn't appreciate Pierce's sense of humor apparently, and were playing for keeps.

Lindsey was helpless in Caleb's arms as he raced toward the river. Several of the Mounties raced after them on foot, while others ran for the dog teams. Even with the girl in his arms, the pursuing police could not gain on the frontiersman.

As Lindsey was carried along, held prisoner in his iron grip, she could feel the great strength of desperation within him. She had disappointed and disobeyed him so many times and yet he still cared about her. His help at other times had been obligatory, but this was different.

When they reached the river, Caleb's team was already in motion. A tall, athletic native man ran beside the lead dog. Caleb leaped down the river bank and placed Lindsey on the sled.

"Hike! Hike!" he shouted, and the team exploded into the harness. The wind was ferocious on the river and Lindsey was not dressed for the cold, but they couldn't stop. It was imperative that they get a good lead on the Mounties.

A hundred yards downriver, another dog team was stationed. The tall native was already there, untying the lead dog. He leaped aboard his sled, and his team was quickly abreast of Caleb's. The native presented a frightening spectacle, dressed in his fur clothing, his wild black hair trailing along in the wind. He was cackling in a language foreign to Lindsey, and it appeared that he was giving Dawson City a piece of his mind.

When the fugitives were well out of rifle range, Caleb slowed the team. On the sled was a bed of caribou skins that the men had arranged for Lindsey. She crawled down between the warm skins and Caleb carefully covered her face.

"Go to sleep now, Lindsey," he advised. "We've got a long ride ahead of us." But of course the girl could not sleep. A thousand questions played havoc in her mind. Where was he taking her? Could they outrun the Mounties? And if they did, would they always be fugitives? She must trust the frontiersman, she decided at last. He was not an impulsive man, and surely must have a plan. She uncovered her face for a moment.

Caleb's team of twelve was running well. They were tall, rangy animals, certainly not fat. Nor were they gaunt. This was the team of wolf hybrids that the miners spoke so highly of. It was said that they were the fastest in the Yukon valley, but the Mounties had fast dog teams of their own. They selected dogs from the finest Husky and Malamute bloodlines from all across Canada, and trained them to perfection. These were the teams which were now in pursuit, two close behind and two farther back.

Several miles from Dawson, Caleb slowed the team to a moderate pace, but a pace they could endure for hours. Occasionally, a tiny light glowed behind them on the river, a lantern on one of the police sleds. The Mounties were dressed for the cold, but even their heavy wool clothing was no match for the arctic wind, which ripped down the bed of the river. While their dog teams were fast and well conditioned, the

Mounties weren't all that excited about catching up with Pierce. His boldness and audacity had taken them by surprise, and a confrontation with the famed explorer might not be pleasant. For the sake of pride however, they continued the chase. His reckless kidnapping of a Canadian prisoner and ransacking the Dawson City jail could not be overlooked.

Lindsey occasionally stole a glance at the frontiersman. The cold was brutal, yet he appeared to take it in stride. When he became chilled, he would step off of the sled and run to keep warm. He would run like this for long periods of time, never releasing his grip on the sled, yet running to lighten the load and conserve the strength of the dogs.

The wind abated a little and the frontiersman, gasping for breath, caught on to the back of the sled. He was drenched with sweat, as he had been running with no rest. The loss of blood from his wound was robbing him of his strength, but their prospects for escape were looking good. After a few moments, he leaned forward and looked down at the girl he had kidnapped.

"Warm enough?" he asked.

"I'm cozy," she said, "but it looks like you're about all in."

"I'm just getting started," he laughed. "We're in for a long haul tonight."

"Are the Mounties still behind us?" she asked.

"They're still about half a mile back," he informed her. "We caught em' by surprise and got a good head start. I think we'll make it, if our sled holds together and if the dogs don't do something crazy." He looked back up the river. "I'll bet old Conway's back there on one of those sleds, giving me a good cussing." He grinned at the thought.

"Caleb, why are you doing this?" she asked. "Why did you come for me?"

"Well, Sam and I were just looking for some fun," he teased. He was quiet for a moment. "I couldn't stand the thought of you wasting away in a filthy Canadian prison somewhere. Besides, Conway's trial was a sorry excuse for justice, in my opinion. They had you figured guilty before it ever began."

"What will happen if they catch us?" she asked.

"I expect there'll be a little gun fight, but I'm sure hoping it doesn't come to that. I've always gotten along pretty good with the Mounties."

The dogs kept up the same grueling pace until the wee hours of the morning. The exhausted girl slept fitfully in the sled while her two guardian angels carried her closer to safety and freedom.

When they had well outdistanced their pursuers, Caleb halted the dog team to give them a breather and rearranged the bedding on the sled. The tall native stopped his team behind Caleb's and approached Lindsey. He stared at her for a moment.

"Are you Pierce's woman?" he asked bluntly. She was startled by his bold question.

"Well, no" she answered. "I mean, not exactly." The native just grunted and stood there staring. "Where are you men taking me?" she inquired.

"Aleyeska," he replied.

Alaska! They were heading for the border then. They were taking her into the heart of Alaska Territory, that wild and lawless region known as the Interior.

Toward first light they passed Fortymile, a little boomtown at the mouth of Fortymile River. Once alive with prospectors, the village was now nearly deserted. Most of the inhabitants had abandoned their claims and headed upriver to Dawson.

Lindsey was awake when the reached the border of Alaska Territory. Caleb stopped the team and looked back up the Yukon toward Dawson and the distant mountains. "Farewell Canada," he lamented softly. "I shall never see you again."

Lindsey considered his words for a minute.

"Caleb, what about your cabin on the Stewart River, and your trapline on the Pelly?" she asked.

"What's done is done," he answered. "Alaska is big enough for me. Besides, Canada's getting too civilized for outlaws like us."

When they were well across the border, which consisted of a small sign on the river nailed to a piece of driftwood, they stopped to build a fire. The frontiersman removed his fur parka and draped it around Lindsey's shoulders.

"Caleb, you're bleeding!" exclaimed Lindsey, when she noticed his arm. The sleeve of his buckskin shirt was stained with blood from his shoulder to his wrist.

"Just a scratch, I believe," he responded.

"That's no scratch, Caleb. You're hurt."

"Well, it doesn't hurt so much, and the bleeding's stopped. I think it might be best if we don't tamper with it."

There were a few supplies in the front of the native's sled, and from this little cache the native pulled out some smoked salmon and tea. Caleb laid the fish on a rock near the fire to warm while the native, whom Caleb called Sam, brewed the tea. The wind had abated and the temperature was rising.

"Chinook come," said the native with the slight hint of a smile.

"What Is a Chinook?" asked Lindsey.

"A warm wind," answered Caleb. "Usually out of the south or sometimes southwest. We'll be moving northwest along the river most of the day, so if Sam's right, we'll have the wind at our backs for a change. Lindsey," he said as he caught her eyes, "There are a lot of things I want to talk to you about, but we'll have to hit the trail soon. I've got a cabin about a day's journey from here. We should get in there tonight, if things go well."

Caleb divided the smoked salmon, and he and Lindsey shared tea from a tin cup. "This salmon is so good," said Lindsey. "I haven't had meat in a month."

"It's squaw candy," said Sam with a chuckle. "We eat it every day. Makes squaw big and fat."

"You'll be eating a lot of it where we're going," said Caleb. Sam's chinook was already beginning to blow when they broke camp.

Inspector Conway was compelled to end the chase at the border. Legally, he had no jurisdiction in Alaska Territory, and he was a man who went by the book. A few more miles across the border were meaningless out here in the wilderness, but he realized he had little chance of catching Pierce. His team was too fast, and this he had proved on his flight from Dawson. And even if he did catch Pierce, Conway realized the frontiersman would put up a fight. Conway was a tough hombre in his own right, but a scrap with Pierce might not be a bargain.

All day the fugitives followed the river to the north and west. Toward dark, they left the river and headed up into the mountains. The trail was steep and rough and had not been used all winter. To make things easier for the dogs, the men strapped on snow shoes and broke out a trail before them.

It was late when the party reached the deserted cabin. It was cold and dark inside, but Caleb soon had a fire going. Sam fed the dogs and tied them while Caleb and the girl unpacked the sled. Lindsey was surprised to find some of her things from her cabin in Dawson stowed in a sack on the sled.

"We stopped by your cabin before we went to the jail," explained Caleb. "Father Judge showed us where you lived. Couldn't take everything, but we picked up a few of your clothes and a couple of candles."

"That's about all I have left," she admitted.

"We really should have a look at that arm of yours," she told Caleb.

"I said it was just a scratch," he told her firmly. "I believe I can take care of myself."

Lindsey was a bit offended at Caleb's sharp remark. She was only trying to help him, to repay the kindness he had shown her. He certainly had every right to be irritable after what he had endured, but his sharp words stung.

"I beg your pardon, Miss Lindsey," he apologized, as if reading her thoughts. "I know you only want to help." He smiled at her. "Let's take a look at it first thing in the morning. I think Sam and I have about had it."

The men were exhausted, and soon collapsed on the floor to sleep, while Lindsey lay on the bunk. The winds of the chinook howled outside the cabin throughout the night. The tops of the tall white spruce and the sturdy birch shook with fury, while the dogs burrowed into the snow for protection from the gusts. The chinook lifted the loose snow from the vicinity and heaved particles against the walls of the cabin. Lindsey listened as the great wind scoured the cabin and blasted debris at its tiny windows.

She listened to the heavy breathing of the frontiersman and his native companion as they slept soundly. Why had he brought her here, up into these cold, desolate mountains? What would it be like to be Caleb's woman? Would his woman move with him from camp to camp for the rest of her life? Would she stay up and worry at night when he didn't come home, when he was out on the trail with his dogs? Would this wretched North Country one day claim the life of the frontiersman, as it had taken the lives of her brother and father?

CHAPTER 9

When she awoke the next morning, a fire crackling in the stove was the only sound. The ferocious winds of the chinook had abated at last. She arose and went to the window. The dogs and sleds were gone, and the men were nowhere to be found. All that remained behind was Caleb's buckskin shirt, soaking in a wooden bucket.

Lindsey felt compelled to go outside and survey her surroundings. The cabin was well built and sturdy, she observed, unlike the makeshift shanties and log shacks she had known in Dawson City. Several ricks of dry firewood leaned against the cabin's north side, like soldiers ready to do battle against the frigid winter. She spied a cache a hundred feet away, a tiny cabin on poles that was used for storing meat. Two other small structures not far from the cabin proved to be a privy and a smokehouse. In the smokehouse were rows of poles, still laden with smoked salmon. She pulled a filet off one of the poles and tasted it. In the four months she had lived in the Yukon, she had not tasted smoked salmon as good as this.

On the south side of the cabin she could see for miles on this clear day. Far below them lay the Yukon River Valley, winding its way north and west between ranges of mountains. Across the river, the sun made a brief appearance between two high, snow-clad mountains and then vanished.

Back in the cabin, Lindsey continued to explore. She found flour and sugar, rice, beans and coffee, dried apples, oatmeal, butter, tins of condensed milk, and much more. Along with the smoked fish, these provisions seemed more than adequate to see them through the rest of the winter.

There were tools in the cabin: axes, saws, an adze, a sledge and several knives. A stack of fur-stretching boards were leaning against one wall and a pile of tanned furs lay nearby. She looked carefully through the stack of wolverine, lynx, beaver, and river otter furs. There were also pelts of marten, silver and red fox and timber wolf, but other species she could not identify.

Above the doorway, a battered lever action rifle rested on two pegs, ready for a crisis. There were cartridge boxes on a crude table in the corner, and under this same table she found a few books. There was an old worn Bible, a book on the methods of mining and several journals. She took one of the journals and sat down on the bunk to read. What she found fascinated her.

They were Caleb's personal diaries. They revealed some of the places he had visited, interesting things he had seen and scrapes he had experienced. He wrote of periods of severe cold, instances of going hungry and encounters with the natives. He wrote not only of his adventures, but of his inner thoughts, his hopes and his observations. As she read through the morning and into the afternoon, she began to get a glimpse of who Caleb Pierce really was.

Darkness descended on the little cabin by mid-afternoon, and Lindsey lit a coal oil lamp to brighten things up. The stillness here was eerie. How she hated the silence and solitude of the north! She brought in a pot of snow from out back and put it on the stove to melt. The young woman washed out Caleb's shirt and hung it behind the stove to dry. As she made supper, she thought of the frontiersman. Would he be gone for a week, a month or even longer? And what did this man want from her? Why had he brought her here? How could she deny him anything he might ask of her? Not only had he saved her life, he had spared her seven years in prison.

A wolf howled not far from the cabin, a deep mournful cry that sent shivers up her spine. Another howled a moment later, closer this time. Soon, a chaotic chorus of barking and howling indicated that a large pack was bearing down on the cabin. With pounding heart, she began to look for things to pile against the door. Then she heard Caleb's voice and realized he had returned with his team of wolf-dogs.

She began to hurry supper as Caleb tended to the dogs, hoping that a hot meal might please him. At last he knocked on the door and she opened it for him.

"Hello, Lindsey," he greeted as he pulled off his fur parka.

"I was wondering about you," she told him. "I didn't know when you were coming back."

"I should have left you a note at least," he apologized. "I'm so used to thinking only of myself. I hope you weren't scared."

"The dogs frightened me. I thought they were wolves," she admitted.

"Whatever you're cooking there smells mighty good," he said, changing the subject.

"I hope you don't mind. I should have asked about using your food."

"That's all for you," he told her. "That's why I brought you up here. I knew there was a good grubstake at this cabin. I killed a caribou today, so we'll have fresh meat for a while. "Oh, and I brought some things from Sam's place, some berries and such."

Caleb came close to Lindsey and touched her cheek with his hand. "You look frail Lindsey," he observed. "This north country has been hard on you. And the loss of your loved ones has wounded you deeply."

Lindsey wanted to cry. Caleb's touch was gentle and his concern for her welfare moved her. He had been on the trail all day, certainly with many struggles and hardships of his own, but was thinking only of her.

"Caleb, you've been so good to me," she told him. "I resented your honesty at first, but I was foolish. We were all a bunch of greedy fools, except for you sir." She hesitated. "I owe my life to you, for what you've done for me and my family."

Caleb turned away and went to the cook stove. "All you owe me is supper," he stated, "and a game of cribbage afterward, if you're up to it."

"That would be lovely," she smiled. "But first, we'll need to take a look at that arm."

"It's mending just fine, Miss Lindsey," he told her.

"Let me look at it, Caleb. I may be a city girl, but I know about such things. My Aunt Ida was a nurse in her younger days, and I learned a bit from her." She paused. "Please let me help you."

"I think that would be all right," he conceded. Pierce realized that the wound needed some attention. He brought her a bottle of iodine and a clean rag. She poured a bit of the iodine into a tin cup and filled it with hot water. Caleb stood before her, not sure of what came next.

"Well?" she asked impatiently.

"Well what?"

"You'll need to take your shirt off, Mr. Pierce," she told him. This terrified the bashful frontiersman.

"I'd rather not. It might not be the honorable thing to do," he told her.

"I need you to either remove your shirt or we'll have to cut your entire sleeve off."

"How about this?" he offered. He slipped out his knife and sliced the sleeve from the wrist to the shoulder.

"You will soon be out of shirts, it appears," she scolded. "Now please sit down."

Lindsey carefully examined the gunshot wound. It was not terrible, but needed a thorough cleaning. The bullet had only grazed Caleb's arm but the wound was deep enough to cause substantial bleeding. All of Pierce's running when they fled Dawson had not helped. The skin was pink around the wound and hot to the touch. Her touch was gentle at first, and the tender, feminine attention was agreeable to the lonely explorer.

"I should get shot more often," he told her. "It kind of hurts, but it has its benefits."

"Yes you should," she agreed. "No point in growing old and grey and having children and grandchildren.

Then came the iodine and the cleansing.

"Ouch!" he exclaimed, but she continued. It was obviously painful and would be to anyone, but the scrubbing was necessary.

"I thought that frontiersmen were supposed to be tough," she said, with a mischievous smile.

"Where did you get that idea?" he inquired. "I'm not accustomed to torture, if that's what you mean.

"Caleb Pierce, I believe that under that hard armor of yours, you're nothing but a little boy."

"I expect you might be right. You're reading me like a book, Miss Lindsey."

Lindsey finished caring for Caleb's wound and then wrapped it carefully with clean cloth. The frontiersman excused himself to get water from the spring, while Lindsey finished supper. He brought in some steaks from the caribou and lay them in a skillet to fry.

"Caribou steaks are best," he explained, "if you cook them in their own fat. There's not much fat on a caribou, especially this time of year, but you'll usually find some on the back and rump. When you shoot a bou', don't shoot the big bulls; shoot a young bull or a barren cow."

"I'll keep that in mind," she said.

Together they sat and ate their fill, and then Lindsey cleared off the table while Caleb brought out the cribbage board.

"I could get used to this," said Caleb. "It's nice to have someone to talk to." He paused. "I don't know how many times I've come home to a cold, empty cabin."

"It's nice," she agreed. "Even with three thousand people in Dawson, I don't think I had a real friend I could trust and talk to, especially when they accused me. Everyone treated me as if I had leprosy, except Father Judge."

"William Judge has always been a good friend to me, Lindsey. He lived over in Fortymile for a while, before the big rush up to Dawson. I'm afraid he won't make it through another winter up here, though. He's really hard on himself."

"Caleb, do you believe I took Joe Hanson's gold?" she asked.

"I know you didn't take it, Lindsey," he answered. "Don't go back to Dawson and kill her, but it was Sue Bennett who stole Hanson's gold."

Lindsey was astonished. "But why?" she asked. "Why would she accuse me?"

"Jealousy," he answered. "I knew her back in Circle City. I heard that she was sweet on me, if you can believe that. We danced a time or two at a saloon over there. She was a pretty girl, but I couldn't pretend to love her." He paused. "Somehow, she got the notion that you and I fancied each other, and she saw red."

"Oh! That's ridiculous!" declared Lindsey.

"Is it?" he asked, and immediately regretted it. "I talk too much," he said, when she turned her eyes away. "Trouble is, I'm out here all alone most of the time. When I get around a friend, and I don't have many, I can't seem to shut up."

"I like it when you talk, Caleb," she replied. "You're the only one who has talked any sense to me since we left Seattle." She paused. "All of this talk about gold and this insane endeavor to conquer the Yukon and get rich has ruined me. I should never have left the city."

"I could never live in a city, Lindsey," he confided. "Even in a little boomtown like Circle or Fortymile. The shouting and cursing and that wretched excuse for music that they play down in the saloons is a vexation to my soul." He paused thoughtfully. "My music is the river running over the rocks and the sounds of the trumpeter swans and geese as they fly south in the fall; the howling of wolves and the wind in the treetops; the loons on the lakes and the mating calls of the moose in late September. That's my music."

"I could never grow accustomed to your music, Caleb," she said. "This stillness terrifies a city girl like me. Every time your sled dogs howl, I cringe inside." She paused. "There's a loneliness here in your mountains, an unearthly something that I can't explain. It seems as if all the forces of nature are against you, desperately trying to kill you. The never-ending cold, the treacherous rivers, the bears and wolves, even the insects are against you here. The ferocious winds, floods, earthquakes and avalanches are all an open grave just waiting for a tenderfoot to happen by. You're a conqueror, Caleb. You've fought all of these things and won, but I'm not as strong as you are."

"Lindsey, this is the way I see it," he countered. "You have to stop fighting this North Country and become a part of it. There's a place for you here in this wilderness if you're patient enough to find it. The same river that killed your brother brings the chinook and silver salmon in the summer and feeds thousands of people. The barren Fortymile country feeds hundreds of thousands of caribou. Steaks from one of these caribou is what we had for supper. The Yukon flats, far to the west of us, is a breeding ground for black flies and no-seeums, but also for ducks, geese and swans."

"Caleb, please don't tell me how wonderful this frontier is," she pleaded. "I don't belong here."

There was a long silence, and then the frontiersman spoke. "I have no money to buy passage home for you, Lindsey. And I wouldn't trust you to any of the freighters that are running the river right now."

"Caleb, I wouldn't ask you to help me any more that you already have. I'll work something out."

"I can get you enough gold this spring to buy passage on a steamer, if you can wait that long. I have a place in the upper Tanana country where I've found some gold. You'd have to help me wash it out though."

"Perhaps I could work my way back on a steamship," she suggested.

"Well, you won't see a steamer here until the first of June," he answered. "And there'll be a thousand broke and homesick cheechakos in Dawson, all begging to work for their passage home." He was silent for a moment. "No Lindsey, you'll need money. If you can just trust me one more time, we'll get you home, if that's what you really want."

"That is what I really want," she said. "I want to go home." She brushed an unruly lock of hair away from her face. "It's as if I've been here forever, Caleb. Going back seems like an impossible dream."

"What's at home for you Lindsey?" asked Caleb.

"I have an aunt and uncle in Seattle," she answered. "I know I could stay with them as long as necessary. Aunt Ida and Uncle Bert are swell. We've always been a close family. Do you have any family, Caleb?"

"No, but I do have some friends along the river here. A few of the prospectors out in the Fortymile country are friendly enough, but most of my friends are natives."

"What happened to your parents, Caleb? I hope you don't mind my asking."

"No, I don't mind," he answered. My parents were really fine folks. They were missionaries down on the lower Yukon... well, really all over the north. We moved all over the place, up and down the rivers, from the Brooks Range to the Wrangells. My mother was a lot younger than my father, but she loved him fiercely. I was almost fourteen when she died. My dad passed on a few years later. Dad was a real woodsman. He learned from the natives how to survive and cope with life in the wilderness. We trapped and built cabins, hunted, fished and ran dogs all over this territory."

"It sounds like you had some wonderful parents," she marveled.

"I sure did. I have a lot of good memories... no regrets." They were silent for a time, each content to bask in the presence of the other. After an enjoyable game of cribbage, Caleb pulled on the fur parka.

"You're not leaving are you?" Lindsey asked.

"I'm heading out to the bunkhouse for the night," he answered.

"Where's the bunkhouse?" she asked.

"Right out yonder," he said. "That building up on the poles. I'll make myself a warm bed up in that old cache."

"Caleb! I can't let you sleep outside. This is your cabin, not mine."

"I'll feel a lot safer out there," he said with a wink. Then he was gone.

CHAPTER

10

Lindsey was up long before daybreak, straightening the cabin and brushing her hair. She washed up and then started breakfast, humming an old tune from the past as she worked. Occasionally, she would peek out of one of the small windows to see if the frontiersman was out and about. There was something different about the girl today, something that even she did not recognize. For the first time in several months, joy, like a tiny flower was springing up in her barren heart.

Caleb was up early, too. Loneliness had been his loyal companion for years, but now it seemed to have vanished. After giving each of the dogs a salmon, he headed for the spring with an axe and two tin pails.

"Mornin', White Eyes," he said to one of the dogs when he returned with the water. He placed the water by the door of the cabin and then broke out the sled and moved it over to the cache. From the cache he brought down sacks of flour, beans, rice and salt. He added tins of coffee and tea to the pile on the sled. After harnessing the team, he went to the cabin.

"Mornin'!" he said with a big smile, as Lindsey opened the door. Lindsey Graham had never looked more beautiful to any man.

"Are you going somewhere?" she asked, dreading the thought of him leaving.

"No. We're going somewhere," he said.

"Where are we going, then?"

"Shopping," he stated with a grin.

"You're joking with me, Caleb," she said, shaking her head.

"We'll see if I am," he nodded back.

After a pleasant breakfast together, Caleb and Lindsey prepared to leave. He brought water for the cabin and filled the wood box while the girl washed the dishes and put them on the shelf. Outside, he made a place for Lindsey to sit amongst the supplies on the sled, and then they were off.

The frontiersman and his team chose a path that led away from the cabin to the north. It wound down gradually out of the mountains and crossed a series of frozen streams. Lindsey marveled at the skills of this man. He cracked no whip over the heads of the dogs like other freighters she had observed. Yet they ran, swift and true, obedient to every word of their master. It was as if they ran with joy and gave their all because of their great love for him.

Caleb had never known such happiness as this. A fine frosty morning, a good, fast team and the prettiest girl in all the North Country were more than any man could ask for. He loved this great wilderness with its pure, untouched forests, and the raw, boulder-strewn mountains. He marveled at the high, jagged peaks where the eagles nested and the mighty Dall rams contended for dominance. He wondered at the extensive herds of caribou that migrated across the barren hills and swollen rivers each year. Caleb Pierce was born in this great land. Here he would live... and here he would die.

On they flew across the hills until they reached Hard Luck Creek. They traveled northwest along the creek toward the Nation River, and reached their destination in the early afternoon. A cluster of makeshift cabins lay nestled quietly in a secluded valley. A canopy of wood smoke hung over the encampment and a score of sled dogs announced the arrival of the newcomers.

Lindsey was hesitant at first, and hung very close to the frontiersman. The natives quickly caught and tied their dogs, and then approached to welcome Caleb. They stared at Lindsey as if she were a novelty, for heretofore Pierce had always traveled alone. There were several young men among the clan, and they eyed Lindsey cautiously. Together with Caleb, they unloaded the sled and carried the supplies into the largest building. It was obvious that they were glad to see him. They pressed around him, shaking his hand and patting him on the back. Lindsey however, was a curiosity to them, and the squaws and young men stared at her and spoke to one another in low tones.

Caleb stated his mission to the elders in their native tongue, and they seemed very pleased. There were nods and gestures of approval among the entire group. There was business to be conducted, but a meal would be shared first in the crude community shelter.

Two of the squaws ladled out generous bowls of stew to Caleb and Lindsey, and then to everyone else. A tiny, brown-eyed girl with a small bowl of her own approached Lindsey and placed a timid hand on her leg. It was a gesture which seemed to say, "Don't worry, I'll be your friend."

Sam Titus joined the group with his beautiful young wife, and crowded in to greet Caleb and Lindsey. His wife, heavy with child, waddled across the room.

"I am Lilly Titus," she said in a friendly manner.

"I'm Lindsey," answered the newcomer with a smile. She turned to Caleb. "This is delicious," she said, indicating the food. "What is it?"

"It's moose head stew," he answered. "It's a delicacy here."

Suddenly, Lindsey was no longer hungry. Her stomach became queasy as she visualized a large pot with a moose head boiling in it. She looked down into the bowl suspiciously, looking for pieces of moose toungue, moose jaw or moose nose. The meat she held in her mouth was tough, and try as she might she couldn't swallow it.

"Are you all right, Miss Lindsey?" asked the frontiersman. "You look a little pale." Lindsey's throat became tight and she felt as if she might choke. She didn't want to offend any of Caleb's friends, but they were starting to look her way. Graciously, she quietly swallowed the meat and placed a hand on Pierce's shoulder.

"Caleb, do you want the rest of mine?" she asked. "I don't feel so good." She turned back toward Lilly with an uneasy smile.

"Sure, I'll eat it," he answered. "It's one of my favorites."

One of the young Athabaskan braves approached Lilly Titus and asked her something in their native tongue. Caleb chuckled at the question, but said nothing.

"You are Pierce's sister?" the native woman inquired of Lindsey, but Lindsey shook her head.

"Are you his woman then?" she asked expectantly. Everyone in the room grew quiet, as they too were curious.

"No. I'm not his woman," Lindsey said, and her answer was translated back to the young brave. He came forward, staring boldly at her and gently touched her face with his hand. Lindsey was terrified.

"You may want to tell him that you are my woman," said Caleb with a grin. "Otherwise, he might stake a claim right here and carry you home to be his squaw."

"I am Caleb's woman," Lindsey said softly to Lilly, who relayed the message. The young man seemed confused.

"Better tell him like you mean it," warned Caleb.

"I am Pierce's woman!" Lindsey shouted then, loud enough for the whole clan to hear. She scooted close to him and took his arm, and the whole clan exploded with laughter. Lindsey had never been so embarrassed in her entire life, and even Caleb blushed a little. *If only Lindsey Graham meant that,* he thought.

"My woman has no clothes," he stated in Athabaskan, and the place erupted with laughter again. "My woman has no warm clothes," he clarified. Lindsey knew they were laughing at her, but she was helpless. "We will trade for warm clothes," he said, waving a hand at the stack of supplies.

They sat for a while longer, and then the squaws shooed their mates and the young men out of the building. Only a few of the women stayed, along with Caleb and Lindsey's little friend with the big, dark eyes. The women also left them, but soon returned, arms laden with fine handmade clothing. There were parkas and jackets of lynx fur and silver fox. Hats of marten and ermine were offered for trade. Dresses of fine white caribou leather trimmed in the finest beadwork astounded the girl from Seattle. Pairs of lovely beaded moccasins, thick warm mukluks, and tall fringed boots of moose hide were stacked on benches.

"Well, pick out anything you like, Miss Lindsey," said the frontiersman. "I'm going to ask around about a hat."

"Everything is so lovely," she said, running her hand over a parka made of lynx.

"They've brought their finest," observed Caleb. "A lot of white women would frown on wearing clothing like this, but we've got plenty of cold weather ahead of us yet. Not only will you be warm from now on, you'll be dressed like an Indian princess."

The shopping then began in earnest. Lindsey carefully chose her new wardrobe while Caleb and the squaws talked price. The beautiful lynx parka, three dresses of the finest tanned caribou leather, and a hat of ermine were selected and brought to Caleb. Gloves of rabbit fur, a pair of caribou skin trousers and a pair of fine moccasins were added. Mukluks, snow boots, such as the natives wore, were a practical addition, as were a pair of knee-high moose hide moccasins.

Lindsey observed as Caleb did business with the women. He seemed determined to give them more than their asking price. He also chose a few other things for her, and some were duplicates of what she had selected.

There were several families represented here, and it dawned on her that he was making sure that each family took home some of the supplies he had brought. Here was a thoughtful, generous man, she observed, so unlike the hordes of greedy people in Dawson.

The rest of the afternoon and evening passed quickly as Lindsey and Caleb lingered in the encampment. Lindsey made a friend of Lilly Titus and the little girl, whose name she learned was Esther. While Caleb and the men spoke of fishing and hunting, Lilly and Lindsey engaged in woman talk.

"Caleb Pierce is a good man," Lilly told her plainly. "Always trade fair, this white man. No whiskey. Only food and good things. Guns to shoot caribou, and knives, axes and saws. No whiskey. He needs a good woman, this Caleb. Good woman like you."

"Like me?" Lindsey countered, astonished. "I'm a cheechako, a tenderfoot. I know nothing of life here in the north."

"You have good heart, Lindsey," said Lilly. "You very good woman, learn fast."

Lindsey pondered the counsel of Lilly Titus on the return trip home. It was dark when they departed the village, but she was not afraid in the company of the frontiersman. She sat in the dogsled, nestled in the warm parka, her lap covered with the warm caribou skins. A great orange moon rose up over the hills and illuminated the snow-covered landscape. How could such a lovely place be so harsh and severe?

She thought of Caleb as they rode on into the night. He was fearless, yet humble; fierce in battle, but gentle in spirit. Everyone revered him, and none dared cross him. He was a legend in the north, from the Mackenzie Mountains to the Copper River Basin. And here was she, Lindsey Graham, alone with him, miles and miles from nowhere.

Foreign emotions began to tug at her soul, heartrending feelings for which she was unprepared and which never should have been. She was falling in love with this rugged frontiersman, and was fighting this love with all her might. She could never stay here in this wretched land. She did not belong here. And she could never ask Caleb to leave this wild place he loved so dearly.

They stopped on a high hill, where the moon shone brightly on the valley below. Hard Luck Creek wound through this valley on its way down to the Nation River. The dogs were uneasy, yipping and howling, but a stern word from Caleb hushed every member of the team.

"Listen Lindsey," he said as he sat down on the sled beside her. There came a deep, long, eerie howl rising up out of the valley below and echoing off the surrounding hills. "That's my music," breathed Caleb with a sigh. "That's an old timer, probably the dominant male of the pack. The females and pups have a higher, more feminine pitch." Then there were other wolf voices, rising up out of the basin. The weird, mysterious melody filled the night and gave Lindsey the chills. She placed her hand on Caleb's arm and moved a bit closer.

"Isn't it odd that people are created so differently?" wondered Lindsey. "The things you love and that make you happy are the very things I hate and that terrify me."

"How can you hate this?" asked Caleb, looking out into the moonlit vastness.

"It's a cruel land," she answered. "The unforgiving cold, the wild animals, the horrible, treacherous rivers and the loneliness frighten me Caleb. This forgotten world of yours is so far from doctors and dentists and medicines and things."

"Are things so important to you, Miss Lindsey?" he asked. Isn't it sufficient to have a place to live, warm clothes and enough to eat?"

"There's so little news of the outside world here. Everyone down in America could die, and you and I wouldn't know it for months. There are no markets here, no stores. I could never get used to this place."

Caleb was totally bewildered. How could anyone not love this country? he wondered. He had hoped that somehow Lindsey might fall in love with Alaska, but the great land had taken her father and brother, and she would never forgive that.

How could he blame her? He knew all too well the dangers that lurked in the wilderness.

There was nothing he could say that would convince her to stay. He had witnessed this homesickness before in the prospectors and transients who haunted Alaska's bush. The desire for home and family would begin to gnaw on a man. The passion to return to civilization would become an unreasonable obsession, until at last, the defeated individual would leave the frontier and return to his former little world. He knew instinctively that Miss Graham was going to leave, but for a while at least, he could pretend that she was his.

CHAPTER

11

It was after noon the following day when Caleb swung his team into Fortymile. The once prosperous boomtown was deserted now, except for a few cabins, a saloon and a little store. The bulk of its inhabitants had rushed to Dawson the previous year when George Carmaak, Skookum Jim and Tagish Charlie had disclosed their legendary discovery.

"How's life, Charlie?" asked Pierce as he entered the store.

"Could be worse," answered the little storekeeper with the fine handlebar moustache. "I hear they're starving in Dawson. Killing their dogs to eat, boiling their boots… anything they can find." He gazed long and hard at Caleb. "Son, I'd be mighty leery about showing your carcass on this side of the border. Mounties were just in here yesterday asking about you."

"How's your grub holding out, Charlie?" asked Caleb, ignoring the warning.

"Well, we've got flour and salmon and not much else, Pierce. None to sell either, I'm afraid. I heard you whipped the devil out of Mike Teague over in Circle. I'd a' give a thousand in gold to watch a fight like that one."

"It wasn't much to see, to be honest about it," said Caleb. "Have you seen or heard of Teague, Charlie?"

"I haven't seen him, but I hear he's been down on the lower Yukon. Whipped up on a priest at Holy Cross, is what I hear. He's sworn to kill you Pierce, so I'd watch my back if I were you. That Mike Teague is a bad hombre, nothing but a bully and a bushwhacker."

"Any freighters coming through?" asked Pierce, as he searched the store with his eyes.

"I've got one coming in tonight from Fort Yukon," the storekeeper replied. "Should have a few things for me, but most of it will go on to Dawson. I can't keep much here in good conscience, with people starving up there."

"Can you send a message to Inspector Conway with your freighter?" asked Pierce.

"I'd be glad to. I know he'd like to hear from you," Charlie answered with a wink.

"Tell him that if he's half a man, to meet me at the border day after tomorrow."

"Are you aiming to settle his hash, Pierce? He's a tough customer. Might get yourself killed," cautioned the little man.

"No. I'm not looking for a fight, Charlie," Pierce answered. I just want to have a talk."

"I'll get word to him pronto," Charlie promised. "Say… how's that young gal you sprung out of the poky? That was about the boldest escapade I've ever heard of. I know you had good reason for what you did. Everybody knows you're an honest man. It's still all the talk up and down the river, and Inspector Conway is mad as hops. If Teague don't get you, that Mountie just might."

"The girl's fine," answered Caleb. I've got her out at one of my trapping cabins, trying to fatten her up. She nearly starved there in Dawson before I got her out."

"They say she's really a looker, son," the older man ventured. "I haven't seen a pretty woman since I left Frisco in "84."

"She's easy to look at, that's for sure," admitted Caleb. "I sure wish I could keep her here, but she's had about all of the north she can handle." He paused. "She wants to go back down to Seattle this spring."

"What's she look like, Pierce? If you don't mind my asking. I haven't seen a woman all winter, and I can't even remember what a pretty girl looks like." What the storekeeper was asking for was a courtesy not uncommon among the men of the north. In the long, dark hours of winter, when the bitter cold forced the miners indoors, they often talked of women.

"Well, I'll do my best to describe her, Charlie, but I'm afraid I won't be able to do her justice," began Caleb. "She's a real lady, he stated. Very beautiful, but not uppity like some of the gals in Dawson. Fresh as a daisy, Charlie, and pure as the new snowfall out yonder." The little storekeeper listened intently, drinking in this first-hand description of the girl he had heard so much about. "She's feminine too," continued Caleb. "All girl, if you know what I mean. She doesn't wear men's clothes like some women I've met up here. You know the type. Can't tell if they're men, or women." Charlie Hawkins nodded in agreement. "But she's not prissy either. I'd have to say she's very feminine, yet capable." Charlie whistled very softly.

"She's got a fine, smooth, musical voice, Charlie. It reminds me of a gentle rain on a tin roof. I could listen to her talk for the rest of my life."

"But what does she look like?" asked the storekeeper. "Physical features, son. You know. Hair, eyes, nose, lips… that sort of thing. Paint me a picture, Pierce."

"All right, Ill try to oblige," he conceded.

"She's exotic looking, I guess you could say. Nothing plain about this one, Charlie. Her eyes are so clear and purty', you might not even notice that they're green."

"But you noticed."

"How could I not?" he asked. "She has a fine, oval face," continued the frontiersman. "Fair countenance. Her face seems to glow somehow."

"Like how?" asked the little man.

"Like with the Glory of God or something,"

"Well, I would'nt know nothing about that missionary stuff, Caleb. Keep going."

"Long, dark brown hair, almost black I'd say, but not quite."

"How long?" demanded the storekeeper.

"Well she keeps it pinned up most of the time, but it's at least down to her waist." Charlie almost choked.

"Why that's enough hair for her and me both," he lamented, rubbing his hand over his balding head. "I love long hair on a woman."

"Her nose is one of her finest features, if you just have to know, Charlie. Elegant is the word I would use, if pretty noses excite you. Like a queen's." Caleb paused, but Hawkins bade him go on.

"She has a fine, delicate neck," he related, "and I've noticed that she has long, slender fingers."

"Skinny fingers don't do a thing for me, Pierce. How about her lips?" Caleb was quickly growing uneasy with this conversation.

"Well I suspect they're soft and sweet, but how would I know?"

"Is she…," Charlie hesitated. "Is she a shapely woman, Caleb?" he asked sheepishly. The frontiersman blushed at Charlie's awkward question.

"Charlie, the shape of a woman isn't really something that honorable men discuss," he answered.

"Who said anything about being honorable?" asked Hawkins in disgust.

"Caleb you are such a naïve pup! You'd better check behind your ears for moisture son." Hawkins was wounded, but he persisted.

"Pierce, you know I'm a lonely old drone. I haven't seen a pretty girl in so long. Humor me just this once, will you?" Pierce weighed his options. Charlie Hawkins was a good friend, and here in the north such friends were hard to come by.

"Well, I reckon you could say she's a shapely woman."

"I knew it!" exclaimed the storekeeper. Charlie Hawkins emitted an unearthly, guttural groan.

"Charlie, are you still in rut or something?" asked Caleb. "I thought the rut was over by mid October."

"Have you ever known me not to be in rut, boy?"

"I s'pose not." Caleb pulled on his parka.

"She's been through a lot, losing her brother and her pa."

"I heard all about that misfortune, and it's sure a shame," said Charlie. "I'd like to see that girl Caleb, but it would be risky to bring her over here right now. Risky for you to be here, too. If the police pull in here, there might be a shooting fracas."

"Yep, I'd best skedaddle. Just get that message to Conway."

"Will do," said the storekeeper.

"Come pay us a visit, Charlie. You know where my trapping cabin is." Pierce paused thoughtfully. "There's some pretty scenery up in my neck of the woods these days."

"I'd like to see that new scenery, Caleb. Now that I've got a good reason, I might be over there in a day or two," he said. And Pierce departed.

It was well after dark when the frontiersman and his dog team reached the little cabin in the mountains. There was a light on inside, so after unharnessing and feeding the dogs, Caleb knocked on the door. Lindsey opened it and let him into the warm cabin. She was clothed in one of her new caribou-skin dresses, adorned with beads and buttons of bone that glimmered in the lantern light.

"How's my Indian princess?" was all Caleb could say as he looked into her eyes. After his long day on the trail, her beauty was breathtaking.

"Indian princess save supper for Brave Warrior," she said with a big smile.

When Lindsey turned to the stove to get his supper, he noticed something strange about her outfit. Between her knee-length dress and her moccasins, she was wearing long johns.

"Now Miss Lindsey, I declare. I'm probably walking on thin ice, but are you wearing my long handles?"

The girl blushed scarlet. "So I am, Mr. Pierce," she answered haughtily. "I found half a dozen pairs in a gunny sack under the bed. As I was running short of undergarments and cannot seem to keep my legs warm in this frigid north, I was hoping you would let me borrow on occasion."

"Permission granted," he said with a grin. "I'd be honored for you to wear my… well…you know."

She sat with him at supper and they conversed. He was a humble man and easy to talk to, possessing a quick wit. She was honest, caring and humorous herself, despite the recent loss of her loved ones.

"How's your arm?" she asked. "I hope you're keeping it clean."

"It's feeling better all the time."

"I've been reading your journals," she confessed, with a glint of mischief in her eyes.

He was surprised. 'You must be desperate for something to read," he replied.

"Actually, I find them fascinating. You've done things that most men only dream of."

"That writing of mine is just a bunch of foolishness," he told her. "Just something I do to keep from getting cabin fever in the winter."

"I wanted to find out something about you... something that I've heard, so I've been doing some investigating."

"I see. Well Lindsey, this sounds serious. Maybe I could just tell you what you want to know and save you a lot of reading."

"Caleb, please tell me if this is none of my business," she began. "You're a mysterious man, and I've heard some rumors. And some of those reports are rather intriguing."

"Well the only rumors I know of that are blowing around about me are these," he began. "Some say that Caleb Pierce is hiding the next big strike. And that one, I must confess, is true. The only other rumor that I know of is that I'm a squaw man, and that I have a different girl in every native village along the Yukon." He smiled. "Is that what's on your mind, Lindsey?"

The girl blushed. "I beg your pardon, Caleb. I had no call to pry into your private affairs. Forgive me."

"Nothing to forgive," he assured her. "It's certainly a valid question and deserves an honest answer." He arose and stoked the wood stove and then returned to his seat. "I wouldn't hesitate to marry a native girl, if I loved her. I've met some that are far too good for the likes of me. But I don't have one stashed in some village along the Yukon, if that's what you mean."

"Have there ever been any women in your life?" she inquired.

"Just one," he replied.

"Can you tell me about her?" she asked.

"That's easy," he began. "She has a nice smile, pretty green eyes, an elegant nose..."

"Caleb, you're teasing me!"

"Big ears, a few missing teeth, hairy arms..."

"Now I know you're talking about me," she said with a little pout. "No. Seriously Caleb, was there ever a special girl that you loved?"

Her question unsettled the frontiersman. For a moment he was vexed, as he searched for adequate words to describe a lost love of the past.

Lindsey graciously changed the subject. "I'm so sorry, Caleb," she apologized. "I had no right to pry. Would you like something more to eat?" she asked rising from the table.

"No, thank you. That was delicious. I'm going hunting tomorrow. There's a big pot up in the cache," Caleb ventured. "If I bring you a moose head, you'll know what to do with it."

Lindsey laughed uneasily, hoping he was not serious.

"I've got a project for you, if you're up to it," he continued.

"What would you like me to do, sir?" she inquired.

"I'm considering sending a load of grub upriver to Dawson. I'd like for you to decide what we'll need to get us through till the first of April, and we'll send the rest up to the priest in Dawson City. I've got some trade goods up in the cache yet, and if I get a moose tomorrow, that will make two loads. I can find Sam Titus and see if he'll haul one."

"Caleb, you men aren't going back into Canada, are you?" she asked.

"No. I've arranged to meet a friend at the border day after tomorrow, and he'll haul it on up to Dawson."

They talked on into the night, making preparations. The frontiersman neglected to mention his foray into Canada that afternoon, or his impending confrontation with the Northwest Mounted Police. At last, Pierce withdrew himself from the cabin and climbed up into the cold, dark cache.

The next day was clear and frigid. Caleb missed breakfast and departed long before daylight with his dog team. Lindsey devoted her day to organizing and sorting their grubstake. Occasionally she would thumb through one of Caleb's journals, searching for a key to this mysterious man's past. He had been deeply hurt by love long ago. That had been easy to see in his tragic countenance. Had she died, this girl whom the frontiersman had loved? Had the great river taken her, as it had taken the life of her brother, Horace?

Caleb returned with his team and a load of moose meat just before dark. He had killed a bull earlier in the morning, and it had taken him the better part of a day to skin and quarter it. He said little as he went about his evening chores, his mind occupied with thoughts of tomorrow and his encounter with Inspector Conway.

Sam Titus pulled in with his dog team after supper. Together, he and Caleb carefully loaded the sleds. Before the men bedded down for the night, Caleb cleaned his hunting rifle and pistol and put extra cartridges and some food in a sack for the trip. He pretended to ignore the girl, but stole occasional glances at her as she tidied up the cabin. She too, looked his way when she was sure he was occupied with his guest. She secretly resented the presence of Sam in a way, for she had grown to love her time spent alone with the frontiersman.

They all rose early the next morning, and while the men harnessed their teams Lindsey prepared breakfast. After Sam had departed from the cabin, the frontiersman approached the girl.

"Don't worry, Lindsey girl," he told her, for he could see that she was troubled. "We'll be back in tonight, but it might be late. There's a rifle over the door there. It's not much to look at, but it shoots just fine."

"I can't shoot a rifle, Caleb," she declared.

"Well, let me show you then." He gave her a short, but thorough briefing on the use of a Winchester. When he was ready to go, he reached out and gently touched her face. He playfully brushed back a dark lock of her rebellious hair, and then he was gone.

The morning passed quickly as Lindsey poured through Caleb's journals. She found no mention of a woman, but there seemed to be a journal missing. Somewhere in the documentation of the history of Caleb Pierce, a year had vanished. She was pondering this discrepancy, when she heard the barking of dogs.

At the window she saw nothing familiar, only a man and a team she did not recognize. She reached for the rifle above the door and waited, her heart pounding.

"Hello the house!" shouted the stranger after he had tied his team. He approached the cabin and pounded on the door.

"What do you want?" asked the frightened voice inside.

"I'm a good friend of Caleb Pierce."

"Come in slow then," she warned.

The man who entered was a small, good-looking sourdough with a friendly face and an elegant handlebar moustache.

"I met Caleb on the river this morning," explained the man. "He said it would be all right if I came up to say how-do. And you can put that rifle down Missy, before you blow a good man's head off. You're scaring me to death with that thing."

"I'm sorry," she said, lowering the rifle. "Sit down if you'd like."

"Don't mind if I do, young lady. My old body can't quite handle a long ride like it used to. My name's Charlie Hawkins, by the way, and I've run the store at Fortymile since gold was first discovered in the district."

"Hi. I'm Lindsey Graham," said the girl, extending her hand.

"Oh, I know all about you, Miss Graham, and so does everybody who is anybody along the river. And you're just as pretty as Pierce described you to be. I know everything that happens along the Yukon ma'am, and what has happened to you and your family is just a shame. This old river is just like a woman. Treat her with respect and you might get along, but take her for granted, and she'll turn on you right now.

And that Mike Teague ought to be horse whipped and hung for what he did to you and your family, robbin' and leavin' you stranded up there at the Five Fingers. If he ever shows his no account face over in Fortymile, you can bet he'll hear from Charlie Hawkins. I'm not afraid of that bush-wackin' hooch runner. Pierce had better watch his back though. I hear that Teague has sworn to kill him. Pierce should have finished the job that night over in Circle City. By not doing so, he may have sealed his own death warrant.

It's a hard life up here, ma'am, and there's no other way to say it. Why, I've seen sixty and seventy below zero, and fifty below many a time. People don't think; that's why they freeze and get frostbit. They just panic. I've seen Pierce take off downriver at fifty below, but I don't worry about him none. He knows the wilderness..." The little man was staring at Lindsey as if to memorize the vision now before him.

"Have you known Caleb long?" she asked, breaking Charlie's meditation.

"I came into this land when he was just a pup," answered Hawkins. "Even then he was all over this country, freighting supplies, trading fur, prospecting and such. Never met a more honester man in this country, other than myself." He paused. "Well Missy, did Caleb ever tell you he had a fine claim over in the Fortymile country?"

"No, he didn't mention it," she responded.

"Of course he didn't. Probably the best claim in the district too, but the whole thing is a sad story and I won't trouble you with it now." He paused to catch his breath and then plundered on. "Caleb discovered this creek up in the hills about thirty miles off the river. He poked around and did a little panning up there and knew he had something special."

"Somebody followed him out there one day. Word got around and pretty soon the whole country was staked, though Caleb's claim was the granddaddy out there. It wasn't like the claims on El Dorado, mind you, but it was substantial." Unconsciously, Hawkins began to twist his moustache.

"Well, there was a boy who came into the country by the name of Jimmy White. Just had the clothes on his back, and not even enough money for a grubstake. Said he was looking for work, so Pierce hired him. They were about the same age, and they really hit it off. Pierce realized there was a lot of gold on that claim, so he partnered up with Jim and they went fifty-fifty.

"They started mining that spring and did real well. We're talking about twenty-five thousand in gold." He paused to let the girl appreciate the monetary value. "That same spring, Bobby Harper started up a saloon and dance hall in Fortymile and brought in half a dozen girls from the outside to dance. They were all nice girls and plain enough, but there was one beauty amongst them, and her name was Klara. I don't recollect her last name, but she was a German girl, tall and quiet. I remember her just like she was sitting here at the table with us, with her pretty blond hair and blue eyes."

"She wasn't a flirt like most of the girls that danced at Harper's. She danced well enough, but her heart wasn't in it. When she met Pierce, they shore fell in love. Well, they spent some time together and figured they'd go back down south and get married in the fall.

"Caleb wasn't one to hang around town though, and went back to work on his claim with Jimmy. The partners worked hard together all summer and into the fall, digging and sluicing up there. Well, the weather started getting bad and they decided to shut down their operation. Caleb sent Jim back to Fortymile with the gold and worked a few days longer, buttoning things up for the winter.

"It'll break your heart when I tell you this, Miss Graham, but when Pierce finally arrived back at Fortymile, his best friend had run off with Klara and twenty-five thousand in gold. There was a steamer taking on wood in town, heading down-river to St. Michael. Jimmy showed her all that gold and she just fell in love with him on the spot. They bought a ticket to who knows where, and nobody's seen them since. Caleb...

the boy just quit his claim and went downriver. He's been on the move ever since. Keeps to himself and doesn't say much."

Lindsey considered this sad revelation of Caleb's past while Charlie prattled on about the history of the Fortymile country. There was no mention in Caleb's journals of his claim near Fortymile, or of a beautiful blond-haired girl.

Even though Charlie liked the sound of his own voice, what he said was very interesting. Lindsey was content to sit and listen throughout the afternoon as he talked of Alaska. He told of the great rivers: the Yukon, the Koyokuk, the Tanana, the Copper and the Kuskokwim. He also spoke of the prospectors, freighters, trappers and the natives. He talked of dark days, earthquakes, blizzards, and avalanches. Then there were rabid sled dogs and wolves of the past, floods and famine and huge fires that burned all summer until the first snows fell.

It was nearly dark when Lindsey made coffee and Hawkins went out to check on the dogs. The storekeeper returned with a gift for Lindsey, something he had been saving for a special occasion. It was a bag of raisins, an imported delicacy in this stark, frozen land. While they nibbled on the raisins, Charlie revealed yet another secret to Lindsey.

"Now Miss Graham," he began, "don't tell that young buck I told you, cause he's liable to clean my plow. I'd sure hate to have him whip me like he done Mike Teague down in Circle." He paused "Pierce and that native pard of his went out to lock horns with Inspector Conway today at the border."

"Conway?" whispered Lindsey as she visualized the stern lawman in the red jacket, and thought of the frontiersman checking the loads in his guns. "But why?"

"I don't know, Missy," answered Hawkins. "You don't ask a man's business up here. I reckon the boy had a score to settle with the law. It's none of my affair," he explained. "But if I were Pierce, I'd leave well enough alone. Them Mounties won't come over on this side of the border searching for him. Why pick a fight with them? That boy'll wind up in a shootin' fracas over there and get hisself killed, sure as the world. He told me to look out for you if he don't make it back, and to see that you get on a steamer after the river breaks up. Yes ma'am, don't be surprised if Pierce doesn't come home tonight, or if that native brings him home in a pine box."

CHAPTER

12

The cold wind on the river didn't hinder the progress of the frontiersman and the native as they mushed toward the border. The trail was hard-packed, having seen heavy use from the freighters all winter. The sleds were heavily loaded, but the dogs pulled them along easily.

As Caleb approached the Canadian border, he discerned the figure of Inspector Conway standing out on the ice. Two hundred yards behind him another Mountie was clinging desperately to two teams of frantic dogs. The frontiersman motioned for Sam to stay back and swung his team toward Conway. He stopped, face-to-face with the lawman.

"Well Pierce. I guess you decided to do us both a favor and turn yourself in," ventured the Mountie with a smirk.

"You guessed wrong," answered Caleb matter of factly. His tone was not hostile, yet Conway discerned that Pierce meant business. "Actually, I thought you might do me a favor and haul these sled loads of grub upriver to Dawson."

The lawman was taken aback by Caleb's boldness. He had mushed down to the border to arrest Pierce, not do him any favors. He considered his predicament, and didn't like it. He had a pistol handy, but so did Pierce. There were rifles back on the sleds, but Pierce had his Winchester just a few feet away.

"It's for William Judge and the hospital," Caleb explained. "If you won't haul it, I'll get a freighter to take it up there," he challenged.

"And what about you, Pierce?" questioned the lawman. "You're a fugitive from justice."

The frontiersman's voice grew cold as ice. "And do you call what you did to Lindsey Graham justice? It was a rigged court and a prejudiced jury. I was there Conway, and there was no justice that day in Dawson. You sentenced an innocent girl to prison."

"What makes you think she was innocent?" asked the lawman.

"Sue Bennett stole Joe Hanson's gold," revealed Caleb. "A couple of the girls at the Monte Carlo know the truth about the incident. I'll give you their names, if you're interested."

"Well I might be, but what's done is done," the Mountie declared. "Sue Bennett left Dawson and went out to Skagway with a freighter a few days ago. She'll be on a steamer heading south in another week. There's no way I could catch her, even if I tried."

"I can catch her and bring her back if you'll keep your goons off me," offered Caleb. "I don't mind a sled race with the Mounties, but I don't want to have to shoot one."

"Thanks for the offer, Pierce, but your services won't be necessary. Let's just leave things as they are."

"Well, what about Miss Graham?" demanded Caleb. "You've slandered her name all up and down the Yukon. You and Sue Bennett and the men of Dawson have ruined her and her father. If you'd had your way, she'd be rotting in a filthy Vancouver prison right now."

The lawman was stunned. He was not accustomed to being harangued by anyone, much less this uncouth outcast of society. Many of the miners despised Pierce, but none dared ever call him a liar. There were indications that Miss Bennett might indeed be the culprit in the Joe Hanson scandal, but if she was, she had covered her tracks well.

"I want Miss Graham's name cleared," demanded Pierce. "I know I've worn out my welcome in Canada, but that girl is nothing but good. She should have every right to go back to Dawson, if she so chooses, though Dawson doesn't deserve her."

The lawman laughed uneasily. "You're not in much of a position to be making demands, Pierce. You're wanted by the Canadian government on several charges yourself. I've got a couple of Mounties back in Dawson that are a bit upset about the way you manhandled them. They want your hide."

"Then I'm the one you're after," replied the frontiersman. "Take me in, if you're man enough. But clear the girl's name, or I'll come after you, and I don't care if you're in Mother England."

The Mountie resented the disdain in Pierce's voice and yet he feared the young man. He had heard countless reports of Pierce's courage, and the power of his insurmountable will. The sourdoughs along the river all revered him, not only for his skills in the wilderness, but for the fact that he was a man of his word. Conway considered Pierce's challenge, but could not bring himself to press the issue further. He felt sick and weak inside as he stared into the cold, clear eyes of this sincere man. The lawman's legs felt as if they might buckle beneath him.

"I don't bargain with criminals," he managed at last.

"All right then," said Caleb, drawing his pistol. "I might as well just shoot you right here, since I've got nothing to lose."

"No! Wait," Conway gasped as he looked down the bore of Pierce's forty-four. "I'll see what I can do," he said.

"Conway," warned Pierce as he thumb-cocked the weapon, "give me your word or I'll shoot you dead." He paused. "You know none of your Mounties could ever track me down out in the hills."

The lawman was between a rock and a hard place. There was no doubt that this menacing frontiersman meant every word he said.

"All right," he conceded at last. "You have my word. But if I ever see you in Canada again, you'll be shot on sight."

"Fair enough," agreed Pierce.

Under gunpoint then, Inspector Conway transferred the supplies and moose meat to the government sleds, while the other Mountie and Sam Titus held their dogs. When the sleds were finally loaded, the two Mounties and their teams struck out east, back toward Dawson.

Inspector Conway, to his credit, kept his word. The Mounties delivered the moose meat and supplies to the hospital at Dawson City, where the Jesuit priest, Father William Judge, lay dying. He called a miners' meeting in Dawson, where he acquitted Miss Graham. She was an innocent woman, they declared, free to come and go as she pleased. Messages were dispatched to Skagway and to the settlements downriver regarding the girl's status, but harshly condemning Pierce. If ever he was discovered on Canadian soil, he was to be shot on sight.

It was long after midnight when the frontiersman and his team reached the cabin on the mountain. He and Sam Titus had parted ways down on the Yukon and the native hurried off toward the encampment on Hard Luck Creek.

Lindsey was beside herself with worry, for the words of Charlie Hawkins had troubled her deeply. The thought of losing Caleb Pierce was more than she could bear. He had been honest and true, risking his own life to help her, taking nothing in return. Would he too, be taken from her?

The barking of his wolf-dogs paralyzed the lovely young woman. She became as one in a dream as she awaited his knock on the cabin door. Then he was there in the doorway, grinning sheepishly, like a young pup hoping to be allowed indoors.

The girl was drawn to him, and the frontiersman took her in his arms and held her close. For a brief moment, nothing existed but the woodsman and the young woman. For a tiny block of time, things were right and good and as they should be.

When she pulled away from him, her eyes were wet with tears. Her lovely black hair shone in the light of the coal oil lantern, and her beaded dress of caribou skin befitted any queen.

"I was so worried," she confessed.

"I told you I'd be back late," he reminded her.

"You went to the border to meet Inspector Conway," she stated.

"Charlie Hawkins tell you that? I'll wring that little geezer's neck," he vowed.

"We had a good, long chat today, although Mr. Hawkins did most of the talking. He told me all about this country and the people here." She paused and began to start supper. "He also spoke of your claim over in the Fortymile district... and about Klara."

Caleb grew quiet, his mood darkening. Like a wounded, cornered animal he searched for refuge from the pain of bitter, distant memories. He found release in the childlike, guileless eyes of Lindsey Graham. When he was in her presence, there was no Klara, and no Jimmy White.

"I'm sorry, Caleb," she sighed. "You must still hurt inside after the way you were betrayed."

The frontiersman was silent for a moment, and then bared his heart to her. "I was devastated at first," he confessed. "I guess I've been bitter since it happened. I wanted so much to be free of the resentment in my heart, but it's been eating away at me for years."

Lindsey approached him again and put a delicate hand on his cheek. Her lovely green eyes were hypnotic. "You can forgive them," she told him. "You've got to forgive them, Caleb. I want you to be free from this." It was as if she was taking the chains from his heart.

"I believe I can," he told her. "I know I need to," he said with a smile.

It was very late when the weary frontiersman reluctantly excused himself from the warm cabin and the good company. Exhausted and shivering, he climbed the ladder to the frigid cache and buried himself in his nest of caribou hides.

Outside the northern lights danced and shimmered across the endless arctic sky. A pack of wolves howled down on the river, their weird music barely audible in the distance. The cabin was dark now where the young woman soundly slept. She was at peace now, secure in the knowledge that her good friend had returned safely.

CHAPTER

13

The next morning started well enough, with a hearty breakfast and good conversation. Miss Graham was soon disheartened, however, by the news that the frontiersman would be heading north up into the Porcupine River country. There was a trap line to run, he told her, and a small cabin there which needed some attention. The lynx and marten were prime and plentiful up north, he explained, but he failed to mention his real reason for leaving. He was becoming too attached to this beautiful girl who had entered his life. Already, his heart ached at the thought of her leaving Alaska. He needed some space and time to think, that he might distance his heart from hers.

After breakfast Caleb began building a sled for Lindsey. It was much smaller than the sleds which he used for freighting supplies. Lindsey had noticed a small pair of sled runners hanging from the rafters in the cabin, along with some other lengths of wood. The sturdy birch runners and cross members had been curing for some time, Caleb told her, but were now ready to use. Using the simple tools available, the frontiersman fashioned the pieces of birch into a fine, light sled. Cross members were securely lashed with strips of rawhide, and a handbrake was installed. This was to be her transportation, he explained, if the need to travel might arise. Crises occasionally occur in the north, he told her, and one must be prepared for the unexpected. He would leave his lead dog White Eyes with her, along with Lobo and Fritz. These magnificent canines, his three best, would be her companions and guardians in his absence.

White Eyes seemed to sense the great responsibility that had been entrusted to him. Like his smitten master, he too was falling in love with the young lady. That wild, savage nature within him had long ago been subdued by his mighty love for the frontiersman.

Lindsey and Caleb spent the remainder of that day and part of the next morning running their dog teams in the hills surrounding the cabin. At first she was terrified to be driving a team of her own, but soon began to enjoy it. White Eyes and his fellows carried the girl and her new sled along with ease. Somewhere along the trail, Lindsey's apprehension became sheer pleasure. Once, in passing, she tossed a well aimed snowball at Caleb, and what began as a formal lesson in dog mushing soon escalated into a fabulous game of chase.

Caleb had run dogs all his life, but was having a bit of trouble with his leaderless team. Mac was an able-bodied substitute for White Eyes, but this position at the front of the team was a whole new experience for him. So while Caleb fought to control his team, Lindsey flew deftly along the trails and easily eluded him.

Evening found Pierce packing his traps and supplies for the trip up the Porcupine River, while Lindsey worried over him. She made sourdough biscuits and bannock bread for his trip, and thick steaks of moose tenderloin for supper. He worried over her too, confirming again his previous instructions for the use of the Winchester. He also placed in her care a leather bag for certain necessities, which consisted of a knife, sulphur matches, a small hatchet, a bit of food and an extra pair of wool socks. She was to keep this bag and the rifle with her whenever she strayed from the cabin.

When Lindsey awoke the next morning, the frontiersman was gone. He had risen early and slipped away into the darkness with his team. She would have despaired except for the comforting presence of the sled dogs. To their delight, she harnessed them later that morning and took them out for an exhilarating run.

Sam Titus and his wife Lilly arrived later in the evening. Lilly was now very heavy with child and exhausted from the rough trail. They were on their way downriver to Fort Yukon, where many of their clan resided. Lindsey scolded Sam for having his pregnant wife out on the trail, but the tall, handsome native only laughed. His people had been nomadic for many years, he explained. To give birth on the trail or in a hunting camp was a common occurrence.

"Where is your man, this Pierce?" asked Lilly, causing Lindsey to blush.

"Well, I guess he's not exactly my man," ventured Lindsey, remembering too late her encounter with Lilly's brother over at their camp, "but he went north, up the Porcupine River to trap."

"Pierce is a good man," said Lilly in a soft voice so that her husband wouldn't overhear. "Good man for pretty white woman."

Lindsey didn't need to be reminded of this, but she didn't argue.

"Yes, he has been very good to me," she admitted. "How is the little girl, Lilly?" she asked, changing the subject.

"She is with her grandmother," answered Lilly. "All the others go to Fort Yukon, but the old woman and her granddaughter, they stay at hunting camp."

"Will they be all right out there alone?" asked Miss Graham.

"Plenty meat, plenty fish, much wood for fire. I want to take the girl to Fort Yukon, but the old woman say no. Poor little girl and crazy old lady, I say."

This information weighed heavily upon Lindsey. It was a disgrace, she decided, to leave an old woman and a little girl alone in this wilderness, no matter how much meat and wood they had. She had a bad feeling about it, but kept her thoughts and comments to herself.

It was nearly midnight when Lindsey was awakened by Lilly's labored breathing. She had insisted that Lilly take her bed, while Sam opted to sleep in the cache. It was fortunate that Sam and Lilly had chosen to stay, as it soon became apparent that the native woman was giving birth. Lindsey lit the lantern and called for Sam, but he did not appear. She put water on the stove to boil and located a few items that might be helpful for a delivery, but the cabin held precious little that might be of assistance. She went to the door and opened it.

"Sam Titus!" she called. "You get in here this minute!" There was no response.

"Him no good!" declared Lilly. "Him not come."

Lindsey wanted to curse the native for abandoning them in this crisis, but she held her tongue. Whether Sam Titus was present or Lindsey was prepared mattered little now, for a new life was coming forth, ready or not. Despite the carefully devised plans of man, nature has a way of working things out.

While the father rested peacefully up in the cache and Lindsey fretted and worried, a tiny native boy was born in the cozy trapper's cabin not far from the Yukon River.

The man child was Lilly's firstborn, yet she endured the birth pangs in quiet dignity. Lindsey had never assisted in childbirth, but let her instincts guide her. Her feelings of helplessness and anxiety changed abruptly with the birth of the baby. A sense of accomplishment flooded her, wonder and awe at the miracle which she now beheld. Deep in her heart, she too longed for a baby, though she would never raise a family in this wretched North Country.

The frontiersman would be honored to know that Lilly Titus had given birth to their son in his cabin. He would be proud of Lindsey. The thought pleased her, and she could hardly wait to tell him the good news.

When Lindsey awoke the following morning, Sam Titus sat with Lilly and their newborn son. He had missed the action, but now had arrived at her side to take all the credit. He was infatuated with the new arrival and spoke softly to him in the Athabaskan language.

Sam and Lilly stayed only another day. Lindsey protested their early departure on the following morning, but they were impatient to be on their way. Sam had a large sled and a good dog team. He tucked his little family under a bed of furs and then they were gone.

Loneliness and longing returned to haunt the cabin on the mountain. Why had the frontiersman deserted her? Was she such poor company or such a liability that she could not go with him? Yet, for Lilly's sake she was glad she had stayed behind.

As the days crawled past, an uneasy fear began to trouble Lindsey. When she took White Eyes and his companions out for their daily run, she thought often of the Indian camp on Hard Luck Creek. The camp must be abandoned now, except for the tiny native girl and her grandmother. Did she dare pay them a visit? The trail through the mountains was steep and dangerous and the weather was fickle. A blizzard in these mountains could mean death for a cheechako like herself.

While Lindsey still considered herself a tenderfoot, in reality she was rapidly becoming a capable young woman. She knew her limitations, but during her short time in the far north she had learned quickly. Six months of hardship and tragedy had been a cruel, but thorough teacher.

CHAPTER 14

On a crisp, cold morning in mid March, Lindsey set out for Hard Luck Creek. She prepared well for the trip, for anything could happen out on the trail. Caleb's journals rehearsed the sad plight of a dozen frontiersmen who made fatal miscalculations as they wandered the cold arctic. For various reasons, they had succumbed to the elements and other hazards that haunted Alaska's back country. A prospector up on the Sheenjek River had run low on ammunition and been killed by wolves. Several others had broken through the thin ice of Alaska's rivers and been swept away by the current to a watery grave. Some had run out of grub and starved, while others had been overcome by spells of severe, deadly cold.

Lindsey bundled up warmly and put some extra bedding on the sled. Carefully, she placed the loaded rifle, some food, her hatchet and her bag of survival necessities among the soft blankets. The wolf-dogs were nearly uncontrollable as she harnessed them to the sled, but at last she was finished and stepped aboard. White Eyes was eager to take to the trail, as were Lobo and Fritz.

The cold air on the girl's face was exhilarating and the beauty of the mountains breathtaking. After an initial burst of speed, White Eyes and his comrades slowed to a brisk but steady pace. Although scenic and spectacular, the trail over the mountains to Hard Luck Creek was also long and grueling. The winding trail crossed numerous unnamed creeks and continued up over a series of large hills. It passed through a narrow mountain canyon where deep snows on the mountainsides threatened to cascade down at any time. It wound along the side of another mountain, where a slip would send them over a precipice and down to their death. How different the trail seemed now without Caleb. He would certainly scold her for her recklessness if he knew where she had gone.

As she pushed on toward Hard Luck Creek, the weather became worse. At first it was just the wind kicking up snow here and there, but then a steady, driving snowstorm slowly engulfed them.

The dogs had been to Sam's camp on Hard Luck Creek numerous times and stayed with the trail, despite the blowing snow. Occasionally, when she grew cold, the girl would light off the sled and run for a few minutes, as she had seen the frontiersman do. The temperature was dropping rapidly. The white trail before her seemed to stretch on and on in the endless swirling landscape. And then she was there.

The encampment on Hard Luck Creek appeared desolate. No one greeted them. Not even a dog barked. The only noise was the shrieking wind and the banging of a battered door as it was slammed back and forth in the blizzard.

Lindsey tied White Eyes and the team to a tree and carefully began to search the cabins. They were humble buildings, tiny little log hovels with dirt floors. Abandoned now, they were cold and ghostly. Where were the old woman and the little girl? she wondered.

There was another little cabin up on a knoll above the settlement. No smoke billowed from the chimney, nor did she see any footprints in the snow as she approached. She almost turned away, but saw something in the snow near the cabin. It was a dead, frozen dog. As she investigated further, she saw others partially buried in the snow. What could have happened? Lindsey pried open the door and entered the dark, cold cabin. Across the cabin there was a mound of moose hides on a makeshift bed frame. She was about to turn away when she saw the bundle of hides move slightly.

"Who's there?" she called, but no one answered. Slowly, she approached the bed and began to peel back the moose skins. Lindsey gasped when she beheld the ghostly, empty eyes of the old woman staring up at her. Cuddled next to her dead grandmother was the tiny native girl. With large, frightened eyes, she looked up at Lindsey.

"Hello, little one," said Lindsey. She held out her arms toward the little girl, but the child cowered away. Lindsey reached for her again and said in a soft voice, "I won't hurt you." I remember you, Esther. Don't you remember me? I came with Caleb Pierce."

Whether she remembered Lindsey or not, she reached out her tiny arms to her. Lindsey took the child in her arms and held her close. The little native girl began to sob uncontrollably. She appeared dirty and neglected, but Lindsey didn't care. They were both alone and frightened in a stark, hostile land, but now they had each other.

"I'm going to take you home with me," Lindsey explained. The child gave no indication that she understood, but clung tenaciously to the young woman. Lindsey wrapped her in a tattered blanket and prepared to leave. She looked around for the girl's belongings but there was nothing, not a rag doll or even an extra dress. Only a small pair of mukluks stood by the door and she took these.

Back at the sled, Lindsey tucked her little charge snugly under the bedding she had brought and untied the dogs. White Eyes was reluctant to head into the teeth of the blizzard, but obeyed at her urging.

The snow was rapidly accumulating and began to drift in the ferocious wind. She must now pass through the driving wind and snow, which blew down from the mountains. It was senseless really, to set off in such a deadly storm, but the girl could not bear the thought of spending the night at the desolate Indian camp.

The dogs now found the going more difficult. Lindsey's first mistake was to challenge the storm. Her second was to trust the dogs to find their way back to the trapper's cabin. Although they were extremely intelligent animals, they were still merely dogs. They felt no urgency to return to the cabin across the mountains, but sought only to get out of the wind. They drifted aimlessly in the blizzard until darkness overtook them.

Lindsey brought the exhausted dog team to a rest beside a high stone bluff that was parallel to a frozen creek. There was a bit of shelter here, a refuge from the howling wind.

She took her bag of necessities from the sled, which contained those items necessary for survival on the trail. She must build a fire now, she reasoned. Without a fire they would surely freeze to death. At the base of the bluff, Lindsey made a valiant attempt at building a fire, but she did not succeed. Her hands quickly became numb after pulling off her gloves, and she fumbled the sulphur matches and tinder into the snow. She recovered the matches and managed to light several of them, but could not ignite what remained of the tinder. She went back to the sled and crawled under the moose and caribou skins where little Esther lay.

"I'm afraid we're lost, little one," she whispered, but the girl did not respond. Lindsey took Esther in her arms and held her close. For the first time in her life, she realized she was responsible for another person's well being. Esther's life was in her fragile, incompetent hands. She had rescued the child, but now they were lost in a deadly blizzard. There would be no rescue from Caleb this time. The closest help would be Charlie Hawkins and the men of Fortymile, but they were far away to the southeast, and which way was that? She wanted to cry and scream and shake her fist at this godforsaken Alaska Territory, but the little native girl she now held close needed her to be strong.

What a horrible nightmare little Esther had already endured. How long had the old woman been dead? From the appearance of things in the cabin, she may have been dead for three or four days, perhaps even as much as a week. The dead dogs indicated that she had been unable to tend to them for several days. Only the thick moose hides at the cabin had saved the little girl, and Lindsey scolded herself for not bringing them along. The moose hides were far warmer than the blankets she had brought.

Lindsey dug out some smoked salmon she had brought, and some fried bread. After they had eaten in silence, she wrapped the young girl in her lynx parka and carefully arranged blankets around them. She peeked out at the dogs, but they had long since burrowed down into the snow, harness and all.

Long after midnight Lindsey awoke. The wind had ceased, but the cold now pressed in around them. Tucked snugly into Lindsey's parka, little Esther slept the sleep of the dead. Lindsey had never experienced such cold. It permeated every layer of her clothing and the bedding on the sled. She could not feel her feet and her body shook uncontrollably. *So this was how it felt to freeze to death.*

Bravely, she pulled herself from the sled and draped a blanket over her shoulders. She tucked the remaining bedding around Esther, leaving only a tiny opening for the girl to breathe. If only this little one might live, thought Lindsey. She marveled at her own thought, realizing she cared not so much for her own life, but for the life of the little native girl.

"God, help us," she whispered softly. "Show me what to do." Immediately Lindsey tripped and fell headlong into the snow, but struggled to her feet. She found what remained of the sulphur matches but the tinder had blown away in the wind. She knew she must make her own tinder now and she dug the hatchet out of the snow. The girl chopped on a nearby spruce tree for a few minutes, producing a handful of chips. She removed her gloves and tried to light the chips, but they were green and would not ignite. Birch bark. It came to her from the far recesses of her weary mind. Caleb had explained to her once that birch bark made an excellent fire starter.

The clouds had disappeared and a three-quarter moon now provided a bit of light. The dogs were up, but they seemed uneasy. They looked anxiously out across the canyon, but remained silent.

River birch and yellow birch grew plentifully along the banks of the frozen creek, and Lindsey gathered handfuls of the paper-like bark. Only two matches remained now, and her hands were shaking so badly that the first match fell from her fingers and disappeared into the snow. The second match shook in her hand, but she held it long enough to ignite a piece of the birch bark. Acrid black smoke began to rise from the tinder as it grew into a tiny flame. Quickly, she chopped and gathered the lower dead limbs from a spruce and added these. As she nursed the growing fire, tears of relief began to stream from her eyes.

Throughout the rest of the night, she gathered wood and fed the fire. She pulled the sled with its precious cargo close to the warming blaze. Periodically she checked on Esther, who was sleeping beautifully. The child would never know of Lindsey Graham's desperate struggle to save her life this night.

The dogs remained alert and uneasy. That which they feared was out there, stalking the darkness.

CHAPTER 15

They came just before dawn, these gaunt marauders with yellow eyes. There were nine in all and they were ravenous, as it had been several days since their last kill. Together they could have easily overcome Lindsey and her dog team, but they were leery and did not attack immediately. The fire was something new, and they approached with caution.

Lindsey, exhausted as she was, eyed the dogs apprehensively. They were restless, fighting the harness now and staring into the darkness. Something was out there, something to be feared. She dared not let the fire die, but she was running low on wood.

A deep, low, mournful cry filled the early morning and was answered by another. Lindsey's dogs howled in return. Fritz leaped in his harness, growling savagely, but White Eyes and Lobo anchored him. There were other howls, some along the valley and two behind them up on the bluff. The forlorn canyon was filled with strange music, the eerie howling of a pack of wolves.

This can't be happening, thought Lindsey as she located the rifle and cartridges. She feared shooting the rifle almost as much as she feared the wolves. She levered a shell into the rifle's chamber and waited, her heart pounding wildly. Fritz was working himself into a savage fury, but White Eyes and Lobo were solemn, as if they knew they were outnumbered. Lindsey stood close to the sled within easy reach of the sleeping child. If the wolves killed them, they would die in each other's arms.

A pair of yellow, evil eyes appeared in the darkness a hundred feet away. Then other eyes could be seen in the flickering firelight. Fritz was frantic, biting and slashing at the harness which held him captive. Fifty feet behind Lindsey, a wolf filled the canyon with his mournful cry. She wheeled with the rifle to see this wolf, which sat on his haunches observing her. He took a few steps toward her and then sat down again. The time had come to start using the rifle.

The gray dawn was giving shape to the wolves. Lindsey raised the Winchester to aim it, but she was shaking so badly she could not hold it still. She pulled the trigger and the rifle discharged, but the wolf remained at his post. She shot again and again, but the rifle bobbed hopelessly in her hands each time. They were now surrounded by wolves.

Esther was awakened by the rifle shots and was attempting to climb out of the sled. Lindsey shoved her down into her warm bed and attempted to remove more cartridges from the box.

Fritz's great desire to protect the young lady from these intruders had gotten the best of him. These wolves were not unlike himself, yet he hated them. Instinctively he discerned what their intentions were, and if they harmed his lovely mistress, it would be over his dead body.

Lobo too, was spoiling for a fight, but his great respect for White Eyes held him back. When and if the lead dog attacked, he would be there by his side. The wizened White Eyes liked a good fight as much as any sled dog, but if he pitched in to fight the pack, who would protect his master's mate?

Morning was breaking on the isolated valley where a life and death drama was unfolding. Lindsey shot several more times at the closing wolves, but managed only to nick one. A large black wolf, surely the alpha male of the pack, was approaching boldly from the front. He was a cunning killer, the leader of the pack now for many seasons. When the pack brought down moose and caribou, it was he who went for the throat.

Fritz lunged once more against the confines of his weakened harness and this time the leather snapped. He shed the harness and kept right on moving, straight for the black wolf. The large alpha male was bowled over by the furious Fritz but was on his feet in a second. As they locked in fierce battle, the other members of the pack joined in to drag him down, as was their custom.

As the battle for the life of Fritz began, White Eyes swung the gang line, pulling Lobo around with him. Lindsey made a desperate grab for the sled and caught hold before it was out of reach. They went flying back along the creek, in what direction Lindsey did not know.

This wolf pack, which had come up from the Nation River, was consumed now in their bloodlust for the noble Fritz. They hated him, though he was their brother and carried a portion of wolf blood in his veins. He was only meat and blood to them now, but as they fell in to devour his body, they let a much larger prize slip away.

It was all Lindsey could do to hang on to the back of the sled as the two dogs raced along. She was clinging precariously to the rifle with one hand, while desperately trying to keep her balance. She placed the Winchester in the sled and chanced a glance behind her. The pack had quickly forgotten about her and was engaged in the gruesome task of ripping Fritz's body to pieces.

Poor Fritz. He had sacrificed himself that the rest of them might escape. What a great loss, Lindsey thought, and yet there was really no alternative. If they had fled as they were doing now, with nothing to keep the pack occupied, they would have all been dragged down and killed.

The frontiersman would grieve for his loyal friend, Fritz. He dearly loved every member of his dog team and they loved their master more than life. Caleb would never blame her for Fritz's death, but she was clearly at fault. This whole mission had been a nightmare, a fiasco... and yet perhaps not. The little native girl was alive.

If only she could have killed or wounded one of the wolves with the rifle. Caleb had told her that they were cannibalistic, occasionally killing and eating their own. A pack of wolves attacking humans was a rare occurrence, according to Caleb. Charlie Hawkins insisted that wolves would never attack people, but Lindsey Graham knew better now. If she ever met the loquacious storekeeper again she would set him straight. Caleb had known two men whom he believed had been killed by wolves, and knew several others who had mysteriously disappeared in the wilderness.

White Eyes' quick thinking and fast legs had saved them for now, but they were still far from home. The dogs were spending their strength rapidly to put distance between their mistress and the danger that lay behind. The snow was deep and fresh, and the dogs had eaten nothing since the previous morning. With Fritz gone, the burden on the other two dogs was now increased.

After a couple of miles the dogs slowed down considerably. Lindsey thought she recognized some of the landmarks along the way, but she could not be certain. White Eyes seemed to know exactly where he was going, though the girl had no clue. She let him navigate. When she could muster a bit of strength, she ran along behind the sled to save the strength of the dogs.

The little native girl was wide awake, but what she was thinking… Lindsey could only wonder. She had wet herself and hadn't eaten since the night before. She must be miserable, Lindsey thought, and yet she seemed content. Periodically she would glance up at Lindsey with those big, dark, innocent eyes and Lindsey's heart would melt. Already, she loved little Esther fiercely. They were two terrified girls lost in this vast, hostile wilderness.

By midmorning Lindsey began to recognize her surroundings. These magnificent wolf-dogs were taking them home. The sun showed itself for a while and the temperature began to moderate. Oh, to see once again the little cabin on the mountain! But the trail never seemed to end. Hour after hour the dogs plodded along, up through the hazardous pass with its mountains laden with fresh, heavy snow and then down into a maze of dark timbered canyons. The trail wound along the ridges and over the long, low spruce-covered hills. Just as darkness was beginning to engulf them once more, they were in sight of the cabin.

Never had a homely log cabin looked so inviting. They arrived safely at last, cheating death not once, but twice. They had survived a blizzard and narrowly escaped being eaten by wolves. Perhaps when she was old and gray, Lindsey Graham, the tenderfoot, would have a story or two of her own to pass along to her grandchildren.

There were fresh tracks in the new-fallen snow at the cabin. Someone had been here, and surely it must be the frontiersman. The cabin was still warm, though the fire had died. Someone had been inside, but there was no note. Occasionally, someone passing through might use a cabin without permission. As long as they cleaned up after themselves and left some dry kindling by the stove, this was considered acceptable.

Lindsey fed the dogs as darkness fell. In the house she pulled Esther out of her wet garments and wrapped her in one of Caleb's flannel shirts. Lindsey was so tired she could barely stand, but managed to make a little supper. Then she and the little girl crawled into bed. Tomorrow would be bath day, she decided, but tonight they must sleep. Her last thought was of the tracks around the cabin. Someone had been here recently, but whom?

CHAPTER

16

It was nearly noon when Lindsey awoke the next day. She was still alone, except for Esther. Caleb must have come home and then gone searching for her. He must still be out on the cold trail, probably worried sick. Her heart ached at the thought of seeing the rugged, handsome frontiersman again.

She set about to do the outside chores as the dogs would be hungry. But they were behaving strangely, much as they had before the attack of the wolves. White Eyes kept looking off in the distance, searching through the trees for something only he could hear. Lobo too, was on edge but the dried fish Lindsey offered him finally caught his attention. They were probably wondering about poor Fritz, she decided.

On the way to the spring she discovered a set of tracks in the snow. She guessed they must be Caleb's prints, knowing that he would have searched around the cabin for her. They were large tracks, almost twice the size of her own, and they penetrated deep, deep into the snow.

After filling the wood box and hauling water to the cabin, she retrieved the rifle and cartridges from the sled.

It was useless to her really, for the terrifying weapon had proved inadequate in her incompetent hands when she had encountered the pack of wolves. Even the loud report of the Winchester had not frightened them away. The rifle had scared Charlie Hawkins though, and that was reason enough for Lindsey to keep it handy.

After supper that evening, Lindsey attempted to give Esther a bath. She placed the wooden washtub by the stove and made a grab for the fleeing girl. Apparently, Esther thought that Lindsey was trying to drown her, for she fought Miss Graham like a mountain lion. She slipped away from Lindsey twice and escaped out of the tub before being captured again by her determined guardian. Giving the child a bath proved to be easier said than done, but in the end Lindsey's strength prevailed. A little swat on Esther's behind convinced the girl to submit to the scrubbing.

What a pitiful little darling she was, sobbing quietly while Lindsey rinsed the soap out of her hair. "You poor thing," murmured Lindsey as she took Esther out and began to dry her off. "And I haven't any clean clothes for you, except for another of Caleb's shirts." She wrapped the little native girl snugly in the tattered flannel shirt. "Tomorrow we'll cut this old thing up and make you a little dress. How would you like that, my love?" Esther did not answer, but melted into Lindsey's bosom. Lindsey sat back in the chair and gently rocked her to sleep.

The dogs were fussing about something outside, but she paid them no mind. They often barked at moose and caribou that wandered these hills at night. When and if Caleb's dog team came in she would know it. They generally made quite a ruckus when they arrived at the cabin.

She drew her own bath water and stepped into the wooden washtub. Oh, to see Uncle Bert and Aunt Ida again! Had they received the letter she had written while back in Dawson regarding the death of her father and Horace? They would be heartbroken, for the families had always been close.

She was nearly finished with her bath when an eerie feeling settled over her. Someone was watching. Lindsey glanced quickly toward the window and for a second, saw an obscure face. Then it was gone. Quickly she stepped out of the tub and wrapped herself in a blanket.

"Caleb, is that you?" she called, but there was no answer. She had been expecting the frontiersman to return, but had not heard his team. What could she expect of him, really? He was a lonely man in this wild land where women were few and far between.

She heard footsteps in the snow in front of the cabin. "Caleb, is that you?" she called again but there was no reply. He was so ashamed that he couldn't answer her, she decided. She went to the door and started to lift the bar. Whoever it was stood right on the other side, waiting to be allowed in. It had to be Caleb. Sam Titus was the only other man who knew of the cabin, and he was in Fort Yukon with his family.

Charlie Hawkins. He also knew of this remote cabin, and he had been quite enamored with Lindsey during his recent visit. The little storekeeper could hardly keep his beady eyes off her that afternoon.

"Caleb, if that's you, please tell me. You're frightening me," she said. Instead of opening the door, she reached up and took down the loaded Winchester from its pegs.

"Get away from that door then, or I'll shoot!" she threatened. She aimed at the wall above the door and squeezed the trigger. After the report of the rifle, she heard a deep voice mumbling and more footsteps. The dogs went wild when they caught sight of the intruder. White Eyes leapt at the end of his chain, growling savagely. Lobo too was in a fit of a rage. Never had Lindsey heard these dogs behave so.

After a few minutes, the vicious barking and growling subsided. Lindsey blew out the lantern and waited, her heart beating wildly. Whoever the intruder was, he had disappeared. She scolded herself for even considering that the frontiersman would dishonor her in this manner. It was obviously someone who was unfamiliar with the dogs.

"Caleb, I need you," she whispered. Had this man of the wilderness deserted her? Was he even now out searching for her, or was he still in the far north, trapping on the Porcupine River? The gunshot had awakened the little girl, so Lindsey took Esther in her arms and lay down beside her. "Everything's going to be all right, darling," she promised, but in her heart she was not so sure.

The following day dawned cold and clear. Lindsey had rested little during the night, fearing the return of the stranger. His tracks from the previous night, which skirted the dog yard, were identical to the ones she had discovered out by the spring. It was he who had been here before, and he had surely been inside the cabin. A faint foul-smelling odor still lingered there. His tracks were huge and bore deep into the snow, much deeper than her own.

Lindsey fed the dogs and filled the wood box, but was reluctant to go to the spring. The dogs were still nervous and uneasy, as they had been the night before. The stranger was camped somewhere on this mountain, or perhaps even as far away as the river valley below. She must be cautious, for good men did not behave in this manner.

She spent the rest of the morning inside, sewing a little flannel dress for Esther. It was not a work of art, but the finished dress fit comfortably and Esther was extremely pleased with her new apparel.

It was nearly noon when the dogs exploded with a ferocious volley of barking. Lindsey found the rifle and crept to the window, hoping desperately that the frontiersman had returned. What she saw nearly caused her heart to fail her, for behind the long team of huskies approaching the cabin was the huge, hulking form of Big Mike Teague. His dogs headed straight for Lobo and White Eyes, but Teague's long blacksnake whip persuaded the leaders to pass on by.

The giant lit off his sled, tied his team and approached the cabin door. "Hello the House!" he boomed, but Lindsey did not answer him.

"I know you're in there, Missy! It's me, your old friend Mike!"

"Go away!" she ordered. "Touch that door and I'll shoot!"

"Now, is that any way to treat a guest Missy?" he cajoled. He held a bottle of hooch in one hand, and from this he took a long pull. "Open up, you spoiled brat!" he yelled. "I'm tired and hungry and I'm about all froze."

"Go away, Mike Teague!" Lindsey threatened. "Caleb's due in any time, and if he finds you here, he won't like it!"

"Well, that's mighty queer. I just saw that four-flusher's camp several days ago way up in the North Country. Good fur up there too. I don't expect he'll be down here anytime soon." He reached for the door and heaved, attempting to break the latch. Lindsey shot into the door, but the slabs of wood were thick and heavy, and would not allow the bullet through.

"Why, you little hussy!" fumed Teague. "I'll fix your wagon!" With that, he leaped onto the wood pile and then up onto the roof.

Lindsey cringed when she heard him walking above her. The rafters sagged and creaked under the weight of his giant frame. Lindsey took the terrified little native girl in her arms and held her close. "Oh dear God," she whispered. "Please help us!"

Under the snow, the roof of the cabin was insulated with caribou moss, or muskeg. Teague began to take handfuls of the muskeg and shove it down the stovepipe. The stove below could no longer draw, and the cabin began to fill with smoke.

Lindsey quickly grabbed a rag and held it over Esther's face, but it did not help. Soon they were both coughing terribly. Teague would show them no mercy, she knew. She would rather die than to let this man put his grimy hands on her, but she must somehow save Esther. When she could take no more, she moved toward the door. No longer able to see, she found the latch with her hands and opened it. She stood for a moment in the doorway still holding the girl. Even in the intense smoke she could smell Mike Teague, who now stood face to face with her.

"You monster!" was all she could say to him.

He cursed her and then backhanded her across the face, knocking both her and the child to the floor. Teague took another pull from his bottle and then stepped inside to open the stove. "That'll learn you, Missy!" he scolded. "You're talkin' mighty uppity for a gal out here in the middle of nowhere."

Lindsey sat on the floor trying to clear her head. Esther was clinging to her, crying softly. The rifle was leaning against the wall by the door, but she dared not reach for it.

Teague quickly had the stove functioning again, and the smoke began to clear. He stretched his enormous hands over the stove to warm them. "You've got a little trigger happy with that carbine, ain't you Missy? It's a good thing you can't hit nothin' with it." He came to her and with one strong arm jerked her to her feet.

"Let go of my arm please," she pleaded, when he did not release her.

"What if I was that no-good Pierce?" he demanded. "You wouldn't mind it so much then, would you Missy?"

"He would never treat a woman this way!" she retorted.

"He's a no-account squaw man is what he is," Teague accused. "Everybody on the river knows that."

"He's the best man in this territory Mike Teague, and you know it!"

"Well, if he had a lick o' sense, he wouldn't have left you up here alone."

Teague was uncomfortably close now and she was trapped in his grip of iron. The overwhelming stench that accompanied him was gagging her.

"Have you ever been kissed, Missy?" he asked, a spirit of lust now gleaming in his eyes. She was so repulsed by him that she could not speak. His beard was matted with food and grease and his bloated face was filthy. He reeked of hootchinoo, tobacco and other substances far less desirable. He crushed her to him and placed his disgusting mouth over hers. She wrenched herself away.

"Let me go!" she cried, half pleading and half demanding, but the giant still held her in his grip of iron. He kissed her again, and this time she could not get away. He released her at last and she turned her head away in shame. Never in her life had she felt so defiled.

"Make me some breakfast Missy," he demanded. "After that, we'll get better acquainted." Teague seated himself at the head of the table and observed as Lindsey slowly began to make biscuits.

"Where'd you get that no-account Injun?" he asked, as his eyes fell on the little native girl. Esther saw the man eying her, and in a panic, ran to hide behind Lindsey's skirt.

"Her grandmother died recently, over on Hard Luck Creek," answered Lindsey. Even as she spoke her eyes were searching the cabin for the rifle. "But she'll grow to be ten times the Alaskan you'll ever be, Mike Teague!"

The giant only laughed. "You know Missy, I think I like your sass after all," he declared.

Little Esther was crying, so Lindsey picked her up and took her back to the bed. "You sit here, my love," she said softly. "Everything's going to be fine. Mama's going to make some biscuits and gravy. Would you like that?"

"Mama huh?" mocked Teague. "Now that's funny." He chuckled at the notion.

Lindsey wept softly to herself as she stirred the gravy in the skillet. Teague continued to mumble and drink from his bottle of whiskey. As Miss Graham was passing by with a tin plate for her unwelcome guest, the huge man made the mistake of slapping her on the backside. The young lady could take no more. She seized the skillet of boiling gravy from the stove and swung it square into Teague's face with all her might. The giant roared with agony and rage.

Lindsey quickly grabbed up Esther and snatched the rifle. She beat him out the door, but Big Mike was right behind her. He was yelling and fuming, still pawing the scalding gravy out of his eyes. Lindsey swung around wildly with the rifle and the little girl, and managed to get a shot off, but she missed.

Then she ran. Still clutching the rifle and Esther, she began cutting down the mountain toward the trail. If she and the child could make it to the river, a freighter might be passing who could help them.

She ran valiantly, but the snow was soft and deep and she broke through often. She was both crying and praying as she ran, continually looking back to see if Teague was following. She had run about three hundred yards, when two strong arms engulfed her.

CHAPTER
17

It was Caleb.

"Whoa there, Miss Lindsey," he drawled, taking the rifle from her. "Where are you going in such a big hurry?"

Lindsey was so relieved, she didn't know whether to laugh or cry. "Oh, Caleb!" she exclaimed, clinging desperately to the frontiersman. Little Esther was confused and squirming in her arms, trying to escape from this unfamiliar man. "It's Mike Teague, Caleb. He's up at the cabin," she managed, trying to catch her breath.

"Did he do this to you?" he asked, as he gently touched the bruise on her face. She nodded.

Caleb stood quiet for a moment considering the situation. "I was coming up from the river," he told her, "and heard a gunshot over at the cabin. I figured I'd better come up here real easy." He paused. "Is there any chance you might have hit Teague?"

"No," answered Lindsey. "I can't hit anything with this rifle. I'm sure he's still up there, Caleb."

"Is that the baby from Sam's hunting camp over by the Nation River?" he asked. She nodded. He started to question her further about the child, but thought better of it. "Lindsey, follow my tracks back down the trail. I left the team tied down there. If I'm not back in half an hour, take off for Fortymile and find Charlie Hawkins. Those men over there will help you."

"You come with me, Caleb," she pleaded. "Please don't make me go alone." She paused, looking deep into his eyes. "You don't have to fight him. Let's make a push downriver to Fort Yukon. I know we can easily outrun him. They've got government men there, and maybe even a lawman."

"Lindsey, you know I can't do that. This is Alaska. Men fight their own battles here. If we run, he'll just show up again in the next town. He's sworn to kill me, girl. Best I confront him face-to-face than to have him ambush me somewhere out in the brush."

"Caleb, I'm afraid he'll kill you!" she exclaimed. He had no words of assurance for her now, for a fight with Mike Teague held no guarantees.

A gunshot rang out from the direction of the cabin. Quickly the frontiersman pulled Lindsey and Esther behind some trees. "Lindsey, be ready to hit the trail. If you see Mike Teague before you see me, take my sled and skedaddle on out of here."

"Caleb, please be careful," she admonished. She pulled his face down to hers and put her lips on his. Abashed, he quickly pulled away.

"Go on now Lindsey," he said. "You're going to get yourself killed if you don't get moving." Caleb checked the loads in his pistol and then started up toward the cabin.

Mike Teague had drunk just enough hooch to make him vicious. Getting slammed in the face with a pan of hot gravy had only added to his fury. He had taken a shot at the girl down in the woods, but his eyesight wasn't as good as it once was. He wasn't worried about losing her though. He could track her down easily enough. When he caught her, he would teach her a lesson she would never forget.

When Teague saw the frontiersman approaching, he quickly unloaded his rifle in Pierce's direction but the man vanished. He was surprised to see Pierce here, for he had passed his camp up on the Porcupine River a week before. He hadn't been anticipating a scrap with the frontiersman, but now that the opportunity presented itself, he would not back down. Teague dearly owed Pierce for the broken wrist he had suffered in their fight at Circle City.

Teague tossed away the empty rifle and pulled a pistol from his waistband. He searched the timber around the cabin with his eyes and listened for the sounds of a man approaching. Like an enormous bull moose he stood, king of the hill, waiting for his challenger to appear.

Caleb had vanished from sight and circled around quietly behind the cabin. He caught hold of the eave and pulled himself up. Teague's dogs went wild, for they caught a glimpse of the man in buckskin as he stalked along the roof. Big Mike knew his adversary was near, but could not locate him until it was too late. The frontiersman came flying off the roof, driving Teague headfirst into the woodpile. Teague was deceivingly quick for a big man and though he was up like a cat, Caleb was gone. He appeared briefly at the smokehouse and drew fire from the drunken giant, but when Teague reached the smokehouse, Caleb had disappeared. A shot rang out from the cabin a moment later, an errant pistol shot that pierced Teague's boot and bore deep into his foot. The big man groaned and hurled obscenities in Pierce's direction. A searing pain from the bullet wound began to slowly creep up his leg. Teague rushed the cabin, discharging a barrage of lead into Caleb's hideout, but it was empty. Big Mike hastily searched the cabin for more cartridges but could find none.

Teague boiled out of the cabin and ran straight for the dog team. He cut loose his entire team of vicious huskies and they immediately attacked White Eyes and Lobo. The frontiersman then appeared in the dog yard and tried desperately to beat back the attackers. He quickly freed his own dogs, and they took their fight down the hill away from the cabin. In the dogfight, Caleb's mackinaw was ripped from him and his pistol lost in the snow.

Teague located a stout pole about five feet long, and with this he attacked the frontiersman. The giant was fighting like a man possessed of a thousand devils, so great was his rage.

Caleb stayed right with Teague, keeping just out of the deadly pole's reach as he waited for an opportunity. The ruffian from the lower Yukon was a powerhouse, but the frontiersman was quick and agile. As he faced Teague, he read his moves, his body language. Try as he might, Teague could not hit Caleb with the club.

No words passed between these arch enemies now. There was nothing to say. There would be no reconciliation, nor would they continue their battle another day. There was only an understanding that this fight would be to the death, and only one of them would walk away.

On one of Teague's wild swings, Caleb managed to catch hold of the pole. Desperately, the giant attempted to wrench it from his hand. Caleb yanked on the pole with his right arm and swung his left fist, landing a stunning blow to Teague's jaw. Then the frontiersman quickly ripped the pole from

Teague's hands. He flung it away from them and closed in on Big Mike.

It was hand-to-hand then, rough and tumble with no holds barred. This was what they really preferred, as it was the true test of a man's physical strength. Teague rained powerful blows upon Pierce, and when the giant connected, his punches racked Pierce's body like the blows of a sledge hammer. Caleb's punches were hard too, fast and well timed. A lesser man would have wilted under Caleb's savage attack, but Teague was considered one of the toughest men in Alaska Territory.

As the fighting continued, the larger man began to grow desperate. He was losing and he knew it. There was a hideout knife in his boot, but he dared not reach for it. If he could just get in a little closer to Pierce...

It happened very quickly and then it was over. Caleb lay on the ground, writhing in pain. The giant had seized Caleb's head and jerked it into his own, head-butting him with all his might. Teague too, was temporarily disoriented by the force of the blow, but he soon began to get his bearings.

An axe lay on a rick of wood under the eave of the cabin, and Teague grabbed it and stood over Caleb. The giant had lived for this hour, for this very moment in which he would take the life of the frontiersman. Caleb Pierce had humiliated him downriver at Circle City, and that had been far more painful than Teague's broken wrist. Pierce was at his mercy now, and Mike Teague reveled in this as one who had his sights trained on a bull caribou.

A noise behind Teague caught the big man's attention, a perilous sound and yet familiar. It was the unmistakable click of a cartridge being chambered into a lever action rifle.

Teague turned to see Lindsey Graham holding the rifle in her trembling hands not twenty feet away.

"Leave him be!" she commanded in a voice far braver than she felt inside. Teague took a step toward her with the axe.

"Put that rifle down," he demanded, but she defied him.

"Take your dogs and leave us alone," she pleaded, but Teague had no such intentions. He chanced a quick glance at the frontiersman and took another step toward her.

"Give me that rifle!" he boomed, "Or I'm going to wrap it around that pretty little neck of yours." This was no idle threat, coming from a man like Mike Teague. He took one more step and reached for the rifle, but Lindsey squeezed the trigger before he could knock it away.

The bullet slammed into the center of Teague's chest, and it staggered him. It bore deep into his body, wreaking havoc on its deadly course. The giant dropped to his knees, stunned and bleeding profusely from the mortal wound. Time ceased to exist. A faint breeze stirred in the tops of the tall white spruce trees that surrounded the cabin. Off in the distance, the dogs continued their fighting but no one heard. Then Mike Teague, still clutching the axe in one hand, pitched face first into the snow, dead.

Lindsey Graham stood only a few feet away, her face ashen and her world reeling. The battered rifle slipped from her trembling hands, but she failed to notice. What had she done? She saw Caleb lying in the snow, clutching his head with both hands. She would have gone to him, but her legs would not carry her. They were weak now and began to buckle under her as her world grew dark.

When she awoke, she was lying on the bunk in the cabin. Caleb sat close by, looking into her eyes and smiling broadly.

He brushed a lock of black hair from her cheek. "Where's the baby, Caleb?" she asked, trying to sit up.

"She's right over yonder, sound asleep," answered Caleb. "She put up a pretty good fuss when I first caught her, but she settled down after a while."

"Your head. How is it?" she asked, taking his big calloused hand in hers. "I saw you there writhing on the ground and knew you were badly hurt."

"I'm still a bit woozy, ma'am, but I'm on the mend now," he answered. "I shore never saw that head-butt coming."

"I killed him, didn't I?" she asked.

"Well, you sure did, Miss Lindsey, and it's fortunate for me. I'd be knocking on the pearly gates right now if you hadn't saved my life." He paused for a moment. "Men like Mike Teague don't live long in this territory. You can only hurt and terrorize people for so long, and then it catches up with you. Teague ruined you and your family, Lindsey," he reminded her. "Stole your money and basically abandoned you there at Five Finger Rapids. You're just one of the dozens that he bullied, beat and stole from."

Caleb looked on as tears began to flow down the girl's cheeks. He marveled at her tender heart and her sorrow over taking the life of an evil man like Teague. "Reckon that makes us about even," declared the frontiersman with a grin. "I pulled you out of the drink back upriver last fall, and you kept that devil from hacking me up with a choppin' axe."

"You busted me out of jail at Dawson too," she reminded him.

"That's right," he responded. "I'd forgotten about that. Maybe you do still owe me." Caleb rose from his chair and went to the door. "I'd better go catch those fool dogs before they all kill each other."

CHAPTER

18

Lindsey was up before the frontiersman returned, tidying the cabin and starting supper. She went to the spring for water, but dared not glance at the body of the fallen giant.

Caleb was everywhere, tying dogs, feeding his team and unloading his sled. His bundles of prime fur went up into the cache, but not before he proudly displayed them for Lindsey. Never had she seen such fine pelts as these that had come from so far north. There were half a dozen wolf hides, a pair of wolverine skins, along with numerous lynx, silver and cross fox, river otter, mink and marten.

Teague's dogs were vicious and difficult to manage, but they had met their match in the frontiersman. Whereas Teague had ruled them with anger and brutality, Caleb now subdued them with wisdom and patience. After the dogs were all tied and fed, he wrapped Teague's body in a canvas tarp. With his chores finished, Caleb headed for the spring to clean up a bit before supper.

Where the spring flowed from the mountain, a small glacier had accumulated over the winter. On the coldest days, it was necessary to chop a hole in the ice to draw water, but with the warmer March weather, it was now open. He took a knife from his scabbard and began to shave off the beard he had accumulated. His thoughts drifted to the kiss Lindsey had given him that very afternoon. What did it mean? Was there a slight chance that she might love him after all?

His foray into the cold arctic had done little to quench his desire for Lindsey Graham. He had intended to distance his heart from the young lady, but thoughts of her had haunted him continually. He dreaded far more than death that terrible day that she would leave him and return to that other world called civilization. His great heart had been broken once before by a good friend and a lovely young woman, and it had taken him years to recover. Knowing Lindsey had healed that gaping wound, but already the thought of losing her was more than he could bear.

The evening with Miss Lindsey was a taste of heaven for the lonely frontiersman. While little Esther played and prowled around the cozy cabin, Lindsey and Caleb swapped stories. She told him of her trip to Hard Luck Creek, of getting lost and of the wolf attack. "It's my fault that Fritz was killed," she confessed sadly. "If only I hadn't set out in that storm."

"I'm just glad you're alive girl, and Esther, too. I should never have left you here alone." He paused for a moment and smiled. "I'm really proud of you, Miss Lindsey. You're quite a lady."

"Well, I've had a good teacher," she returned, "the best man on the river."

The frontiersman blushed. "Don't know about that last part," he said humbly.

"Oh! Guess what!" she beamed. "I almost forgot to tell you." She proceeded to convey to him the details of Sam and

Lilly's visit and of the birth of their son. Caleb listened intently, not so much to the account of the birth, but to the music of Lindsey's heart. Her voice was clear and melodious, her words were well chosen and appropriate. She seemed to cast her spell upon him again, that mysterious, supernatural force called love. He had fled to the north to dissociate his heart from hers, but now in a moment, he had become hopelessly ensnared.

Lindsey too, had feelings for this man of the wilderness, but she fought them. She would be returning to her own world in a few months and could not afford to become emotionally involved with Caleb Pierce. If only she could persuade him to return with her to Seattle! But city life would never do for the frontiersman. This man who had wandered the lonely reaches of Alaska and the Yukon would die like a caged animal in the confines of a city like Seattle.

The following morning saw the frontiersman and his makeshift family harnessing the dog team and mushing for Hard Luck Creek. Caleb would have preferred to go alone to retrieve the old woman's body, but Lindsey was not about to be abandoned again. Pierce added four of Teague's dogs to his own team for the trip, which did not sit well with White Eyes and the others. They were jealous and resentful of Teague's dogs, but aside from an occasional snarl, they tolerated the newcomers.

Caleb tucked Lindsey and little Esther under the warm moose skins on the sled and they departed. It was a glorious day, except for the grim task of hauling the old woman's body home. They arrived at the desolate encampment in the early afternoon, and while Lindsey occupied the child, Caleb wrapped and loaded the body onto the sled.

They were still on the trail when darkness fell, but the stars gave light enough to see. Occasionally, Lindsey would glance at the frontiersman as he rode on the back of the sled or ran along behind. At one point, he stopped on a barren ridge to gaze out over a lonely valley.

"What do you see, Caleb?" asked Lindsey as she stepped off the sled to stand beside him.

"Nothing in particular," he answered, "I just wanted to stop for a while." There was a long silence as the man and woman gazed out across the rugged landscape. "Reckon there's any hope for you and me, Miss Lindsey?" he asked. "I had pretty much resigned myself to being alone when you return to Seattle, but then you kissed me yesterday."

She did not answer immediately. Why had she kissed him? It was an impulse really, and yet she knew it was born out of love. Her mind was telling her that this relationship would never do, but her heart was whispering something else.

"Caleb, I do care for you a great deal," she began. "I've got feelings in my heart, emotions that I can't even understand." She paused. "You're a good man, Caleb. You're kind and honest and strong of spirit. You belong here. We both know that. But I don't... I can't live here. This is a man's country Caleb, not a woman's."

Her words were like a dagger in the lonely frontiersman's heart. Try as he might, he just could not accept the fact that she was not his woman, and never would be. What a fool he was to fall in love with her over and over again, and each time he fell his love became deeper and stronger. He was courting a heartbreak far greater than the one that had nearly killed him a few years before, and yet he was powerless to stop it. How could he not love this young woman? Love wasn't an earthly force that a man might control, but if was like the mighty Yukon. It flowed where it pleased and there was just no stopping it.

"We'd best head on in, Miss Lindsey," he suggested after a moment. "It's getting late."

The next day was spent packing at the little cabin. It was expedient that they travel downriver and then into the upper Tanana country before the river ice became treacherous. The furs Caleb had trapped were loaded onto Mike Teague's sled, along with the giant's massive corpse. Into the other sled were loaded the tools, traps, bedding and what remained of the supplies. To top off the load, Caleb lashed on the body of Esther's grandmother, which would go downriver as far as Fort Yukon.

Long before daybreak, they departed from the trapper's cabin and descended out of the mountains to the river valley below. Lindsey would miss the frontiersman's cabin, as it had been a refuge from a hostile world. Nor would she ever forget it, for here she had killed a man.

When they reached the Yukon they turned upriver, heading south and east toward Fortymile. The wind howled along the river now, but Lindsey scarcely noticed. She had traversed this country once before and recalled their flight from Dawson. Now they must visit Charlie Hawkins, the storekeeper at Fortymile, to sell Caleb's furs and to turn in the body of Mike Teague.

It was a long, grueling trek upriver, as the late winter snows had drifted and packed hard across the trail. Caleb was accustomed to handling a sled on the trail all day, but Lindsey was not. By the time they reached the border, the girl was stiff and sore but did not mention it to Caleb. Lindsey insisted that Pierce stay at the border with his dogs, for he was a wanted man in Canada. They switched dog teams, and she drove Teague's sled, his dogs, and his frozen body on into Fortymile.

Lindsey tied Teague's team outside, and then entered the humble store. Such was Charlie Hawkins' rapture at the sight of her, that for once in his life he was speechless.

"Good day, Mr. Hawkins," greeted Lindsey as she approached him.

"Well! Miss Graham," he said at last. "What an honor to have such a lovely young lady in the humble village of Fortymile." He looked toward the door to make certain Caleb Pierce was not with her. "Will you marry me, Lindsey dear? I've been thinking on it for months now, and I feel that you and I are destined for one another. The days are short, but the nights are oh so long and lonely in this desolate place."

Lindsey was taken aback by his bold proposal and blushed scarlet.

"Mr. Hawkins! I hardly know you. I don't think I could..."

"Well, I just thought I'd ask. Most women would jump at the opportunity to marry a good-looking chap like me."

"I'm planning on leaving after spring breakup," she told him. "I'm going back down to Seattle."

"That's not a problem, Miss Graham," he offered. "I'd be glad to escort you... even pay your way. We could go out with the next freighter that comes through."

"Thank you, but that won't be necessary, Mr. Hawkins. I already have plans to stay with Caleb until late May or early June. We're heading downriver toward the Tanana, to prospect for gold."

"That no-good frontiersman is going to get you killed, Miss Graham. You've already had several close calls. If you follow him out into that upper Tanana country, you'll never come out alive. That Tanana River is one of the worst in the territory, with quicksand, sweepers and whirlpools that'll just swallow a canoe."

"I don't think Caleb would put me in jeopardy, Mr. Hawkins."

"That fool kid ain't got a lick of sense, Miss Graham. Girls like you ain't meant to be traipsin' all over kingdom come, and runnin' on the rivers. A girl like you oughta just sit around the house and look pretty. You got no business handlin' dog teams and fishin' and runnin' traplines like the native women here."

"For your information, Mr. Hawkins," she began, her voice turning to ice. "I only wish I possessed half the skills that the native women along the river do."

"I still say Pierce is a fool," continued Hawkins boldly. "If he had any sense, he'd follow you back down to Seattle and settle in down there."

"Mr. Hawkins," she reasoned, but words suddenly eluded her, for the frontiersman stood in the doorway.

The color quickly drained from Hawkins' face as Caleb approached the counter. "Pierce," he apologized, "I didn't mean..."

"You're right Charlie," Caleb said with a soft smile. "I am a fool." He paused. "This is my home. It's all I know. What would I do in Seattle, Charlie? Be a salesman or work in a factory?"

"Caleb, I didn't mean..."

"Forget it Charlie. No harm done nor offense taken." He reached across the counter and clamped a big hand on the little storekeeper's shoulder. "I've a bit of fur out on the sled if you're buying, and Mike Teague's frozen carcass if you're in the mood for some company."

"Teague's dead?" asked Hawkins in amazement.

"Yeah. I had quite a tussle with him up at my cabin a few days ago. He was about to use a choppin' axe on my head when the girl here shot him graveyard dead with my old Winchester. She saved my life."

Hawkins stood spellbound. What big news this was, and he was likely the first to know. Mike Teague, long considered to be the toughest, meanest man in Alaska Territory, had been killed by a woman!

"Well, the Mounties will be tickled to hear that," he said. "They've been looking for that bully for two months or more. I guess he killed a good man over on the Pelly this winter, and Inspector Conway has been after him."

"The incident at my cabin was self-defense," Caleb explained

"Sounds like it to me Pierce, but the Mounties will want to question Miss Graham. They'll be by here tomorrow."

"We're heading downriver tonight," Caleb told him.

"Tonight?" questioned Hawkins. "I was just getting reacquainted with the young lady here."

"We need to get downriver before the ice gets bad," explained Pierce. "And we have a lot of miles to cover."

The frontiersman brought his furs inside and Hawkins looked each one over carefully. Normally, he would have argued price for the furs, but wouldn't dare to haggle in Miss Graham's presence. He offered top price for the hides, to Caleb's surprise and Lindsey's delight. He talked continuously of the news on the river, the riches of the Klondike and the starvation in Dawson. Caleb paid him no mind, as he was accustomed to Charlie's way. The little storekeeper would never stop gossiping until they had departed.

It was well after dark when they pulled out of Fortymile and back onto the river. Teague's sled and the dog team were left behind in the border town, which left Caleb's big freighting sled heavily loaded. With Esther still sound asleep and Lindsey sitting in the sled, the frontiersman mushed on across the border and back into Alaska Territory.

A million stars provided adequate light to navigate the trail to Fort Yukon. Lindsey was content to ride along quietly, occasionally stealing a glance at the mighty frontiersman.

After a few hours on the trail, Caleb pulled off alongside the river and made camp. While he fed the dogs and built a fire, Lindsey tended to Esther and prepared supper. The frontiersman fashioned a large, warming fire and then made a bed of soft spruce boughs and caribou skins beside it for Lindsey and the child. After they ate, they sat and talked for a while.

"We'll be about three weeks or more on the trail," he told her. "We'll stop in Fort Yukon to see Sam and Lilly and their new youngin."

A light, warm wind sighed in the treetops above them. Lindsey looked admiringly over at Esther, who was already sleeping soundly. "She has never said a word to me, Caleb," Lindsey confided sadly. "She has never laughed or smiled... she seldom cries either. Just stares at me with those big, sad eyes."

"She's been through a lot, Lindsey. Probably doesn't know a word of English either."

"Caleb, I love that little girl so much," she lamented. "Would I be wrong to take her back to Seattle with me?"

The frontiersman took a stick and stirred the fire, then laid it across the flames. "I'll tell you the truth Lindsey, though it may be hard for you to bear. Love's a strange thing," he said. "I know how much you love this little one, with a selfless love that never seeks its own. It's a love that would do what's best for the girl, even if it tears your heart in two." He paused. "Here she can live among her own, as God intended. She can live in honor and dignity. You know how she would be treated in a city like that, among white people. This is her home, just as Seattle is yours."

Caleb looked into Lindsey's big, dark eyes and saw a tear trickle down her cheek. Some motherly instinct within her had bonded with this little one, and the thought of giving Esther up was heart wrenching.

"I think it's in every woman to want children, Lindsey," he told her. "You've done right by her, if anyone has. You saved her life, just as you did mine. When no one else in the world cared about her, you did. You have every right to take her back with you, but..." he hesitated.

"But what?"

"She belongs here," he said with finality. He stoked the fire and walked a hundred yards upriver to make his bed.

CHAPTER 19

The days which followed seemed endless. The long, grueling hours behind the dogs on the trail became days, and the days became a week. At Fort Yukon, they spent a day and a night. Caleb and Sam Titus burned and dug a pit down through the permafrost for the burial of the old woman's body. Members of her clan immediately set out to kill a moose for her potlatch, a celebration of her passing into the next life.

Little Esther seemed to blossom in the presence of Lilly, but who wouldn't? Lilly's joy was contagious and seemed to draw the little native girl out of her shell. Soon, she was smiling and laughing and babbling in her native tongue.

Lindsey was delighted to see the girl so happy, but her heart was already aching at the thought of losing her. Sam and Lilly insisted that Esther stay with them for she was of their clan, and among their people the Titus family was relatively prosperous.

Sam Titus had a friend who had salmon to spare, and Caleb purchased as much as they could haul. There was still food in Fort Yukon, unlike the towns upriver, Dawson and Fortymile. No luxuries could be found such as sugar or molasses, but they were able to secure flour, salt, coffee, bacon, beans, a bag of rice and a few tins of butter.

As they departed from Fort Yukon the following morning, Lindsey hid her tear-stained countenance from the Titus family. Big Sam stood with a stoic face on the porch of their humble home, while Lilly smiled and waved. Little Esther stood beside the young native woman, who now held her tiny hand.

Lindsey's emotions overcame her as the rapid pace of the wolf-dogs began to separate her from the little native girl. A brilliant sunrise overtook them and turned the gloomy riverbed into a picturesque snow-covered highway. After a time, she emerged from her despair and leaned against the back of the sled to absorb the warm sun. The dogs had slowed considerably by this time and had settled into a pace they could maintain for hours.

Caleb knelt down behind the girl and placed a reassuring hand on her shoulder. "You did the right thing, Lindsey," he said softly. "She'll be better off with her own people."

"Yes," she sighed. "I know she'll be happy."

As the hours and days crawled slowly by, Caleb and Lindsey ventured ever deeper into the magnificent wilderness. Each day the sun lingered a bit longer than the previous day, and the temperatures began to rise ever so slowly.

Two days downriver from Fort Yukon, the frontiersman swung his team away from the river and headed due south. There was no packed trail here to follow as there had been on the river, but only an ancient, forgotten trapline known only to Caleb.

When the snow became deep, Pierce would strap on his snowshoes and break trail for the dogs. The girl's admiration for this man of the wilderness seemed to grow with each day she spent with him. He was quiet, always choosing his words carefully. When he did speak, his words were meaningful. He was in his element here and enjoyed showing Lindsey his beautiful world.

He stopped often to point out a band of caribou in the distance or their tracks in the snow. Caribou were curious creatures, he told her, and would often approach if they didn't catch your scent. Each set of animal tracks told a different story, he explained, and he unraveled these mysteries of nature for Lindsey. The scrapes on a young aspen tree were from a young bull moose rubbing the velvet from his antlers. The scratches on a poplar might be those of a black bear marking his territory. Bark chewed from the heights of a tall spruce was a porcupine's handiwork. He knew the habits of each creature, what they were useful for and where they could be found. He noticed anything out of the ordinary and saw many things that Lindsey couldn't.

If circumstances had been different, this man and woman would have made a remarkable pair. The comely young maiden with long, black hair, so gracious, elegant and feminine, would have complemented nicely the handsome rugged frontiersman. But the quest now was for gold, not for love. Gold enough to purchase Miss Graham's passage home was the imminent objective.

The trail was steep and dangerous in places and the sled was heavily loaded. The old trapline followed bleak, barren ridges for miles, where stunted stands of black spruce contended with the elements for survival. It skirted enormous boulder fields where thousands of tons of granite had been strewn haphazardly by an ancient force. Occasionally the trail descended from the ridges and plunged down into a quiet valley where the snow was deeper and the timber taller.

The days were long and the trail was difficult, but something within the girl seemed to rise to the challenge. Caleb made her as comfortable as he could, taking a break now and then from the trail to share a bit of knowledge or an observation. She made no effort to impress him now, for he knew her weaknesses. They had been through difficulties and endured tragedy, and now there was no pretense between them. There was only reality. She trusted Pierce implicitly. He had not failed her. He was a man of honor and a man of his word.

Each night when they made camp, Pierce tied the lead dog, White Eyes, near Lindsey's bed to watch over her. Then he would disappear into the trees to make a bed of his own, well out of sight but not out of hearing. Occasionally a wolf howled off in the distance while she lay awake, and White Eyes would stand and growl softly. Lindsey would immediately shudder and snuggle deeper into her bedroll. The howl of a wolf was musical in a way, she decided.

After days of toil in the high country, they descended into a beautiful river valley surrounded by birch-covered hills. When they reached a small frozen riverbed, Caleb halted the dogs.

"Is this the Tanana?" asked Lindsey hopefully.

"No," he replied with a smile, "but we're getting close."

"But this is a river, isn't it?"

"The Chena River, Lindsey."

"This is a beautiful valley, Caleb," she observed.

"It is. You should see it in the summer or fall." He looked back toward the timber-covered hills. "I fear that one day this valley will be another Dawson City."

"Why is that sir?" she asked.

"There is gold here," he answered. "The creeks up in the hills around here are rich in color. Some prospector will happen by in a few years and find it." He paused. "Then they'll move in here and rip this valley and these hills apart to get it. They'll foul the creeks and kill the fish and every moose and caribou within a hundred miles of here."

"Caleb, why don't we look for gold here?" she suggested. "Must we go on, deeper into this rugged country?"

"Miss Lindsey, I have a few places I would like to show you yet, if you're agreeable. If you will trust me one last time, I promise you won't be disappointed."

"Mr. Pierce, if there is one person in this world that I do trust, it is you. I am at your mercy, and yet I know I am in capable hands."

After a few miles on the Chena River, they came at last to the dangerous Tanana. This was a braided waterway, whose name in Athabaskan meant Two Rivers." Far to the south and east, the Chisana and the Nebesna flowed out of the Wrangell Mountains to merge and form the mighty Tanana.

Just as Charlie Hawkins had prophesied, the Tanana was a formidable opponent from the beginning. It wasn't the hard-packed drifts of snow and ice or the massive log jams and debris that slowed them, but thin ice. Hot springs that boiled up out of the riverbed warmed these waters, causing unpredictable ice conditions and open water in places.

The patient frontiersman took no chances where Miss Graham's safety was concerned and was forced to detour around these dangerous pockets time and again. They made camp at the mouth of the Salcha River and then pressed on upriver the following day.

Another grueling day on the Tanana brought them into a land of beautiful, birch-covered hills and a large lake. They stopped early that evening and Caleb made a fine camp on a ridge overlooking the frozen landscape. Otter and beaver inhabited this lake, as was evidenced by their tracks and several holes out on the ice.

"Miss Lindsey, would you like to try your hand at ice fishing?" asked Pierce, as he rummaged through his gear on the sled. He found a pair of rigged lines and a piece of salt pork for bait. Together they walked out onto the ice and dropped their lines into the holes. After a time, Lindsey was rewarded with action on her line and jerked a nice grayling up through the hole and onto the ice. Caleb rebaited her line, and she immediately caught another.

"You're quite a fisherman," declared Pierce, as he again prepared her line. "You're already two ahead of me." Lindsey was suddenly captivated by this new skill she had learned.

"Beginner's luck, I believe," she ventured.

They sat patiently for a few minutes, hoping for another grayling or two. Suddenly, Lindsey's line became alive again, as the struggling fish underneath threatened to pull her down through the hole.

"Caleb, I can't hold him," she exclaimed, as her hooked victim jerked viciously on the other end of the line. The frontiersman was quickly at her side, observing and encouraging her as she fought the big lunker for several minutes. The girl gasped in amazement when Pierce finally pulled a large lake trout up through the hole and landed him at her feet.

"Well, we've got supper, thanks to you," he said. "That old fella must weigh twelve or fifteen pounds."

"I love fishing," Lindsey suddenly decided. "I mean this is really the first time I've ever fished, but it's quite enjoyable."

"It's humiliating, not to mention embarrassing," drawled Pierce. "You caught supper and I got skunked!" he pulled his inactive line up out of the hole. "Rascals stole my bait," he observed with a twinkle in his eye.

As they were carrying the fish up from the lake, a thought occurred to Lindsey. "Caleb, you never baited your line! Did you?"

"Sure I did," he teased.

At a nameless creek the following day, the frontiersman and Miss Graham abandoned the Tanana and followed the little tributary northward. A trapline paralleled the frozen creek for thirty miles, but the trapline had not seen traffic yet this winter. White Eyes and his canine companions seemed more eager now, for they sensed their long trek across the Interior was nearly over.

They made their last camp in the late afternoon, as they wouldn't have time to make it over the mountains to the Goodpastor by nightfall. Caleb rationed out the last of the salmon to the dogs, saving only enough for the following morning. "We'll have a tough day tomorrow," he warned the girl that evening. "We're sure to find some deep snows up on top."

Although Lindsey was anxious to attack the mountain the following morning and end their long trip, the frontiersman displayed no such urgency. He was seldom in a hurry, content to enjoy each moment as it floated slowly by.

Toward midmorning, they broke camp and began to slowly ascend up into the high country once again. They picked their way slowly and carefully upward, following a dangerous, obscure pathway that twisted and turned up the side of the mountain. The trail clung tenaciously to the mountain on the left, but dropped off sharply on the right until the valley was barely visible a thousand feet below. Still, they ascended up to the tree line, where ancient, deformed black spruce trees stood, blasted and coated now with layers of snow and ice.

For a time, they were on top of the world it seemed, as they followed yet another alpine ridge along for miles. Ahead of them to the north, the mountains rose up rugged and majestic. Behind them, the hills sloped gently down toward the Tanana basin. They skirted a high peak and then began a steep descent that continued for several miles. As they descended out of the high country and into another world, Lindsey and Caleb slowed the dogs and sled the best they could.

So this was Caleb's world, thought Lindsey as she beheld some of the most beautiful scenery she had ever seen. This forlorn country, known only to the frontiersman and perhaps a few natives was breathtaking. It was rugged and pure, and quiet like Pierce himself. Timber-covered ridges stretched in all directions, rising up toward the surrounding mountains. Dozens of deep, brush-choked canyons plunged down toward the Goodpastor River, which meandered through the valley below.

The man and woman followed the Goodpastor north for a few miles and then crossed the river. Up on a wooded knoll overlooking the valley was a log cabin.

"We're home, Miss Lindsey," announced the frontiersman as they pulled to a stop in front of a sturdy log structure.

The fleeting sun of early April provided a bit of warmth as they unpacked the sled and tended to the dogs. There was kindling and tinder beside the wood stove, left there by Pierce many months before. Lindsey quickly had a fire going and began to explore the cabin. Things were a bit dusty, for the winds that blew out of the mountains here often kicked up the silt along the river.

Despite a coating of dust, this cabin was certainly the finest she had seen in the north. It was large and finely crafted of straight, peeled timbers. A ladder led up to a sizeable loft that was illuminated by a small glass window. There was a small table in the loft and a sturdy handmade bed covered with soft caribou hides.

Downstairs a wood cookstove dominated one corner, with a pitcher pump nearby. A fine set of handmade chairs and a handsome table stood in the center of the cabin. A larger glass window gave light and provided a view of the lonely valley and frozen river.

Outside the cabin were smaller, less noble log buildings, which included a smokehouse, a privy and a cache mounted high up on a set of poles. Lindsey sat on the porch for a moment while Caleb finished his chores. When he was done, he sat down beside her and looked out across the valley.

"Well, what do you think of this country, Miss Lindsey?" asked the frontiersman.

"It's absolutely breathtaking," she breathed. "So pristine and pure."

"It's even prettier when the snow melts," he told her. "It's quiet and peaceful now, but when the river breaks up, it just fills the whole valley with its music."

"Where is the gold, Caleb?" she asked.

Pierce took a handful of snow and fashioned it into a ball. "It's all around us," he answered. "I believe this whole mountain behind us is full of gold. These little creeks that flow on either side and down to the river are where I've been panning these past two years."

"A whole mountain full of gold," sighed the girl. "How will you ever get it all out?"

"I don't intend to touch it, Miss Lindsey. We'll get enough to meet our needs out of the creeks. I can't bear the thought of tearing up this country, even for gold."

"I do agree it would be a shame to have a town like Dawson in this valley," she said.

The howl of a wolf from upriver drifted toward them on the evening breeze, causing a small commotion among the sled dogs.

"That was eerie," observed the girl. "I don't think I could ever get accustomed to hearing those lonely cries."

Caleb tossed the snowball he had fashioned toward one of the dogs. "It grows on you after a while."

They sat talking on the porch for a time, each enjoying the company of the other. "Caleb, this cabin is very nice," she said as she arose to go in. "It's the best cabin I've seen here in the north, certainly better than any in Dawson."

"Sam Titus helped me build it about three years ago. That was before he and Lilly jumped the broom. I was prospecting up here about five years ago and found some good, clear color in one of these creeks," he continued. "The more I panned, the more I realized that this could be the next big strike. But after what happened over in Fortymile, the way they tore that country up over there, I decided to keep quiet about it." The frontiersman shook his head sadly.

"It wasn't just the way people destroyed the land, but it was the greed that bothered me. People started jumping one another's claims and fighting over claim boundaries. And then, when Jimmy and Klara took off with all of our gold we had panned, I just got sick of it all. I vowed if I ever found good color again, I'd keep quiet about it."

"Sam comes up here once in a while to dig around, but he's not a greedy man. He and I hauled all of this stuff in here for the cabin a few years ago, and he helped me stack the logs and put on the roof." He paused. "I thought if I ever tired of trapping and running the rivers, I might retreat to this pretty little valley."

"Mr. Pierce," said Lindsey earnestly, "I'm honored that you've chosen to share your beautiful valley for a time. Your secret is safe with me."

CHAPTER 20

Winter seemed to hold Caleb's beautiful valley in its grip forever. Each day the sun stayed longer, but the cold temperatures continued. Caleb and Lindsey started up a trapline to occupy their time, and fished for grayling and pike through the ice on the river.

Small bands of caribou wandered through the valley occasionally, remnants of the great Fortymile herd that roamed from the Alaska Range to the Mackenzie Mountains in Canada. Moose were abundant along the Goodpastor, and Dall sheep patrolled the ramparts of the surrounding mountains. Black bears and grizzlies were growing restless in their dens and were beginning to venture forth to feed on whatever they might find.

Ever so slowly winter began to release its hold on the upper Goodpastor and the snow began to melt. As the days grew longer and warmer, great flocks of Canadian geese and sandhill cranes filled the skies, hurrying on to their nesting grounds farther north. Trumpeter and Tundra swans passed over in smaller flocks, along with fleet-flying ducks of many species.

The snows in the mountains became tiny streams that flowed ever downward toward the Goodpastor. The river, in turn, became a torrent that carried along with it slabs of ice and tons of wood debris.

In late April, a native from Healy Lake, a friend of the frontiersman, came and took the dogs. He would care for them until the fall, when Pierce would come back upriver.

By early May, the snow was gone. Caleb took Lindsey out to one of the creeks that flowed alongside the mountain he was sure held the mother lode. Here on the creek, above a small beaver pond, they began panning. "I've done most of my work over on the other creek," he explained to Lindsey. "I'm not sure exactly what we'll find here. I've never really panned much over on this side."

The frontiersman's first pan yielded two small nuggets. Lindsey's yielded a larger one and a bit of dust. By midday, they were both doing quite well. Already, the little pouch tied to Lindsey's waist was beginning to bulge. "Lindsey, you're doing a fine job of this on your own," said Caleb. "I think if we split up, we may find something even better. I'll need to purchase a grubstake when we get to the Yukon River, so I'd best pan a little for myself."

"Fine with me, Caleb," she responded. "How much gold should I take?"

"How much do you want?" he asked.

"Enough to pay for my passage home and perhaps a bit to help my aunt and uncle."

"Well, I've no claim on it," he said. "It's all up for grabs."

As Lindsey moved upstream, the gravel in her pans began to grow richer. Caleb disappeared and left her to her work. She moved quickly further up the creek, growing more excited as she walked. Suddenly, memories of her brother flooded her mind. If only Horace were here to see this, she thought.

She climbed out of the creek bed and sat on the hill for a while. A beaver was hard at work in the little slough a hundred yards below. Lindsey worked hard all afternoon, and then returned to the cabin alone. Caleb was there, and supper was on the stove. "I got tired of digging and went down to the river to wet a hook," he told her. "How did you do?"

Lindsey showed him the small leather poke, bulging now with gold dust and nuggets. Caleb whistled softly. "That'll buy your passage home," he said.

"I'd like to get more if I can," she said hopefully.

"I can understand that," he replied. "Take all you want. We can build a rocker box if you like. It would make things a bit faster for you."

"No. No thank you, Caleb. I've found a great spot above the beaver lodge."

Gold fever seemed to seize the girl in the weeks that followed. She panned enough gold for her passage home several times over, yet still continued her quest for riches. The frontiersman was content to let her dig, for each day she lingered was another day spent together.

In the early days of June, salmon arrived in the Goodpastor River. They were tired and spent, having traveled over a thousand miles up the Yukon and the Tanana. These were the Chinook salmon, the largest of the five species, some weighing thirty pounds or more.

It was on the day that the salmon returned that Lindsey announced that she was ready to go home to Seattle. Her stash of gold was growing heavy and would be worth a fortune. Charlie Hawkins had told them in Fortymile that the price of gold had escalated to thirty dollars an ounce.

The tearing of Lindsey's heart began in earnest now, for a part of her dearly loved the frontiersman and his beautiful, wild world. The longing for civilization, for her friends and family, pulled at her from the other direction.

It was with heavy hearts that Caleb and Lindsey set things in order at the cabin on the upper Goodpastor and packed their things for the trip downriver. Caleb's heart was aching mightily, for he had held secret hopes that this girl might fall in love with his little valley. He would have wept, except that men of the north, explorers and adventurers, were above such displays of emotion. It was not considered manly so they kept their wounded feelings bottled up inside, where they festered and infected the heart.

Behind a facade of cheerfulness, Pierce packed Miss Graham's meager belongings and her heavy treasure into the freight canoe. He fashioned a comfortable seat for her in the front and would have shoved off, but she had disappeared.

He found her up in a clearing, looking across the valley toward the cabin, which was dwarfed by the mountain behind. "Caleb, I hope I'm doing the right thing," she said. "I love this little valley. It has to be the prettiest place on earth."

"I'm going to call it 'Lindsey's Valley'," offered the frontiersman. "Whenever I come back up here, I'll always remember the time I spent with you."

"I'll never see it again," she sighed. "I'm such a fool to be leaving you, but I can't help myself." She began to cry.

"I just want you to be happy," he told her. "Charlie Hawkins is right, Lindsey, this is a hard country, even for a man. The cold, the mosquitos and no-seeums. Hauling wood and water, and the long miles on the trail... wolves and bears always causing trouble, and then the riffraff that are drifting in here after gold. Cabin fever and loneliness... with no womenfolk to talk to. This is no kind of life for a fine woman like you."

They returned to the river after a time and shoved off into the swift current of the Goodpastor. Lindsey had not been on the water since the previous fall, when the tragic accident had occurred at Five Finger Rapids. Immediately, she thought of her brother, Horace, and of being rescued out the belly of the mighty Yukon by the frontiersman.

Things were different now. Even in the waters of this turbulent river there was peace. Caleb Pierce feared nothing in this wilderness, for he understood the earth, the seasons, and the dangers that lurked along the trails and rivers. But he feared those things he could not comprehend. Man's lust for gold and the things he would do to obtain the yellow metal was disturbing to Pierce. Man's carelessness for this great land and the wildlife that inhabited the Interior plagued him as well. The callousness and the brutality that drove men to hurt and kill each other was something new, which came with the gold seekers.

For hours they drifted in the current of the river. While Caleb skillfully guided the canoe, the girl rested and watched for wildlife. Her vigilance was rewarded with sightings of moose and caribou, beaver and otter. She also spied a grizzly with twin cubs and many species of migratory waterfowl.

Late that evening, they pitched camp on the banks of the Goodpastor, for they still had not reached the Tanana River, which flowed northwesterly toward the Yukon. Navigating the Tanana would prove to be more difficult, for its hazards never seemed to end. Log jams, gravel bars, whirlpools and sweepers were ever- present dangers.

While the Goodpastor was clear and clean, the Tanana was brown and murky, laden with glacial silt. Salmon had to rest in its tributaries to clean the silt from their gills on their long journey to their spawning grounds.

The trip down the Tanana to the Yukon was long and tedious. The days of early June were nearly without darkness. Every hour on the water brought Lindsey closer to the Yukon, where she would catch a steamer for home.

They talked often; she, of what remained of her family, the booming city of Seattle and of her old friends. He talked of Alaska and the Yukon Territory, of hard times and good times of the past, and places he yet wanted to see.

"Lindsey, what's the first thing you plan to do when you get to Seattle? He asked one afternoon as the floated along. The girl thought for a moment.

I'm going shopping with Aunt Ida," she responded. "I'll have to buy some new clothes. The only store bought dress I have left is so tattered I won't be able to wear it again."

"I think you look mighty fetching in your caribou skin dress, Lindsey."

"You flatter me, Caleb," she scolded, but the compliment pleased her. "What else would you do?" he asked.

"I will probably go to the market and buy some fruit. I haven't had an apple in almost a year," she answered. "They grow a lot of them in Washington. And some ice cream would be heavenly. Caleb, have ever had ice cream?"

"I expect not," he answered. "What's it taste like?"

"It's sweeter than honey," she told him. "There are shops down in Seattle that sell different flavors of it."

"I'd like to try some one day," he told her. "I've heard about it, but Charlie Hawkins says he can't get it."

"How about horehound candy, Caleb? Or peppermint? It's nothing but pure sugar.

"Well it sounds awful good, but I've never had any. Sam Titus says that when the white man brought sugar up here and traded it to his people, they lost their strength. He won't eat it, and he's as strong as a moose." They said nothing for a time and then Lindsey broke the silence.

"And what are your plans, Caleb?"

"I thought I might head south after this, down into the Alaska Range. Did I ever tell you about Denali, Lindsey?" he asked.

"No, you never mentioned it. What is it?"

"It's just a mountain. It's to the south and west of us a hundred miles or so. The natives call it Denali. In their language, it means 'The High One.' It's the highest mountain around here.

"I'd like to see it," she told him.

"If you ever come back to Alaska Lindsey, I'll take you there," promised the frontiersman.

I won't be coming back, she thought, but didn't have the heart to say it aloud.

On the ninth day of June, they reached the village of Tanana, which had been built at the confluence of the Tanana and the Yukon. It wasn't much of a town in Lindsey's estimation, certainly nothing like Seattle. There was only a little trading post, half a dozen dilapidated log cabins and a large dock for loading cordwood. Fortunately, a steamer headed for the outside was due in that evening. The frontiersman had determined that a prolonged departure for Miss Graham would be agony. A rapid departure would not be painless, but would be merciful. They had been in the village only four hours when the steamer Duchess arrived and docked to take on wood. The Duchess was crowded with a myriad of refugees from Dawson, along with the lucky handful who had struck it rich.

Lindsey looked on as Caleb labored to secure passage for her on the steamer. They were already overcrowded, but a generous tip to the captain finally changed his mind. Lindsey's small fortune of gold dust and nuggets was placed under lock and key in the captain's quarters at Caleb's request. Caleb also located an old friend on the steamer who was headed outside, and entreated him to look out for the girl.

All too soon the cordwood was loaded for the boilers, and the whistle blew for departure. The girl stood looking at the man in buckskin, groping for words. Hearts were breaking as each sought the courage to meet the other's gaze. The girl was crying, but the frontiersman was stoic, mustering all his strength to contain his emotions. Never had Lindsey been so unsure of herself.

"Oh! Caleb," she cried, as she flung herself into his arms. She held him as if she would never let him go. A small crowd was staring at the beautiful girl in the caribou skin dress, clinging to the man of the north.

"I love you," she whispered softly, but he heard her clearly.

"And I love you, Lindsey," he said as he crushed her in his arms. "I'll always love you."

The stewards were pushing to depart and were growing impatient with Caleb. At last he released her and reached up, brushing back a rebellious lock of dark hair from her face. Then he walked down the gangplank and didn't stop.

Lindsey watched the frontiersman as the steamship moved out into the current, hoping that he might turn and wave. He did not look back, but continued walking. As he walked away from the river, great tears streamed down his face. He did not stop walking until he was far from town.

CHAPTER 21

The bustling city of Seattle welcomed the Duchess and her passengers home with open arms. Gold fever was raging all along the West Coast, and every available vessel, some barely seaworthy, was heading north to the Klondike. Thousands of people had arrived in Seattle from points east, all bursting with confidence, to equip themselves and embark on the perilous journey north.

Lindsey was shocked when the little steamship pulled into port. Seattle was far different from the little city she had abandoned only a year before. Throngs of people lined the wharf now, cheering and waving. There were people everywhere, and stacks of tools and supplies as far as she could see. The port was choked with ships and barges, many of which were being loaded for the long journey north to the Klondike. She should have been glad to be home, but this did not resemble the home she remembered.

What would Aunt Ida say when she saw the dress she was wearing? A year before the caribou dress she now wore would have shamed her. It had drawn strange looks and even a few comments from the steamship crew and its passengers. There was a time in her life when she wouldn't be caught dead in it, but things had changed. The frontiersman had called her his Indian Princess the first time she had worn it. He had told her that she looked fetching in it just a month ago, and this pleased her. Caleb always meant what he said and knew a fetching woman when he saw one. If Caleb Pierce liked it, then she would wear it in dignity.

The Duchess was the third steamship to arrive from the Klondike that summer, and like the two previous vessels, brought back many disillusioned passengers and only a handful of successful gold hunters. The reports of the unsuccessful were spurned by the gold-crazy populace, who watched and cheered as the few wealthy dragged their heavy boxes of gold down the gangplank.

Miss Graham's take was modest compared to a few, who suddenly found themselves to be filthy rich. Her accomplishment was newsworthy, however, for she was a single woman. She was ushered along with the others to the nearest bank where her collection of dust and nuggets was weighed and measured. The price of gold had soared to thirty-five dollars per troy ounce, which left Lindsey Graham a moderately wealthy woman.

Uncle Bert and Aunt Ida were thrilled to see their lovely niece again, and not because she was suddenly rich and famous. She had always been a delight to them, for they had never been blessed with children of their own. They welcomed their wayward niece into their home.

Her return to the big city was glorious at first, as she was hailed "Queen of the Klondike" by her admirers. Old friends were suddenly best friends, and distant relatives were now not so distant. There was a steady stream at Aunt Ida's place of gentlemen callers, relatives, and many would-be prospectors soliciting her advice. Time and time again she told the exciting stories of her time in the beautiful, rugged North Country.

Always, she spoke with reverence of the frontiersman. The man who was a legend in the North Country became a legend in Seattle as well. True to her word, she never mentioned Caleb's little valley on the upper Goodpastor.

Lindsey Graham was on top of the world that summer. The finest, wealthiest men in Seattle were beating a path to her door. Invitations to parties, dances, and various social functions arrived daily. Uncle Bert and Aunt Ida, who considered themselves "just simple folks," were vaulted into the upper echelon of Seattle society.

Seattle was not the same city Lindsey Graham had left behind just a year before. Gold fever was rapidly driving this city to madness. Tens of thousands had arrived here and most of these people were heading north. Day and night they roamed the streets, as all of the hotels and boarding houses were packed. Stacks of goods lined the streets and strings of luckless, worn out horses were paraded through town on their way out to the wharf. These would be loaded onto the steamships heading north, and would soon be in service on the harrowing Dead Horse Trail.

Crime escalated in Seattle as gangsters and ruffians moved into town and set up shop. Good, strong dogs were bringing a hundred dollars each, and many were stolen from Seattle residents and smuggled onto the departing steamers for use in the north. Theft was an everyday occurrence now and more heinous offenses than this were not unheard of.

Gold was the talk of Seattle, as it was in San Francisco and Vancouver. It was the chief topic in every crowded saloon and filtered into every conversation. Peddlers and outfitters sold tools and implements specifically designed for use in the gold fields such as Yukon stoves, Klondike picks and shovels, Yukon boots and Klondike gold pans. There were people everywhere, and not a quiet moment to be found. No, Seattle was not the same and never would be again.

Lindsey's days were busy and full, but after a time she began to grow tired of the city's rapid pace. The noises of Seattle, the trains that raced through the town at all hours of the night and the constant honking of the horns of motorcars vexed her. It seemed there were always visitors at Aunt Ida's. Each night she fell into bed exhausted, relieved to be free from people for a few hours. Often, as she lay awake on her soft bed, she would think of the noble frontiersman, and wonder where he might be. Was he out on the trail somewhere, cold and alone, shivering to keep warm? He would be listening for the lonely howls of the timber wolves, and the song of his own heart would not be so different.

She was of age to marry of course, and had already received several proposals since her return, but the thought sickened her. Aunt Ida, bless her heart, was continually parading a lineup of young men before her for her consideration. Lindsey was cordial and polite, but the endless stream of strangers was just a blur.

As the summer slipped away, despite the best efforts of friends and family to cheer her, the girl grew despondent. She longed for her quiet time at night when she could escape the world around her. She thought of Caleb Pierce often. She longed now for his peaceful, tranquil world where there was still a bit of sanity.

Where was he? Was he thinking of her? He had said that he would always love her. His words seemed to tear at her soul now, for she knew he had spoken the truth. He had never been one to speak flippantly, but chose his words carefully, and meant what he said.

She began to realize the magnitude of her mistake as the leaves on the trees began to turn colors. The cold winds of October came in from the ocean and tossed the leaves from the trees into the city streets. She too, had meant what she said on the steamer in Tanana. She really had loved, and still did love this man of the north. He was ever in her thoughts now, and often in her dreams. She loved him and yet had forsaken him for the miserable life she was currently living.

It was not only Caleb she missed. She longed now for the endless clear skies and the pristine rivers of Alaska. The simple people like Sam and Lilly, the rugged mountains and the even the dangers of life in the bush called to her.

Her world here in Seattle seemed so small and structured and finite now. It seemed that there was no purpose to living other than living itself. She felt like a caged animal on a treadmill going nowhere. Even if she returned to Alaska Territory, the chances of finding Caleb were slim to none. He avoided most of the towns and the people there, except for the handful who knew him as a friend.

A steady rain was falling. Lindsey woke up to the sound of the rain on the roof, and it soothed her troubled soul. She lay awake for a couple of hours, listening to the rain and thinking. She dressed herself and brushed her long, black hair, as she had promised to go to the market with Aunt Ida today. She was freshening up when her aunt came to her room.

"Lindsey dear, do come quickly. There's a gentleman here to see you."

"Please send him away, Aunt Ida," she pleaded. "I don't want to see anyone today."

The plump aunt disappeared momentarily, but soon returned. "He says he's came a long way to see you Lindsey, and it's pouring outside."

"All right. I'll be right there."

When she entered the living room, Caleb Pierce stood in the doorway, soaked to the skin. He looked like a half-drowned puppy, hoping to be let in the house. She ran quickly across the room and into his strong arms. He held her there for a moment, rocking her ever so slightly and trying not to crush her in his strong arms. She was warm and soft and smelled nice, while he was cold and wet and didn't smell quite as nice.

Aunt Ida busied herself in the kitchen and left her pretty niece unchaperoned yet safe in the arms of the Alaska frontiersman.

"Caleb, I really do love you," she told him through a blur of tears. "And I want to go back to Alaska with you."

"I'm willin' to stay here Lindsey, as long as you'll be my wife."

She looked up into his eyes. "I will be your wife, Caleb, but I want to go back up north with you. We both know you belong in Alaska. I know now that Alaska is where I belong too."

He kissed her then and held her close, as the cold Seattle rain played a sweet song of love on the tin roof.

- END -

Lightning Source UK Ltd.
Milton Keynes UK
UKHW021017210820
368606UK00012B/985

CHRISTMAS TALES FROM THE FARM

The Yorkshire Shepherdess

PUFFIN

DISCLAIMER: Frozen bodies of water are dangerous and you should not attempt to walk or skate on a frozen lake.

PUFFIN BOOKS

UK | USA | Canada | Ireland | Australia
India | New Zealand | South Africa

Puffin Books is part of the Penguin Random House group of companies whose addresses can be found at global.penguinrandomhouse.com.

www.penguin.co.uk   www.puffin.co.uk   www.ladybird.co.uk

First published 2025

001

Text copyright © Amanda Owen, 2025
Additional material and research by Corinne Lucas
Illustrations copyright © Becca Hall, 2025

The moral right of the author has been asserted

Penguin Random House values and supports copyright. Copyright fuels creativity, encourages diverse voices, promotes freedom of expression and supports a vibrant culture. Thank you for purchasing an authorized edition of this book and for respecting intellectual property laws by not reproducing, scanning or distributing any part of it by any means without permission. You are supporting authors and enabling Penguin Random House to continue to publish books for everyone. No part of this book may be used or reproduced in any manner for the purpose of training artificial intelligence technologies or systems. In accordance with Article 4(3) of the DSM Directive 2019/790, Penguin Random House expressly reserves this work from the text and data mining exception.

Set in 11.5/16.5pt Sabon LT Pro
Typeset by Six Red Marbles UK, Thetford, Norfolk
Printed and bound in Great Britain by Clays Ltd, Elcograf S.p.A.

The authorized representative in the EEA is Penguin Random House Ireland, Morrison Chambers, 32 Nassau Street, Dublin D02 YH68

A CIP catalogue record for this book is available from the British Library

ISBN: 978–0–241–65725–6

All correspondence to:
Puffin Books
Penguin Random House Children's
One Embassy Gardens, 8 Viaduct Gardens, London SW11 7BW

Penguin Random House is committed to a sustainable future for our business, our readers and our planet. This book is made from Forest Stewardship Council® certified paper.

A dedication for the distractors.

For those that gnawed at my feet, tugged at my sleeve, stole my pens, and chewed both my hair and charging cable. Demanded food and attention; belched, farted and sought to ruin the ambience of whatever peaceful corner of the farm I claimed, giving me inspiration, irritation and fleas in the process.

And to the animals on the farm also, without whom I would have no story.

Contents

Introduction	1
The Runaway Reindeer	5
Chicken for Christmas	21
Chalky the Arctic Terrier	35
The Greatest (Gift) Of All Time	49
Goodbye, Little Joe	63
Three Yuletide Yarns, Two Spotted Sheep and a New Year's Miracle	79
Our Winter Olympics	93
Guess Hoo?	107
A Snowy Game of Hide and Sheep	121
An Owen-Family Christmas	137
Glossary	155
Acknowledgements	165
Quiz	167

Introduction

Dear Reader,

Welcome to Christmas at Ravenseat Farm.

My name is Amanda Owen, but I'm also known generally as the 'Yorkshire Shepherdess'.

I am a shepherdess, writer and mother of nine children – Raven, Reuben, Miles, Edith, Violet, Sidney, Annas, Clementine and the youngest, Nancy. We live at Ravenseat Farm in the Yorkshire Dales, England, with the children's dad, Clive, as well as a **menagerie** of animals – sheep, cows, chickens, dogs, horses, goats and more.

Each and every day on the farm we keep to a strict schedule set by the needs of our animals, and the seasons too. There are always plenty of jobs to be getting on with, but we all muck in together and that's what makes it so fun. From shepherding the sheep (and the children too!) to feeding, lambing, homework, fetching, carrying, digging and more. We feel so lucky to live among lots of green space where the children can grow, learn and play, and we get to see the British countryside at its finest all year round.

With springtime come the newborn lambs. The **moorland** birds fly home to the hills to lay their eggs on the ground. The hay meadows start to grow, and the fields shine with yellow marsh marigolds, nodding their heads in the gentle breeze. The skylarks bring their song, and it's a hopeful time of new life and fresh starts.

Summer bathes the hazy mountainous peaks in a golden glow. In the valleys below you'll find a maze of **drystone walls** to get lost among. The sheep are shorn of their thick wool, making them look clean and white against the bright green of the land. Summer holidays are here, and the children love nothing more than bathing the ponies in the **beck**, splashing in the **tarn** or using the long hours of sunshine to go on adventures and picnics across the nearby **moors**.

In autumn, the birds leave the hills and head

to lowlands and warmer climates. The moors lose their colour as the **bracken** turns a rich burnt umber, and the bright purple of the heather flowers begins to fade. Now is the time to prepare for the colder months that lay ahead, and we shepherds start bringing our flocks down from the hills to mate.

And at the end of the year, in the depths of winter, we face howling winds, sub-zero temperatures and lightless days. Here the weather makes its own rules, and never-ending rain and deep, deep snow can become some of our biggest challenges.

But winter, and Christmas especially, is also a special time of joy and adventure at Ravenseat. Whether that's discovering animals who have come to the farm to shelter from the weather, like the barn owls you can read all about in 'Guess Hoo', or the festive family traditions we've followed for years, like our own version of the Winter Olympics (turn to page 93 for more on those). And of course it can be a hard time too, like when my sheepdog Kate and I had to play a snowy game of hide and *sheep* in the deep winter snow, which you can discover on page 121.

But above everything, winter and Christmas at Ravenseat Farm is a time for family, friends and farming. And so, I thought it would be a good idea to write this collection of short stories and share just some of our festive fun and frolics with you.

I hope you enjoy the book and, however you choose to spend it, I hope you have a wonderful Christmas.

Amanda x

The Runaway Reindeer

The countdown to Christmas was underway. The children had two weeks off school and high hopes for snow and a visit from Santa.

We'd had great fun decorating the living room with berry-laden branches of holly and small pine cones plucked from the conifer trees that stood below the farmhouse. And our faithful Christmas tree had once again been uprooted from its mossy bank beside the river and now sat next to the draughty living-room door, shimmering with gaudy tinsel and a thoroughly random selection of baubles.

The week-long build-up to Christmas Day followed the same pattern every year. Miles would untangle the knot of fairy lights that probably wouldn't work.

Reuben would have 'borrowed' (and not returned) the large turkey roasting tray to catch oil from beneath a tractor. And I would carefully fill our shared advent calendar with chocolate treats, which would almost immediately be stolen by a thief or two.

As well as the usual daily chores around the farm – the feeding of the cows and sheep and mucking out of the horses – we made great plans for a festive extravaganza of delicious food, homemade presents, crackers and karaoke. We also got out the board games, though we only truly felt *bored* when we were stuck in the house for any length of time; we are an outdoorsy family to the core.

The Christmas parish party was another thing to look forward to. Held in the village hall, it was an opportunity for the children to dress up in their most flamboyant outfits and meet up with friends. Laden with tins of mince pies, cake and homemade pizza, they would gallop in, looking forward to a night of party games like pass-the-parcel and musical chairs.

I looked forward to it too, as I could stay home for a night of peace and quiet (which is quite rare on a busy farm). A few hours alone also gave me chance to wrap gifts and get ready for the big day, away from prying eyes. Clive would reluctantly stay at the village hall, acting as guardian, referee and peacemaker, ready to provide tissues for snotty noses, sticking plasters for minor injuries and encouragement where needed.

The party always began with a gentle round of bingo and ended with the kinds of chaotic games that often end in tears. There was lots of homemade food to eat and then afterwards a disco. And every year, around halfway through the party, Santa would arrive with a gift for each of the children.

But this time, Santa's visit included a surprise – he was bringing along not only an elf but three four-legged helpers . . .

Reindeers: tame ones that the children could stroke and feed.

The children were beside themselves with excitement, ready to ask Santa and his elf all their questions. I dreaded to think what they might be; living on a working farm meant that they were very practical, so it could be anything, such as:

'Do reindeer get **foot-rot?**' or,

'Do they need to have **eartags?**'

Clemmy and Annas had filled a couple of small bags with **sheep nuts** that they hoped the woolly visitors would find irresistible.

'Which reindeers will Santa bring?' Clemmy asked.

'I have no idea,' I said, wracking my brain for their names. 'Rudolph, maybe?'

'No, no, no,' replied Annas. 'I've heard that only the girls are coming.'

Back at the party, Santa took centre stage while his three reindeer stood patiently beside him wearing smart red-leather collars with silver bells. They nuzzled Annas's and Clemmy's hands, and became all the children could talk about for the next few days.

But Santa's visit wasn't to be the most exciting thing that happened that year . . .

It was 23 December and the weather was bright and cold, perfect for the sheep that were happily grazing at the moor without a care in the world.

With only a couple of days left before Christmas, it seemed that everything was unusually calm. Both the household and farm were running smoothly, and I was completely prepared and unflustered – it almost felt too good to be true. In previous years we'd had to deal with various disasters – a mouse taking up residence in the dairy on Christmas Day, the oven conking out while cooking the festive dinner and, worse still, *head lice* (which was only noticed when I was helping the children put on their paper hats).

The oldest two children had finished work for the year at last: Reuben had temporarily stopped all his digging jobs – people really didn't want to have a noisy digger on their land during the Christmas holidays – and Raven was back from university, making the farmhouse a *full* house.

The younger children were happily crafting Christmas stockings for the sheepdogs and the horses. But for the older ones, everything being quite so orderly just wasn't what they were used to.

'You seem to have everything under total control this year,' mused Raven who was busy crocheting.

'Absolutely I have,' I said, smiling.

'Feels a bit weird if you ask me,' she replied.

'Maybe after all these years I have finally cracked it,' I said, trying not to sound too smug.

'We've had some good Christmases over the years,' said Reuben wistfully.

'Do you remember that time I fell asleep with a chocolate orange in my bed?' said Raven.

'OK! That's enough of that. What shall we do?' asked Miles.

There was silence.

All the farm jobs had been done, and the house was completely tidied.

'Erm,' I pondered. 'I'm sure that there's plenty to get on with . . .'

'I never thought that I'd ever say this,' chipped in Sid, 'but I'm bored.'

Raven focused on her crochet, Miles and Sidney

sloped off upstairs, Edith and Violet went to make cups of tea.

Suddenly Reuben's phone rang, cutting through the silence like a knife. He answered and listened carefully to whoever was on the line, occasionally agreeing with whatever the caller was saying.

'Yep, yep ... Really? How on earth did that happen?'

I flashed him a curious look, but he just put his finger over his lips and left the room so he could carry on the conversation.

I stoked up the fire and was just plumping up Chalky's dog bed when Reuben strode back in.

'You'll never guess what,' he teased.

Clive looked up from his newspaper, peering over his glasses. 'Now what's happened?' he asked.

'You know the reindeer that came to the parish party? Well, one of them has escaped, gone on the run, headed for the hills!'

'No way,' I said. 'Really?'

'Yes, really, and guess who they want to find and catch her? None other than yours truly.'

By now the whole family had gathered and were quizzing Reuben on what exactly had happened.

It seemed that the reindeer had a very busy schedule in the run-up to Christmas, with many venues to visit alongside Santa. Somehow, in their haste to pack up after the parish party, a gate had been left open . . .

. . . and the most curious (or naughty) reindeer had made a *very low-speed getaway*!

The elf – who was also the reindeer's keeper – had done his best to tempt her back, but she was quite determined to continue on her adventure. Out of the village hall and into the darkness she had plodded, turning her back on her two friends and heading to . . . well, nobody knew where!

'Oh my goodness, this is soooooo exciting,' exclaimed Annas.

'An escaped reindeer?' added Edith. 'How unbelievably festive.'

'You couldn't make it up!' I said, shaking my head.

And the children had so many questions:

Where was the reindeer now?

Had there been any sightings?

If we did find her, how were we going to capture her safely?

Reuben was in his element – an exciting new challenge had just come his way.

'We need to make an action plan,' he mused.

This needed to be kept quiet; the last thing any reindeer in unfamiliar surroundings needed was to be scared by lots of people going to find it.

'Why can't we just grab her? If we can get close enough,' asked Violet.

'Well, I *have* been up close to them, and I know that they are very big and strong,' said Clemmy.

'And they can move very quickly,' stated Nancy firmly.

'How do you know that?' asked Edith.

'Because they pull Santa's sleigh around the world on Christmas Eve!' Nancy replied.

There were nods of agreement all around.

'Good ol' Santa is going to be missing one of his team this year,' said Clive.

Apparently the last time the reindeer had been seen was the previous evening, after the party at the village hall. Surely any sensible animal with a sense of adventure would head away from humans and towards the open countryside? There had been no reports of a reindeer roaming the streets, and nobody in the village had awoken to one in their garden, so it seemed that she could only have come in our direction, towards the wild moors.

'I'm going out to look for her,' announced Reuben, who was already putting his wellies on to a chorus of, 'Can I come?'

We decided that it would be safest for the oldest boys to have a scout around, to see whether they could get a rough idea as to her whereabouts and mood.

Would she be scared? Was she hungry? Lonely? Until we had answers to these questions we couldn't make any firm plans.

Already Nancy, Annas and Clemmy's Christmas-stocking project had been abandoned for more exciting tasks: making HAVE YOU SEEN THIS REINDEER? and WANTED posters, complete with mugshots of cartoon reindeers that they copied from Christmas cards.

While everyone was focused on their jobs, I quietly asked Clive his thoughts.

We both agreed that if the boys did actually manage to find the reindeer, then we would have to think very carefully about how to capture her. Perhaps we could use food or another reindeer to tempt her into a pen?

Clive went back to reading his newspaper; he was pleased that the children had been set a surprise festive challenge that would keep them busy (and out of his way!).

Edith, Violet and Raven were now searching online for reindeer facts: what was their natural **habitat** like? What do they like to eat? What kind of noise do they make? Sheeps bleat, horses neigh, but could we find a recording of a reindeer sound and use it to call her over to us?

Though I kept it to myself, I wondered how Santa's reindeer would cope with the harsh Swaledale terrain. She was a world away from the comfort and warmth of the Christmas grottoes and shopping centres she was used to.

It soon became clear from the girls' research that I needn't have worried; if the reindeer had in fact headed on to the moors, she would have accidentally stumbled upon her perfect habitat. Reindeers prefer open, sparse alpine land, just like the moors. They eat moss and lichen, which we have plenty of. The only thing she was lacking at that time was snow, but that was soon to come! And as for noise, well, we found plenty of videos of reindeer grunting, but decided not to use them in case it scared her, or worse – made her angry!

I smiled. This was certainly an education for all of us.

Hours went by. The winter days were short, and sunlight was in short supply. Night would soon fall, and the moors would be blanketed in its inky darkness.

I stood in the doorway of the farmhouse, looking upwards to the hills. Being outside at night at Christmas is a soothing experience; under the starlit skies peace hangs in the air. It's an unworldly quiet, interrupted only by the screeches of owls and the distant *blargh* of sheep.

My moment of calm was soon broken by the sound of the boys returning from their mission. They were empty-handed but had positive news – they'd spotted the runaway reindeer!

They had taken their motorbikes to the highest point of the moor and had spied a lone figure against the distant skyline. Initially it had been difficult to confirm it was our festive fugitive, because colour-wise she looked just like one of our sheep.

But as the boys moved closer the reindeer had suddenly raised her head, and her impressive antlers gave the game away.

'She looked like the stag on the front of a biscuit tin,' said Sid, painting a perfect mental picture for us all.

As the boys warmed up over mugs of tea, the reindeer was the *only* topic of conversation. The girls had finished fact-finding and shared more of what they'd learned. Reindeers, rather like sheep, are natural wanderers and can cover great distances. They are also blessed with thick fur coats to keep them warm against the bitter cold.

'I tell you what, Mum,' said Reuben. 'She isn't half speedy –'

'And she can jump!' added Miles.

'I thought that they could fly?' Nancy chimed in.

This all sounded very positive for the reindeer's well-being on our cold moors but also like it may be challenging to catch up with her! 'Might it struggle to find enough food?' I wondered aloud.

'It's got its teeth with it, hasn't it?' said Clive dryly.

'True! I was hoping we could lure her to us with the sheep nuts that Clem fed her at the party. If we could persuade her to go into one of the sheep folds that are dotted around the moor, then maybe we could lasso her and then walk her back to the farm?'

'That's a possibility, I suppose,' said Miles.

'A remote one,' said Clive.

'Well, have you got any better ideas?' challenged Miles.

'Yes, a net,' stated Reuben.

Raven decided to share some of her newfound expertise in all things reindeer with the boys.

'They have amazing eyesight,' she said. 'And they can travel at up to forty miles an hour. There's no way that it would walk into a net.'

'We could just chase it until it got tired and lay down?' suggested Reuben.

'I think that you'd get tired and lie down before it did!' laughed Raven.

It was time for me to state the obvious. 'I don't suppose that she might just remember that she is a tame reindeer and come to us, if we called for her?'

Everyone nodded. Though it was time for bed, we agreed to try out our plan as soon as we could.

The main focus for Christmas that year became how to catch a reindeer.

Reuben called the elf from the party and quizzed him on how reindeers' minds work. Would borrowing another reindeer work to tempt her into a pen? Could a reindeer get stuck in a **bog**? And the all-important question: what was 'our' reindeer's name?

The answers were as follows: another reindeer would not help (and there was no way that he was going to risk losing a second); reindeer are flat-footed and so unlikely to sink into a bog . . .

And her name was Chloe.

He added that if Chloe was troubling us then he could arrange for her to be shot! There was a look of horror on everyone's faces at this suggestion.

Reuben was quick to point out that he meant *shot with a tranquilliser dart* to make Chloe sleepy and therefore easier to catch, but Reuben had insisted that there really was no need, because she wasn't bothering us at all.

Though we tried shouting her name across the moors to call her over to us, Chloe stubbornly remained a fugitive at large. So as a family we decided that we would watch out for her as best we could, and see if her solitary mood changed over time – perhaps in time she would even make friends with our flock of sheep?

We spotted Chloe most days after that. She would pose majestically, nose in the air, tendrils of windgrass caught up in her velveteen antlers. We took pictures of her with a long-lens camera, and stared through binoculars looking for any signs of injury, illness or a thawing of her frosty attitude.

But as time went on it became clear that Chloe had decided to go back to being a wild creature. Her days of pulling Santa's sleigh had been forgotten.

We saw Chloe properly for the last time a week or so later. She was stood stock still and looked towards us, bright eyes flashing, before turning and energetically springing between **peat haggs**.

Since then there has, in these parts, been occasional reports of sightings of anything from a red deer to a caribou, glimpses of an elk or even – allegedly – a moose.

And every Christmas I hope that we might be blessed with another festive visit, not only from Santa and the snow, but also from Chloe. It would be magical to look up to the moors where the land meets the sky and see the outline of a runaway reindeer, enjoying her freedom.

Chicken for Christmas

Here at Ravenseat Farm we feel lucky to have so much green space around us: fresh air, wide skies and a freedom in nature that other people perhaps might not have. Although this is normal for us, I do still occasionally remind the children (and myself) just how blessed we are.

I also sometimes tell them about my childhood growing up in a town and how, as a youngster, I really wanted for nothing. I enjoyed doing many of the same things that they do: reading, drawing, playing out in the garden and whizzing down the street on a bicycle or roller skates.

My safe place as a child was my bedroom, because from its window I could watch the world go by. There were heydays and grey days, but it seemed from my bedroom view that the world didn't sleep, that there was hustle and bustle day and night.

But there was one thing guaranteed to bring everything to a standstill: snow.

For a short while a blanket of snow would silence it all and make everything clean and fresh. It didn't have to be very deep: just a few centimetres was enough to cause everything in town to grind to a halt. Roads would be closed, and schools too, which was an added bonus. The children nod in agreement whenever they hear this – they love a snow-day too.

Now that my home is a remote hill farm, high in the Yorkshire Dales, heavy snowfall is normal, but I still love it just as much as I did when I was a child. Being cut off from the world still has the same soothing effect on me, even though it makes the daily chores around the farm much more difficult than usual.

Being prepared for bad weather is key. During the summer we stock our shelves at home with food, tins, bottles and the essentials (teabags!), ready for the winter to come, in case we get snowed in.

The farm is a world away from where I grew up. There are no supermarkets within short walking distance, and to my children the idea of 'just popping to the shop' seems ridiculous. But with a little planning we can be self-sufficient and that is something that I take great pride in: if we want milk, then we milk the house cow, Buttercup. If we need bread, then we bake it. And if the children want sweeties or chocolate . . . well, then they just have to find where I've hidden them!

There are a number of mouths that need feeding – not just the human ones. Sheep, cows, horses, dogs and chickens too. We begin preparing the animals' winter food in summertime. Exactly as the saying goes, we *make hay while the sun shines*, making as much as the weather and land allow. There are lots of wildflowers among the meadow grass, baked dry in the blisteringly hot sunshine and folded into sweet-smelling hay **bales**. Then the bales are stacked and stored in the barns, until the hungry winter months arrive.

So if you don't actually need to go anywhere, then the idea of being 'snowed in' on the farm could be seen instead as the world being 'snowed out'.

The children agree with this, and being unable to get to school doesn't trouble them one bit. Any mention of the snow plough heading in our direction doesn't exactly create a positive response from them, though it doesn't necessarily mean an end to their snow-day either.

With no other houses around to shield us, our home's barren, windswept position leaves us exposed to the very worst storms that can batter us from all directions. And just because the road is cleared of snow it doesn't necessarily mean that it'll remain that way. Even if it stops snowing, once the wind picks up again then the previously settled flakes begin to swirl and pile up, and through long periods of bad winter weather we can be visited by the county council's snow plough every day.

On the day of this story, the whole family was working around the farmyard when I heard the low rumble of the bright yellow machine and saw its orange flashing light slowly moving down the road towards us. This was my cue to make a pot of tea and rummage around for a biscuit. By the time the driver had pushed the snow down to the packhorse bridge, I was waiting for him with a mid-morning **brew**.

'You'll be busy now, what with this weather forecast,' I said from ground level, as I passed up the enamel cup.

'Yes, I never stop on these bad days,' said Jack the snow-plough man. 'As fast as I clear those top roads they fill back in with more snow.'

'We're all right here though,' I replied. 'School is closed for now and the children are turning their hand to winter sports.'

I often joke that the Winter Olympics could be held at Ravenseat. The children ski, snowboard, skate and have even pinched a sweeping brush and had a go at curling on the shore of the frozen tarn.

While Jack and I were chattering I saw Clem out of the corner of my eye. She was holding on to Tony the Pony's lead rope while he sprung around, clearly thrilled at being brought out of the stable. Tony was trying his hardest to roll and dance, just as Clem was trying equally hard to *not* let him roll and dance in the soft, powdery snow.

'Looks like there's a tug of war going on!' commented Jack, nodding towards the scene. Even from this distance I could see Clem's face was puce in colour, determined as she was to keep control of her wayward pony.

'Well you've heard the saying, *just hold yer horses*,' I smiled.

By now Jack had drained his cup and demolished the biscuit. 'Well, that's me fed and watered,' he said. 'Tell you what though, not only am I clearing the roads, I'm on feeding duty too.'

'Who, or what, are you feeding?' I asked.

'Well . . .!' he chuckled.

Jack explained that, each morning of this particular snowy spell, he had driven to the border between Yorkshire and Cumbria and then turned his plough round before making his way back.

On the first day he had set out very early to try

and clear the roads. It was still dark, and the plough's beacon flashed bright orange across the open moorland, briefly lighting up his frozen surroundings. Jack began to carefully turn the vehicle round, not wishing to get stuck in such an isolated place.

'It was so cold,' he said. 'Proper Baltic up there.'

Suddenly he spotted something during one of the plough's flashes of light. Something *huddled* under a bower of ice-laden rush stalks, the only thing that provided any shelter from the ghastly wind.

It was a small flock of **bantam** chickens!

Jack had wound his window down, inviting a raw blast of cold air and a smattering of ice into his warm cab, as he peered at the birds. There were no human footprints in the snow around them, no signs of anyone or anything really, just half a dozen small chickens; it was their brightly coloured feathers that had made them noticeable against the white snow.

I was completely startled. It didn't make any sense that right there, in no-man's land, miles and miles away from anything, was a flock of chickens.

We've taken in our fair share of stray or (as is more likely to be the case) abandoned animals at Ravenseat Farm. It's usually cats or dogs. We often don't know the full story behind these sorry cases, so have to presume that the pet owners have made the difficult decision to 'set them free'.

'Are the chickens still there?' I asked Jack.

'Yes. Every morning I go over, turn the plough round and throw them some crusts from my sandwiches before I head back. They look for me coming now.'

Poor chickens! They would be hungering, as apart from Jack's bread there would be nothing around for them to eat; the ground was frozen rock-solid right now, and there was no sign of this hard winter ending.

'It's such a shame,' he said, shaking his head. 'They look a good type.'

'Could they be caught?' I asked. We already had chickens, so it would be no trouble to have a few more.

'Oh, yes,' he said. 'Definitely. If you get me a box then I'll pick them up for you tomorrow. I'd be happy to see them go to a good home.'

Our flock of chickens consisted of ex-barn hens, all brown, with the exception of our oldest hen, Linda. She was a cream-and-black coloured chicken with a fearless attitude; everybody and everything on the farm stayed out of her way. She would even take a running jump and flap her wings to get over the barn door and help herself to the bull's corn. Talk about ruffled feathers! Not even 1.5 tonnes of solid beef was a match for our mother hen. So long as Linda was around, no harm would come to any chicken in her flock.

The next day the children could hardly contain themselves. They were delighted at the prospect of the new arrivals, so the chicken puns came thick and fast.

'I'm so *egg*-cited,' Violet laughed to collective groans.

Reuben pointed out that we were just waiting for a delivery of *chilli* chicken.

A piercing shriek from Sidney announced that the plough was coming down the road. I got on with making some tea while the children scrambled to pull on their wellies, winter overtrousers, hats and coats.

Down at the bridge the snow plough was quickly surrounded by the children who, under normal circumstances, would be less than pleased at Jack's arrival. I handed over the tea and biscuits and was given a slightly soggy box in return. It was surprisingly light, but from within I could hear a low, gentle crooning.

The children jumped up and down wanting to open the box there and then, but there was a real danger that it would fall apart and we would be left playing chase the chicken across the moors!

So we trooped over the fields towards the henhouse with the box, the children kicking up snow as they went, or scooping up handfuls to make snowballs; I marvelled at their energy as I breathlessly waded through the deep drifts.

'Home to roost!' I announced, placing the box on the floor as the children crammed through the henhouse door.

Miles, the self-styled manager of our 'poultry unit' (as we grandly called it), opened the box and began lifting out its occupants.

We were all extremely surprised at what we saw.

'Wow! That's a Silver Spangled Hamburg. This is a Golden Sebright. That could be a lavender-laced . . . summat!' said Miles, excitedly reeling off the breeds.

'They're not so big,' said Sidney.

They were bantams, a smaller variety of chicken, but perfectly formed.

'This one's a cockerel,' said Miles, as he held a slightly confused-looking, beady-eyed male chicken in his hands. 'He's the one with biggest comb on his head and the longer tail feathers.'

There was no panic from the new birds, and only a questioning look from resident mother hen, Linda, who perched beside the hay-filled nest boxes.

'Will they be all right?' asked Violet.

I assured her that, having survived for days in Arctic conditions, they were clearly tough enough to withstand some henpecking from naughty Linda.

'She will *get in a flap* I'm sure.' I laughed at my own joke while Sidney rolled his eyes. 'But they'll settle, once the *pecking* order has been established.'

Leaving the new chickens to make friends with the old ones, we trailed back to the farmhouse, wondering how someone could have abandoned them in such a harsh place. They really were fine birds, not your average chickens. And, although the effects of hunger and cold weather had probably made them a bit weak, they were still surprisingly friendly and tame.

'Maybe they escaped, or were stolen?' suggested Sidney as we trooped into the warm kitchen, the door held open by a waiting Clive.

'We'll never know why,' he said. 'But someone else's loss is our gain.'

'More eggs!' said Violet.

And so the chickens soon made themselves at home that Christmas and breathed new life and sparkle into our once colourless flock.

Slowly but surely the snow melted, and the land awoke from its wintry slumber.

Where once we'd had to wade through huge drifts and sidestep frozen, icy gutters, now we strolled through the first rush of green growth that filled everyone with positivity and hope after the long, cold winter.

The chickens could roam freely now too, and we would visit them twice daily with corn and mixed crumbs.

Springtime is also egg time. Our original chicken crew were old girls, stuck in their ways; we'd hear their celebratory *cluck* and know an egg had been laid neatly in their nest box.

But the not-so-new wild and carefree bantams did not want to use a nest box, no matter how snug and comfortable it was. Sometimes we would hunt high and low, knowing full well that an egg **clutch** sat hidden, somewhere.

But where?

The challenge was to find *all* the eggs, and we spotted them in all sorts of places – under a picnic bench, even behind a toilet bowl. Everyone enjoyed this task, such a simple pleasure made even better as we now had a variety of eggs to collect: not just the average beige type but small, perfectly white ones, blue-tinged eggs and occasionally brown, freckled ones too.

I'd smile watching Nancy kneeling beside a nest box. Inside, a hen would be concentrating on squeezing out an egg. Nancy would slowly slide her hand beneath the unsuspecting bird and carefully lift out the prize. Then, gently cupping it in the palms of her hands, she would bring it up to her cheek to feel the warmth of the freshly laid egg.

Summer came and went. Sheep were sheared, hay was made and time flew, but our chickens didn't. They had no intention of leaving the nest: with five-star accommodation and complete freedom to do what they liked, they were happy to stay with us.

Before we knew it, our local village show was coming up again. Clive was preparing the sheep for competition, Reuben was polishing up his tractors, Sidney was getting ready to run the **fell** race across the moors, and the girls and I made an assortment of yummy cakes and pies for the home-baking section.

Every year Miles would compete with half a dozen of our best eggs. It wasn't the most demanding of contests but, nevertheless, finding and matching six *absolutely* identical eggs could be difficult.

Before now, the only animals allowed to attend the show were sheep – specifically Swaledale sheep, the native breed of this area. So it was with great *egg*citement that Miles announced that the show had added a new section to the competition.

'There's two new classes, Mum,' he said, looking up from the show schedule.

'For what?' I enquired.

'Chickens!' It was his turn to squawk. 'Best hen and best cockerel, and overall champion.'

'Who are you taking?' I asked. 'Surely not Linda?'

'The Golden Sebright cockerel,' he announced, smiling as he filled in the entry form. 'He might be small in size, but he has a big personality.'

I pointed out that the judge wouldn't pick a winner

based on the character of the chicken; it was all about looks.

For the first time since he arrived at Ravenseat in a soggy cardboard box, the little cockerel was captured and then catapulted into the limelight in one fell swoop. He was certainly ready for the village show, as he strutted towards the front of his cage to pose and cast a steely eye over his feathered competitors, all of which were at least twice his size.

With his chest puffed out and his shoulders pulled back, he flapped his wings and let out a belter of a *cockadoodledoo*!

And with that, he won! Best in class and then overall champion.

The judge came to find Miles to congratulate him.

'Fantastic bantam chicken,' he said, shaking Miles's hand enthusiastically. 'It's rare to find a tiny bird with so much personality. He is marvellous.'

We didn't win much else that day – just a few rosettes here and there – but we were over the moon with our prize-winning chicken.

From being abandoned by the roadside at Christmas to becoming a village-show champion by late summer, it was a triumph that made our hearts sing.

And that's certainly something to crow about.

Chalky the Arctic Terrier

If being sensible ever played a part in deciding who exactly came to live at Ravenseat Farm, then maybe we wouldn't have quite so many mouths to feed.

But with a big family, and a lot of space around us – fields, pastures, barns and stables – I find it difficult, nigh on *impossible,* not to welcome yet another four-legged friend into our home. Though actually, having four legs isn't necessary either, considering that our farm includes peacocks (two legs) and a giant land snail (no legs at all).

I could, of course, blame the children for an unreasonable amount of pester power . . . but truthfully I'm as guilty as them of enjoying the chaos and work (and expense) that our animals bring us.

And no farm would be complete without a collection of canines.

As well as being dear companions, our dogs play an important part in running our farm. Whether that's the border collies who herd the sheep, or the terriers who control the rodents, their hard work, no matter how small, is always appreciated.

Terriers like to hunt – specifically mice and rats – and with a keen nose and a sharp eye they have a sixth sense for where any might be hiding. Nosing through straw and burrowing beneath the dusty hay bales in the barn, nothing holds these determined little dogs back from catching farmyard pests that, if left alone, could ruin our animal feed and spread disease.

A pair of terriers seems to be the best number to have at any one time, especially as these little dogs would occasionally fight – and not just play fighting either!

Pippen was a Jack Russell crossed with a border terrier, thick set with short legs. She was as heavy as a brick and just as inflexible. Her tan-and-black coat was smooth and self-cleaning, shedding all traces of mud no matter what grotty adventure she had been upon. She had never been a very sociable pup, preferring to have as little to do with humankind as possible. A tummy scratch would be enjoyed, as would some leftovers from dinner, but she'd ignore all of that if there was something more exciting happening outside.

Chalky was also a Jack Russell. She was small in size – though taller than Pippen – with a wiry, white coat – hence why we called her the Arctic Terrier. Or at least she was white sometimes . . . from a distance. Her bright colour stood out when she was nosing through the brown rushes in the fields, or when she was pacing back and forth beside the entrance to an earthy rabbit burrow. But on closer inspection she was a delicate shade of eggshell or ivory (or beige, taupe or just dirty in less polite terms). She was a dog that wouldn't be tamed or tidied, and wouldn't walk on a lead. She'd never had to, so why start now?

Terriers are, by nature, independent souls, happy to roam the farm without rules. We never shut ours in the house, and so they enjoy a freedom that the other animals simply don't. You would assume then, as we did, that there was plenty to keep them entertained at Ravenseat, without ever needing to leave the farm.

But one day, cheeky Chalky decided to wander . . .

Not too far in terms of distance, at least the first few times – just far enough to mean that we'd receive helpful phone calls from our neighbours. They'd have spotted Chalky mingling with the hikers that pass through the farm and then, later in the day after finishing their walk, meet outside the pub in our nearest village...

... four miles away.

We discussed it as a family, but none of us could understand why Chalky should just decide to take off. She certainly wasn't lacking in any home comforts; she was just a little dog who enjoyed a big adventure!

Sometimes we would spot Chalky scurrying towards hikers on the footpath across the valley. They would stop, turn round and try to discourage her from following their group, flicking their arms towards her and telling her to go home. She took no notice whatsoever.

Even Clive bellowing, *'CHALKY!'* from the farmyard had no effect!

She was microchipped, and wore a collar engraved with her name and our phone number. And so we resigned ourselves to the fact that, if Chalky was not lying by the fireside by teatime, then we could expect a call from the pub to fetch her. As a farm dog, she wore a safety collar, designed to snap if it got caught up in a fence. But Chalky didn't need a fence; she could 'lose' (or remove) the collar without one. Whether she did this on purpose, or they just came off *accidentally*, we will never know, but we came to accept that a collarless dog was still better than a missing one.

It wasn't long before curious Chalky had discovered other places to explore, further down the dale. Campsites, bed and breakfasts, hotels ... In fact, anywhere that walkers went, she would go too.

She soon made a name for herself locally and, as awareness of her adventures grew, so too did the circle of people that would come to her rescue.

The owner of a local glamping site called to say that Chalky was currently lounging in one of their hot tubs, in the company of their Labrador. Luckily for Chalky, he stressed that there was no rush for us to pick her up, and he wouldn't be charging us for her mini-break.

The postman would arrive with our letters, parcels and one *special* delivery of a first-class terrier.

And Daryl, the school-bus driver, would bring the children home with an extra passenger on board – Chalky – who insisted on taking the front seat. What's more, the children who would normally fight tooth and nail to sit up there would allow it! After being dropped off they would scamper over the bridge and up to the farmyard together, all in a hurry to tell us where Chalky had been found this time.

'She was at the campsite at Muker,' Edith reported, as she made herself tea and Chalky snuffled around for a morsel of toast.

Chalky's adventures, and fame, began to spread far and wide. Tan Hill – England's highest pub,

almost *seven* miles away from Ravenseat – was a favourite of hers, and Chalky became an honorary regular there. Raven would show me pictures she had found online of Chalky, nosing for crisps dropped by the customers at the bar, or sat contentedly by the open fire.

For a while we accepted her behaviour, until one day . . .

Feeling brave from her many quests, Chalky took things a step further – literally – by crossing a line and straying into Wensleydale! A place known for its rolling hills, dairy cows and the famous cheese that Gromit loves so much – *sixteen* miles away.

Unfortunately for Chalky, she was unknown in those parts and ended up in a crate at the local vets. She had been taken there by a well-meaning local who told the vet that if the friendly little unkempt dog went unclaimed, they would take her home. Having 'lost' her collar *again*, thankfully it was her microchip that saved her this time, providing the vet with our address so that we could rescue her.

Christmastime brought with it a break in Chalky's off-farm activities. With fewer walkers around to lead her astray she was happy to stay home at Ravenseat, and gift us with her presence. She enjoyed frolicking outside with Pippen, rolling in the powdery white snow (which really showed up how beige her coat had got), and digging frantically at the frozen ground with her front paws for who knows what.

No wintry weather was too bad for our terriers; their energy was off the scale. The mischievous pair would run for miles over the snow behind our **quad bike** as we went to **fodder** the sheep. And though they couldn't match the speed of the sheepdogs, still they shared their love for chasing sheep.

But what Chalky and Pippen didn't have was any herding skills whatsoever. They wanted to help, but were always in the wrong place at the wrong time, which made the sheep go the wrong way. Clive would try and call the terriers to him, but they ignored him, bouncing along in their usual joyful manner, snapping at the heels of the bigger dogs.

Kate and Bill – our sheepdogs – could only tolerate this 'help' so much. Bill would turn round, snarl and bare his teeth, causing Pippen to slink off, *sheepishly*, with her tail tucked between her legs. Chalky would roll on to her back in surrender as Bill stood triumphantly over her, thinking that he had taught her who was the boss. He was wrong, of course, because as soon as work resumed the terrible terriers would just carry on in their naughty way.

As Chalky grew older she did not grow wiser. If anything she grew braver, seeking adventures further and further from home. Sometimes she would latch on to a new group of walkers and, when the time came for them to go home, Chalky would look sad, shake and shiver to pull at their heartstrings. We can only imagine the conversations they had about her:

'What should we do? We can't leave her here!'

'She must be a stray – look at her scruffy coat. And she has no collar . . .'

As winter drew to a close, the groups of walkers returned to the dales, causing Chalky's wanderlust to also return. The whole family would discuss at teatime when and where the last sighting of her had been and then wait for the call requesting us to come pick her up.

Believe me, we tried very hard to understand how Chalky's mind worked. Especially when she disappeared for the longest stretch so far.

It was a late winter day, the frost was sparkling on the moors and, while there remained a chill in the air, the sun was shining weakly through the clouds. Pippen was outside, chasing rabbits through the bracken, but Chalky wasn't with her; Chalky was nowhere to be seen.

I wasn't particularly worried, since this was very normal Chalky behaviour after all, and we all went about our chores on the farm, expecting the usual late-afternoon phone call from the village pub to say that Chalky was ready for her taxi.

But the call didn't come that day. And it didn't come the next day either.

By the end of two weeks, we were more than a little worried for our cheeky terrier. We eagerly waited for the news that Chalky was at the campsite at Keld, Muker or beyond. We quizzed Daryl, the school-bus driver, and the postman for any reported sightings from down the dale. We rang round our neighbours and searched the farm thoroughly, checking in every cupboard and under every pile of straw. The reality was that the farm and the moors are so big that we just couldn't search absolutely everywhere. Sheep and even cows have been known to disappear in Swaledale. It's a treacherous land with bottomless bogs, deep caves and tall cliffs. And there are so many barns and outbuildings dotted all around, Chalky could have easily found herself inside any one of these and become trapped.

The only family member who didn't seem concerned by Chalky's absence was Pippen. She was making the most of not having to share the best spot by the fire. The children were baffled that Pippen wasn't showing any loyalty to her companion!

'She's happy to fill Chalky's space by the looks of things,' said Reuben, looking at a contented Pippen dozing on the ever-present pile of farm coats in the porch.

'Can't we just follow her? She'll take us to Chalky,' said Miles.

'Nah,' I said. 'There are heroic dogs who save lives, but Pippen isn't one of them.'

'I want Chalky back,' said Annas sadly. 'I miss her.'

'You didn't say that when she left dirty paw marks all over your bed,' said Edith.

'Or when Daryl blamed Chalky for the infestation of fleas on the school bus!' added Violet.

'That was really bad,' I admitted. 'Everyone was itching and Chalky got the blame.'

'Aye, such happy memories,' said Clive, maybe a touch sarcastically.

'I hate not knowing; we're always going to wonder what happened to her,' said Raven.

We were all starting to feel that Chalky might be gone forever.

Chalky was loved by so many local people that it made sense to write an announcement to be posted online. It would be a celebration of our adventurous but disloyal dog. The final chapter in cheeky Chalky's story. News soon travelled far and wide, maybe even further than Chalky had, and we had many kind replies and presents, like dog shampoo and even sausages!

The next few days passed by under a bit of a cloud. Everyone was feeling sad about Chalky, and had taken to giving Pippen, Kate and Bill lots of extra attention and titbits in her absence, which of course delighted them.

It was early evening, all the farm chores had been done, dinner was in the oven and the family were in the living room. Pippen was practically smouldering in front of the fire – a true hot dog.

Suddenly Clive's phone rang loudly with a number he didn't recognize, making us all jump. He squinted at the screen as the children demanded, 'Just answer it!'

'Hello?' said Clive quizzically. 'Aye, it is. How can I help you?' As Clive continued the call, we were all trying to guess what was going on.

'Really? Champion! Thanks for letting us know.'

No one could believe what had happened.

The caller was a woman who lived in Cumbria, nearly *twenty* miles away!

She'd recently gone to a rehoming kennels to adopt a dog and had chosen a beige-coloured terrier with pleading eyes and a cheery personality. The dog had been found in a local Cumbrian pub, looking lonely and bedraggled. She didn't have a collar and her microchip was broken, so the lady had taken her home and named the dog Twiglet.

But a few days later the woman had spotted Chalky's mugshot online, and started to wonder about Twiglet's *real* identity . . .

Feeling sad about the possibility of having to give up

her new pet, she still knew that it was the right thing to do. And so the lady called Clive to find out whether Chalky and Twiglet were in fact the same dog.

Finally, after some frank discussions and proof that Chalky was Twiglet and vice versa – the smattering of brown spots on one of her ears sealing the deal – we got our Chalky back.

The children were beyond delighted, and we thought that Chalky might give us a sign that she was happy to be home with her loving family too. Maybe I did catch a brief, sweet moment between Chalky and Pippen as they left the farmhouse together, their matching stumpy tails held high. No doubt they had lots to catch up on and were off to tackle the new rodents that had taken up residence in the barn during her absence.

Had Chalky learned her lesson? Absolutely not. If anything, it merely increased her appetite for adventure, and she went on a lot more quests over the years.

Nowadays Chalky's travels are almost over. Old age has crept up on her and, although she still wanders about the farmyard, she spends considerably more time sleeping by the fire. Even so, the lure of a bright winter's day will still tempt her outside for a roll in the powdery white snow.

And during her fireside slumbers she'll be dreaming of turkey leftovers with a smattering of gravy from the Christmas roasting tray, or perhaps a few crumbs of Wensleydale cheese. Her ears will twitch, and her legs will paddle back and forth as though running up hill and over dale.

In Chalky's mind at least, the adventure never ends.

The Greatest (Gift) Of All Time

I remember a time when the word 'goat' meant a bearded, spiky-horned, nimble-footed animal with a love for causing mischief. But nowadays G.O.A.T. stands for something entirely different – Greatest Of All Time – and I've got to say that Reuben, my eldest son, felt like he was the *greatest brother of all time* when he decided that he wanted to get the three little ones – Annas, Clem and Nancy – early Christmas presents.

Being a young man of many talents, Reuben is frequently asked to do all kinds of odd jobs on our farm and beyond, from fixing machinery and digging ponds to even rescuing animals. And one winter, in early December, he and his friend Sonny had been tasked with loading *forty-eight* pygmy goats into their van and finding them new homes.

After they'd picked them up, he rang me and said, 'Do you think the little ones would like a goat each?'

You might think that with a farm full of animals the last thing I would want is more mouths to feed, but I've always said that everything is entirely the opposite of what you'd expect at Ravenseat.

It comes back to my own childhood days, when I had a very small front garden, a slightly bigger back garden and a driveway, and was surrounded by houses and busy roads. I could only dream about having the random selection of animals I do now. Once I asked my parents for a pony, but they rightly refused, explaining, 'We don't have the room. You can have a guinea pig instead.' Eventually we agreed on a small dog.

These days, with loads more room, I feel like I haven't got any excuse to say no, particularly to my children. So when they ask, 'Can we have a horse?' the answer, more often than not, is, 'Why not? Yes!' And over the years, as more and more requests have come in, so too have the animals in our family.

'Can I have a cow?'

'Yes.'

'Can I have a sheep?'

'We've got lots of them already, but yes.'

'Can I have a peacock?'

'Yep.'

'How about a hamster?'

'No, because one of the bigger animals will eat it.'

So when I got Reuben's phone call asking for permission for goats, it felt like a reasonable request – though we didn't tell Clive because from previous dealings with them it was clear that he really wasn't a big fan.

I'd brought a goat with me when I first moved to Ravenseat, all those years ago. She was a beige, brown and white Toggenburg, the kind you'd find in Switzerland. She had bad legs, a bad temper, was badly behaved and loved nothing more than leading the sheep astray. She was called Flymo, after the brand of lawn mowers, because she nibbled the grass and kept it short. But it wasn't just the greenery that she liked to munch; she liked eating clothes off the washing line too. In all honesty I have to agree with Clive: she was a total and utter nightmare.

Then, thanks to my inability to turn any animal away, we ended up with a *second* goat and that just made things even worse. Flymo and Randy would hang about the yard like a couple of bored teenagers looking for trouble, though it wasn't with people that they would pick a fight, it was with their own reflections.

This wasn't too much of a problem on a day-to-day basis, because our trucks were too dirty for them to ever be able to see themselves in. But if we had visitors, especially ones with nice shiny, clean cars, they would soon catch sight of two equally handsome goats staring back at them, square up and set to, launching headlong into what obviously was their own reflections! The result was often a trip to the garage and a large bill . . .

So goats really weren't the flavour of the month as far as Clive was concerned, but I always reckoned that it was better to ask for forgiveness than permission. And when Reuben called and asked the question, I said without hesitation, 'Of course we'd love some goats! Just do it.'

We managed to keep this a secret from the girls for one whole day. And then, after loading Annas, Clem and Nancy into the pick-up all wrapped up in their winter woollies, they were ready for their mysterious outing to Sonny's farm. Reuben was just as excited as they were!

When they arrived, the girls jumped out of the pick-up and, on going into the barn, were met by . . . a sea of knee-high goats!

The sweet-faced, soft-haired pygmy goats were the perfect size to cuddle, and squeals of glee erupted from the girls as they wasted no time getting snuggles in. The excitement reached fever pitch when Reuben revealed the real reason for the visit – for them to pick one each as an early Christmas present, and bring them home to Ravenseat (so long as he didn't have to wrap them up).

On their return to the farm, I gathered everyone into the yard (apart from Clive) to meet the latest additions to our ever-growing menagerie. The girls leaped out and Reuben, who was dressed in fluorescent orange like some sort of safety-conscious Santa, opened the back door of the truck and proudly introduced us to:

Rocky, chosen by Clemmy, who was tan and white; Billy, picked by Annas, the black-and-white one; and finally a dirty white goat, who was a bit on the large size for a pygmy, who for some reason was named after the farm's owner, Sonny. That one was Nancy's.

We immediately scooped them up, cooing over their size and dainty faces. Between cuddles, I caught sight of Reuben leaning against his truck smiling, almost smugly, to himself. It was going to be very hard to top this gift come Christmas Day.

This wholesome moment threatened to be short-lived however as I spotted some not-so-cute-looking, tiny but spiky horns atop the goats' heads, the perfect size to poke an affectionate cuddler in both eyes. I headed inside, hastily searching for wine bottle corks to skewer on to the ends of their horns to prevent any incidents. Thankfully, the goats were tame enough to potter about without any ridiculous cork accessories.

Despite all of Clive's doubts (based on our previous experiences with Flymo and Randy), these sweet little goats bucked the trend. Instead of *baaa*-d attitudes, Billy, Rocky and Sonny had a springy joy about them and brought an early festive feel to the farm that year with their playful antics.

Over the coming weeks, as we approached the Christmas holidays, the newcomers settled in nicely, and I have to credit my children for this. They adored the goats and the goats adored them back, following them everywhere – indoors, outdoors, it didn't matter. It was an open house as far as the goats were concerned – where the children went, the **kids** went!

This did cause a bit of a problem when it came to doing their business, without being too rude about it. Pygmy goats do rabbit-like droppings that are small and round and dry. And that's great, because on a farm in winter everything is wet and most of the poo you encounter is more of the runny type. So mini, pellety poos that can literally be swept up are very welcome around these parts.

The children quickly noticed that when the goats' tiny tails began waggling at speed, a little sprinkling of pellets would soon follow. And, ever the practical one, Nancy discovered that if she took the end off the Henry Hoover, she could cut out a step in the cleaning-up process!

It wasn't just the two-legged among us that the goats won over. They also developed an understanding with the other animals. When I went and fed the horses, the goats weaved between them, scampering up to the **manger,** standing on their back legs and eating right out of the horses' feed bowl. You could see the horses give them a bit of side eye, but then they just carried on.

The goats would go to any lengths to get an extra bite of food ... and it was starting to show! After the children, food was the main focus of the goats' attention. Most days, once they'd seen the children off to school, I would hear *pitter patter, pitter patter* as Rocky, Billy and Sonny came back up to the house. We had a large feed bin in the yard with a sliding door on the bottom. It slowly released flakes of cereal, which were quickly gobbled up by the three greedy goats. So, while still officially pygmy goats in name, their rolypoly bellies were starting to suggest otherwise!

Goats will famously eat anything. But with Sonny, Rocky and Billy, even this mischief was done in a way that brought a smile to our faces.

It was a few days before Christmas and, having got to know them over the past couple of weeks, we thought we knew most of the goats' tricks by now. But how wrong we were . . .

We normally have friends dropping by at this time of year so that we can wish each other a Merry Christmas, and usually share whatever festive fare I have in the pantry. One day a friend came by and, as she climbed out of her car, I spotted something unheard of round these parts – fancy designer wellies! And this particular pair were made by Jimmy Choo.

As she came into the house, she kicked her wellies off at the porch door, as we all do. While we chatted, the children started munching on the mince pies and cake – when there's nine of you, eating sweet treats can be competitive. If you don't get in there fast, you won't get any!

I soon became distracted by a strange sight. The children were looking towards the windows, sticking their tongues out and pulling faces. Looking straight back at them, with equally ridiculous expressions, were the goats. They were staring hopefully at our snacks through the window panes, *their* tongues furiously licking the glass, clearly hoping to get a taste!

Soon it was time for farewells, but I realized with horror that the goats had given up on the sweets and moved on to something far more tasty: my friend's wellies! The goats never bothered with ours, which were dirty and splattered with muck. But her Jimmy

Choos were spotless. And true to their name, they were now *chew*ed. You had to laugh: the Choos got chewed! I sheepishly apologized and waved her off. Needless to say, she hasn't been back for a Christmas visit since.

There was just one last thing to do before the big day. As is tradition in our house on Christmas Eve, the children each write a letter to Santa, letting him know what presents they would like to receive. They then send them up the chimney, the flames carrying their wishes to Santa and his elves. This year, Annas, Clemmy and Nancy had all requested the same thing – goat coats!

Come Christmas morning, having no patience to wait until later in the day like we normally do, the girls excitedly unwrapped their gifts and were delighted to see that Santa had indeed delivered three fluorescent jackets: a yellow one for Rocky, an orange one for Billy and a light turquoise one for Sonny. Although they were a little bit snug across their expanding tummies, for the rest of the holidays the goats skipped about the farm spreading sunshine in more ways than one.

And helpfully, if I lost one of my children, all I needed to do was look for a flash of neon and I knew Annas, Clemmy and Nancy wouldn't be far away.

Following the children everywhere doesn't *always* end well for the goats . . .

As to be expected at this time of year, and much to the children's delight, heavy snow was forecast between Christmas and New Year. With the snow keeping us at home for the next few days, the children enthusiastically dove head-first into all the winter activities that Ravenseat has to offer: sledging, skiing, snowboarding and ice-skating.

The goats also enjoyed the cold blast – it seemed that nothing could dampen their high spirits. They would come out of the stable each morning, positively dancing in the snow, their bristled hair dusted with snowflakes.

One particularly cold, icy morning, the goats followed us down to the **ford**. The children were suitably dressed in hats, gloves and ice-skates, and as soon as we had checked that the ice was thick and strong enough for them to skate safely, they began gliding over it. By the time the goats' little legs had caught up with us, the children were already on the other side of the ford. Instead of stopping where they were, as they normally did, you could see the goats thinking, *Hmm! Usually there's running water here, and we wouldn't go across. But today it's frozen, so we'll come too!*

Everyone stopped to stare as the goats took a couple of tentative steps on to the ice.

'Look at that,' said Clemmy, pointing. 'I didn't know goats could skate.'

'Neither did I,' I said.

But we spoke too soon. The goats remained upright until about halfway across the ford, before their legs did the splits and the chaos began.

'Sonny's down,' observed Reuben.

'No, no, he's OK,' I assured the girls, who were looking a bit panicked. 'Look, he's back on his feet... sort of.'

But my relief was short lived. Instead of turning round and heading to the safety of the shore, the goats skittered up river, where the ice was thinner...

'Go back, go back!' we all started shouting, frantically waving our arms. But our noise just seemed to encourage them on.

As they shuffled upstream, the ice started to crack under the weight of our tubby pygmy goats!

You've never heard shrieks like it – from the goats, the children and me.

'They're going to fall in!' screamed Nancy.

'Nah, they'll be fine,' I tried to reassure her, as I started preparing myself for a *very* cold swim. Rescuing goats out of an icy river was not on my Christmas to-do list.

Miles was laughing so hard, tears streamed down his face.

'Miles,' I muttered, 'it's not funny. I need you to do summat!'

'All right, keep your hair on. I don't even think they need rescuing,' he replied as he started unfastening his skates.

'This is not the time to get cold feet!' I joked. Miles just rolled his eyes in reply.

Thankfully, before anyone had to risk frostbite, the goats' common sense kicked in and they made a U-turn. They took one faltering step after another and, with a last little leap, they finally made it back to solid ground. And the funny thing was, they simply shook themselves off and waited patiently for us to follow, like nothing had ever happened.

I, on the other hand, needed a sit down and a warm drink after the panic of it all. So we skated our way back across the thick ice, and were reunited with our three slightly soggy friends. We all agreed that maybe the goats shouldn't join us for the snowboarding session that afternoon – I could picture them icing up like giant snowballs, or getting stuck in drifts. Although there was no chance we could ever lose them with their high-vis jackets!

So this Christmas, any visitors to Ravenseat should watch out for our three cheeky goats, because wherever they go mischief will surely follow.

And who's the G.O.A.T.? Well Sonny, Billy and Rocky are, of course.

They're our Greatest (Gifts) Of All Time.

Goodbye, Little Joe

We are lucky here at Ravenseat Farm to share the land with a host of animals, two legged and four. Each comes with its own personality and quirks, from Chalky the dog to Coco the sheep. And sometimes, without us even realizing, they make their way into our hearts. We love welcoming all sorts here, but sometimes we have to say goodbye to them too. This is a story about one of our favourites (if I'm allowed to say that): a horse called Little Joe, how he came to live with us, and how we learned to say goodbye.

Horses are friendly creatures, and ours lived in pairs. Josie and Princess – our two **piebald** and **skewbald** horses – shared one half of the old stables, and our two **Shetland ponies** – Tony and Little Joe – shared the other. Tony the Pony and Little Joe were not the best of friends *all* of the time – they would bicker, usually over food – but within minutes they'd have made up with a bit of mutual grooming.

Little Joe was an old boy of forty years, which is a jolly good age for a pony. And, although his teeth were worn and his eyes misty, he had a zest for life that made him seem like a much younger pony.

Joe had come to stay with us, not as a fresh-faced youngster, but as a mature horse with a mysterious past. He had belonged to one of our friends and neighbours, Susan, who was a vet. She had seen him with some children from the traveller community, who were visiting the annual **Appleby Horse Fair**. What began as a casual interest in this pony soon became a sale, such was the skill of those young entrepreneurs!

Perfect for teaching her grandchildren to ride, Joe soon enjoyed a new life with Susan and her Fell ponies. But ponies eventually outgrow their young riders, and after a decade of loyal service Susan had to – reluctantly – look for a new home for Little Joe.

Raven had been introduced to my horses at a very young age; I'd been plopping her on Josie and Princess's big, flat backs in a wicker-basket saddle since she was a baby. What I didn't have was a small pony for her to learn to ride independently when she was big enough . . . but I knew someone who did!

We never officially bought Little Joe from Susan; he came to us on loan. *Permanently,* as Clive never stopped reminding me. 'Little Joe is on the longest holiday I've ever known,' he'd say.

Joe would spend summers outside, joining Tony, Princess and Josie on the moor. Here he could be truly free to wander as he pleased. The sun on Little Joe's back would warm him through, and he would soon shed his raggedy, grey-flecked coat to reveal a sleeker, blacker shine. And grazing on the lush new moorland grass would always put some spring back into his step.

But every year, as Christmas approached, we would worry about Little Joe. The cold, the mud and the bare fields . . . Though we made the most of the festive season, it could be hard enough to stay upbeat ourselves when the days were so short on sunshine.

The stables have wooden dividers between them called stalls, corner hay racks above, and mangers below for feed. They are not the most modern of dwellings but we like them, as do the horses, because they provide them with shelter, warmth and comfort. And the horses provide us with warmth and comfort in turn, especially during the cold winter months, as nestled under their thick, wiry manes are warm fuzzy necks to thaw our hands and cheeks as we bury our faces into their softness, breathing in their wonderful smell.

It was here that Little Joe and his horsey friends would spend their Christmas and the harshest winter months, happily munching their way through armfuls of the softest green meadow hay and nosing through a carpet of deep straw bedding. As we went about our daily chores in the farmyard I would often peep over the top door to see what was happening. Sometimes I was met with a blank stare from a munching pony, but other times I would hear the deep rumble of a snoring horse, happily dreaming away.

When it got *very* cold, we would blanket Joe in the stable and then add a waterproof rug when he wanted to go outside. He hated wearing the rug and would do everything he could to remove it – wriggling and writhing, itching and rolling, scraping alongside walls and fences, whatever he could do to rid himself of it. Over time his rugs became colourful patchworks of glued-on fabric to repair the rips and tears, the whole outfit kept in place with baler **twine**.

Joe may well have been small in stature but he was huge in terms of the amount of destruction he could cause. He had a naughty streak and led the other horses astray, teaching them how to squeeze through hedge gaps, duck beneath bridges and, worst of all, how to tip-toe over a **cattle grid**.

He would create new exits from the fields by itching his bottom on walls and fences, leaving behind gaps that he could then squeeze through. As the air turned blue with Clive's angry words I would deny that Little Joe was responsible, pretending that his small size meant he couldn't possibly be guilty of such destruction. Unfortunately, Joe would always leave telltale strands of his wiry black tail hair at the scene of the crime, so there'd be no mistaking who exactly was to blame.

And so, this affectionate little chaos monster became, for the next fifteen years, a beloved member of our growing family.

Little Joe taught each one of the children how to ride, how to fall off and how to do a super-quick emergency dismount. He tolerated them bandaging him from head to hoof, adding plaits to his mane and nail polish to his hooves, and even dressing him up as one of Santa's reindeer.

Reuben was far less interested in playing hairdressers, preferring to think about how Little Joe could be useful to us. He built Joe a sledge to pull children and logs across the snow, and Joe willingly played along for a while. Then, when he had had enough, he just stopped, refusing to move until the children left him alone.

Just as Joe's appetite for being naughty never went away, neither did his hunger for adventure.

As we put the **tack** on the other horses to prepare for a late winter's-day ride, Joe would look excitedly towards the bridle rack. Here, among the leather **reins, halters** and girths, was Joe's well-worn **bridle**. It stood out from the others with a velvet, red-and-gold **browband** and rosettes on the sides, and had been snapped and restitched many times after he had catapulted his daydreaming rider over his head when performing a sudden stop.

'You don't want to come out with us, Joe!' we'd say to him as the other horses stomped and literally champed at the bit, impatient at just how long the preparations were taking. 'It's Baltic out there!'

'I'll put him back in the stable while we're gone,' I'd tell the children. 'He'll have a fine old time – he has a rack stuffed full of hay and a sweet **treacle lick** too, and he won't have to share any of it with Tony.'

Unfortunately Little Joe made it plain he felt he was getting the short end of the straw. As we left the farmyard for our ride his whinnying would begin. Looking back over my shoulder I would see his black, whiskered **muzzle** and two flared nostrils peeping over the lower half of the stable door. On really cold days you could see the steam rising from them – he was literally fuming at missing out!

One afternoon I was trotting up the road on Josie, accompanied by Violet on Princess and Clemmy on

Tony, when we realized Joe had escaped through a broken stable door. We stopped, looking back over our shoulders to see him determinedly trotting through the melting snow in our direction.

'Here comes Joe!' said Violet.

'What should we do with him?' asked Clemmy.

I weighed up our options: should we turn round, dismount our horses, try to catch Little Joe and tow him back to the stable (with him digging his heels in), or just let him tag along, riderless?

We went for the second option; it seemed kinder (and easier).

From that moment on, Little Joe joined us on all our rides out, walking along behind, or stopping to nibble the early buds of green grass through the icy slush. Wherever we went, Joe followed along too, lagging behind at an ever-increasing distance. I liked to think that he was happiest travelling at his own pace, taking whatever paths he wanted. Sometimes he might up his speed and break into a trot on the downhills, and at other times he was dawdling about miles away and barely visible.

It certainly added something new to our rides, working out where and when Little Joe would turn up and what shortcuts he would take to reach us. Nothing would stand in his way – he'd tiptoe around bogs, wade through undergrowth and once even trailed through a neighbour's garden, leaving a telltale dollop on their neat lawn.

He was a true master at cutting corners.

Little Joe's escapes were legendary, but there was no escaping old age. As he got older he would sleep more, lying down in the straw, ears occasionally twitching, contentedly sighing. We imagined that he was dreaming of his younger days. He would sometimes need a helping hand to get back on his feet – a well-timed shove beneath his shoulder would have him up and about, shaking off any pieces of straw before he shuffled over to the feed **trough** to check if breakfast had been served.

It was a foul, late-winter morning. Grey clouds rolled in from the moors, bringing showers of sleet, and we had retreated into the kitchen to warm up after a busy couple of hours feeding the animals. I stared out of the window into the farmyard, hoping that the day would brighten and the wind would drop before we set off with bales of hay for the waiting moorland sheep.

The smaller children had sensibly decided to stay indoors. Their oldest sister, Raven, was studying, nose in a textbook, and Edith and Violet were on tea duty, handing out mugs to me and their windswept brothers who, one by one, had joined us inside, stamping the snow off their boots and removing their damp woollen hats.

'What a day!' I said, closing my eyes.

'Awful, so hard on the animals,' said Clive.

'And us,' I muttered.

At that moment the door swung open, and a red-faced Sidney stood on the threshold.

'Joe's lying down,' he said breathlessly.

'Oh?' I said. 'Have you tried to get him up?'

'Yes,' he replied. 'But I can't.'

'Don't worry,' I said. 'It sometimes takes a little *oomph*.'

'And you're just a weakling, Sid,' added a smirking Miles.

I left the house, leaving the boys to playfully bicker.

I scooted across the yard and dived through the stable door. It was much warmer in there, and I took a moment to enjoy the familiar horsey smell.

But there, right in front of me, lay Little Joe – only this time the spark had left his kindly eyes.

I stared hard, looking for the faintest rise and fall of his chest. Bending down, I gently stroked the soft hair on his neck, still warm to the touch. It felt unreal that the pony who had wolfed down his breakfast only hours ago was now gone.

As farmers, the general belief is that you are familiar with life and death and that, because of your work, you're hardened to it. But I say that if you aren't touched by it, then you're in the wrong job. You can't fight the cycle of nature, but it still bothers you greatly. And you can't change the outcome either, but with our animals – especially one of Joe's age – you feel torn. You've done your best, and they've had a good life, but there's this tug in your heart between being practical about it and feeling genuinely sad for their passing.

As I crouched there in the stable, considering how I was going to break the news to the children, I felt the softness of a warm muzzle on my arm. Of course, I had forgotten about his stablemate, Tony the Pony! I looked into Tony's face for any sign of emotion. He looked at me curiously and then went back to nuzzling my arm. I thought that perhaps he was trying to comfort me, to show me that he understood that Little Joe had left us and then I realized: he could smell the mints in my shirt pocket.

I heaved myself up and looked down on Little Joe. Tony had now assumed position as guard of honour, crunching his mint and probably rather hoping that he would get Joe's too.

Slowly, I walked back to the house.

'I have something to tell you all,' I announced.

'Is he up?' asked Clive.

'No,' I said. 'And he's not going to be.'

It took a minute for what I had said to sink in, though I suspect that my face said it all.

Sidney looked shocked, Miles frowned and Clive looked crestfallen.

'What? Do you mean that . . .?' Reuben's words trailed off.

I nodded. I just couldn't bring myself to say it.

'You need a hole digging?' offered Reuben.

Tactless, some might say – but it was exactly what was needed to lighten the mood.

A procession of children made their way over to the stable, where a gentle stillness and calm had descended. Everyone shed a tear as we remembered our lovely Joe.

Clive and Reuben talked quietly about how to get Joe out of the stable, through the doorway and up the field to his final resting place.

'You need to get busy making a headstone and a memory box,' I said to the others.

Raven nodded, struggling to hold back her tears. She explained to Nancy how she had led Little Joe for many a mile with Nancy on his back, in the exact same basket saddle that Raven had once used.

'He was in good order, **t'owd** lad,' Clive said.

'Yes, he was super sturdy for a pony so long in the tooth,' I replied.

'He didn't have many teeth,' said Clem matter-of-factly.

'Didn't stop him eating though.'

Tony was nibbling hay while being cuddled by Annas. I expected that he was in for some serious pampering soon, now he was the main focus of the children's horsey affections.

Josie and Princess knew their daily schedule well, and so were very aware that something was wrong. We made a point of bringing them to see Joe to say goodbye. We watched them sniff curiously at him, and saw Tony paw the ground in an attempt to raise him. I was grateful for the icy raindrops that disguised my tears.

Joe lay peacefully in the stable while we prepared to bury him. Edith and Violet filled an empty metal biscuit tin with photographs and his favourite mints, and made him a crown of primroses, the only flowers that had emerged from the winter gloom so far. Annas and Nancy carefully brushed and tidied his mane and plaited his **forelock**, while Clem picked the dirt from his hooves and oiled them. He had tolerated these glow-ups while he was alive, and it seemed entirely fitting that he was going to gallop off to horsey heaven clad in the colourful contents of the children's jewellery box.

Sid and Miles went to find a headstone, and Reuben used his digger to make a hole in the frozen ground beside the small ridge in the High Bobby Dale field. This had been Joe's favourite place. From here he would stand and watch Raven, Edith and Violet excitedly approaching, hoping to take him for a ride. They would tramp up the field with a halter and bulging pockets of minty treats. Depending on what mood he was in he'd either eat the treats and go with them or eat the treats and gallop off. If it was the latter, the glum trio would stomp back down to the gate empty-handed, while Joe stood on the ridge, neck extended, ears joyfully pricked, his wild, flowing mane dancing in the breeze.

'I swear that he was laughing at us,' Raven said, smiling at the memory.

It was a sombre occasion as we all gathered around Little Joe's grave to say our final goodbyes. For a moment there was a break in the wintry greyness and the sun cast a light across the ramshackle funeral attendees of terriers, horses and humans.

There really was only one more thing to do.

There's an old saying in the Dales, though we're not sure where it's truly come from:

The best horses in heaven, they have no tail.
This is the rule we know without fail.

With that, as is as our tradition, Raven stepped forward with a pair of shears. Holding Joe's wiry, thick tail carefully in her hand, she cut it before he was lowered into his grave and gently covered over with soil, the spot marked by a rectangular boulder. We walked away, the horses stayed, the terriers rolled in something smelly, and, eventually, life on the farm carried on.

But every year, as we get the house ready for Christmas, I turn to the stone shelf by the fireplace. Sitting among the ramshackle collection of objects we keep in memory of some of our brilliant animals is a slate heart, painted with flowers, and in the middle, his name, *Little Joe*. I give it a dust and smile at it fondly, remembering the pony that brought us so much chaos and so much joy.

And that's his tale.

Three Yuletide Yarns, Two Spotted Sheep and a New Year's Miracle

I woke with a start.

'What was that?' I muttered, still half asleep.

Over the years, I've become familiar with the many sounds of Ravenseat Farm. I can tell cries of laughter from angry tears, and bleats of hunger from hazard. But the noise that awoke me on this cold midwinter night was unlike anything I'd heard before.

There it was again, a low and echoey sound carried through the sky on the relentless wind. *What is that?* I wondered.

Being mid-December, it was a little late in the year for Hallowe'eny goings-on!

I pulled the bedcovers higher to chase away the shivers that had come over me.

Too cold and tired to investigate, and confident the noise didn't belong to anyone or anything in need of urgent help, I went back to sleep. But it was a fitful night and the mysterious sound continued until my alarm went off at 6.30 a.m. It was time to get up, even though the sun wouldn't rise for hours.

Downstairs in the kitchen, my bleary-eyed children emerged one by one, and the house filled with the usual morning sounds: kettle boiling, plates clattering, toast popping and cereal crunching. Among the routine chatter about the jobs and plans for the day, Clem yawned and said, 'I didn't sleep very well.'

Sid, stifling a yawn of his own, added, 'Me neither. I kept being woken up.'

'Why was that, then?' asked a very fresh-looking Miles, who had clearly slept through it all.

'Well, there was this really funny noise. Did anyone else hear it?' asked Sid.

The rest of us chimed in that we'd heard it too, and the children had many theories about what it could have been.

'It sounded like an owl to me,' said Clem.

'Maybe it was Santa, come early!' suggested Nancy, the youngest.

'Don't be silly,' laughed Edith, swiftly bursting that bubble. 'Although maybe it was Chloe the reindeer, feeling a bit lonely now it's nearly Christmas.'

No one could settle on what had made the noise, though we all agreed that it wasn't a sound usually heard on the farm. But with a busy day ahead of us Annas moved the conversation on to another topic:

'Where are Coco and Chanel?'

Coco and Chanel had come to live with us at the start of December and had swiftly become part of our family's morning routine.

As is usually the case when you live on a farm, if you're going to get a gift, it will probably have four legs. And Clem and Annas had received their Christmas presents early that year – two Dutch Spotted sheep, made even more special because they were both in lamb. It was like buy one get one free – in December, Clem and Annas each got a sheep, then come lambing time in spring, they'd each get another!

The girls had called them Coco and Chanel after a famous French clothing designer on account of their beautiful, thick, soft fleeces. Our usual sheep, Swaledales, have very oily, grey wool. But a Dutch Spotted's fleece is fluffy and luscious. Coco belonged to Clem and was white and brown, and Annas's sheep was Chanel, who was black and brown.

And never has a luxury designer name been more suited to two sheep. Coco and Chanel quickly became very, very spoilt, receiving a lot of petting from the girls. I couldn't blame Clem and Annas, as their sheep had sweet natures, coming to greet you as you approached the gate and letting you stroke them.

Although I suspect the sheep might have had an ulterior motive, because Coco and Chanel were also very greedy. And despite how round their endless appetites had made them, they still managed to squeeze through unbelievably small spaces or barge into the house on their quest for more food.

Coco and Chanel never strayed too far. The other sheep liked to explore the land, but not these two. They were a very homely pair, with seemingly no wild desire to be out on the moor. They had learned where the feed bin and the house were, but that was the limit of their roaming (not like Chalky the dog!).

Instead, they joined a flock of misfit sheep we kept nearer the house, each with a backstory of their own. If you happen to go to a farm, you'll often find a little flock of weird sheep somewhere, that are different from the everyday ones the farmers deal with. We called ours 'crusties' – older sheep that had earned the right to not be sold on, and instead were living out their years in peace. It was an honour saved for a special few.

What we were yet to know was that Coco and Chanel had gifts of their own for us, and our Christmas that year was marked by three tales of chaos, each more surprising than the last.

Confident that we'd bump into Coco and Chanel on our rounds, the children and I piled into the porch, pulled on our wellies and set off, taking hay and feed to the sheep, cows and horses. But we didn't make it far before we heard that deep noise again.

Heading in the direction of the sound, we came across Annas's sheep, Chanel, with a mop bucket stuck on her head! Her unladylike grunts were echoing in the plastic, making an awful din.

Being the greedy sheep she was, Chanel had found the mop bucket and clearly decided that she would stick her head in it, in case there was a bit of food at the bottom. Finding it empty, she must have then tried to pull her head back out, swinging it around until she literally wedged the bucket over the top of her big brow, with the handle jammed behind her ears. It looked like she was wearing a helmet from a suit of armour. And the sound was something else. No wonder it had woken most of us up!

The mystery of the ghostly noise in the night was solved.

The children were laughing so hard they could barely breathe. 'Look at that! Look at that!' they gasped as the silly sheep ran up and down the field, trying to get it off. She looked ridiculous.

Once they'd composed themselves a little, we set about trying to get the bucket off her head. But everyone had a different opinion on how to remove it. Some thought you needed to pull the bucket; others thought it was Chanel who needed pulling. At one point Miles declared, 'It's no good! We'll have to cut it off,' and started heading to the tool shed for shears.

'No, ye cannot do that,' Clive warned. 'If the gal moves, you'll go with her **lug**.'

After much pulling, twisting and turning, I found the right angle and, with a heck of a heave, the bucket popped off, revealing a dazed-looking Chanel. She soon recovered and carried on looking for food like nothing had happened, while I was exhausted from a night of bad sleep and wrestling a sheep before 8 a.m.!

After that fiasco, I decided the rest of the children needed less troublesome Christmas presents, so I spent the following weeks finishing the festive shopping – buying model animals and miniature machinery for the younger ones, and books and practical clothing for the older ones.

Next on the Christmas to-do list was to decorate the house, something I like us all to do together as a family, although I hadn't planned on inviting Coco and Chanel.

This job always started down in one of the fields, where we'd dig up the fir tree we'd replanted the year before. Snow had already fallen and it was a bit of a battle breaking up the frozen ground to release the roots. After a good effort from the lads, we'd freed the tree, dragged it up the yard and through the open door into the house, leaving behind a trail of soil and pine needles. Now there was just the simple job of putting it up.

Well, I say put the tree up, but actually I mean *hang* it up because, after too many years of something charging into the house to try and scratch against it, eat it or climb up it, leaving a scattering of broken baubles and tangled tinsel in their wake, we stopped putting our tree in a bucket on the floor.

You wouldn't find a star or an angel at the top of our tree; instead, there was some baler twine. Reuben and I used it to attach the tree to one of the living-room ceiling's wooden beams. We'd try and get the height right so the tree sat perfectly on the floor, but we'd usually get a bit fed up and this year was no exception. We tied it up, hoping no one would notice that it was hovering a few inches off the ground.

While we were hanging up the tree, and the little ones were sorting through the decorations, Sidney said, 'I'll sort the lights out.'

'Great,' I replied, 'but do plug them in before you spend the next five hours unravelling them only for them not to work.'

So off Sid went to find a spare plug to test them. 'They work,' he hollered back, and began the thankless task of untangling the lights, looping them around Violet's outstretched hands.

In the middle of all of this, no one gave much thought to the open front door or the line of dropped pine needles, like a trail of breadcrumbs, leading straight inside. Usually, grass is the thing sheep like to eat, but at certain times of year, particularly when there's snow on the ground, they'll nibble away at the bark on the trees. Never ones to miss out on a free meal, Coco and Chanel came barging into the house.

We stood no chance of stopping these two bulldozers, who will absolutely flatten you to get to food. They spotted the tree and charged.

What followed was like a scene from the TV show *Gladiators*. Coco and Chanel crashed into the tree and it started swinging like a giant pendulum, bashing the two sheep as it went back and forth.

The house erupted with noise as the children were rolling about laughing. I started shouting at Coco and

Chanel to *get out*, but they didn't listen. I had to shove them for all I was worth because they've got a leg on each corner, like a table. They're so hard to budge. And they always come in a pair, so it's not just one sheep I had to manhandle outside, but two! After *another* wrestling match, I finally got them back outside and quickly shut the door.

In the chaos of getting the sheep out something must have happened to the fairy lights because they didn't work the next time Sid plugged them in. It was the last straw, and so we abandoned decorating the tree for the evening and went to bed.

Hoping that this was the last of their antics, I spent the next few days adorning the tree with some working lights, lots of gaudy tinsel and the random assortment of decorations we'd collected over the years – things the children have made, mismatching baubles and chocolates. Ours certainly wasn't an orderly, colour-co-ordinated tree, but it was decorated with memories, the way we liked it.

With the preparations complete we just had to wait for the big day. Christmas rolled around with no more nonsense from Coco and Chanel, and we settled into our usual routine of letters to Santa on Christmas Eve, the challenge of roasting a turkey big enough to feed eleven people and spending as much time out in the snow as possible while the children were off school. We were lucky to have many white Christmases at Ravenseat and – as long as I was prepared – I loved it when it snowed.

There were the usual jobs to do on the farm, of course, but in December we were pretty much in maintenance mode with the sheep, keeping them warm and fed. Most were in lamb, but not due until early April, and they were happy enough as long as they had plenty to eat and the snow wasn't too deep.

We set out on New Year's Day with bales of summer-scented hay, trudging through a fresh covering of deep snow on our rounds, working up to the moor and then back down to the house past our weird little flock of crusties.

When we came to their field, I knew something was wrong straight away because Coco and Chanel weren't waiting by the gates for their feed. And where they should have been were *lots* of hoofprints and flattened snow instead.

'What's been going on here?' I said to Clive.

'Well, I don't know,' he replied. 'It's only January; far too soon for lambs.'

But I could see the signs in the snow, clear as day. The sheep had gone round and round in circles; it's something that a **ewe** does when she's in labour. We needed to investigate – quick!

We abandoned our fodder and headed through the gate. Working our way round the back of the shepherd's hut we came across Ravenseat's own little Christmas miracle – Coco and Chanel had lambed not one but two lambs each, about three months earlier than expected. And they did it all without any help and in a snow drift!

We once had a ewe lamb in February, and we thought that was unbelievable. So to have *two* lamb on the first day of January was unheard of. And we were completely unprepared. Each spring we would do lots of work ahead of lambing time. The children particularly loved to build the 'sheep hospital', which was their fond name for the buildings where we would take the newborn lambs and their mothers to check them over.

It's not just the lack of preparation that had me concerned. Lambs are born in spring for a reason. There's grass on the ground, which the sheep need to eat to help their milk supply. And it's a lot warmer too.

A snow drift has to rank as one of the worst places to give birth. But this was another reason why Coco and Chanel had flattened the snow. For lambs to survive, they need to be able to stand up within 10–15 minutes of being born so they can find their feet and latch on to the ewe. They desperately need that first suckle of fatty milk, called **colostrum**, that gives them energy. Without that they won't survive, especially in temperatures well below zero like we were experiencing that day. So they definitely didn't want to be stuck in a pile of snow, unable to stand.

It was amazing that all four lambs had survived. It just shows what good mothers Coco and Chanel are.

Once the immediate shock of it all wore off, it was action stations.

'Right, OK,' I said. 'We need to bring them in, out of the cold. You lot head to the stable and bed up with plenty of fresh straw,' I instructed Clemmy and Annas, handing out the jobs that needed doing. 'Violet, nip up to the freezer and check if we have spare colostrum milk in case these lambs need a top up.'

And, knowing how good Edith is with sheep, 'Help me get these lambs into the stable,' I asked.

Quick as we could, we all got to work and in no time at all the lambs, Coco and Chanel were out of the wet snow and cosy in the warm stable.

Sid and Miles had appeared by this point, attracted by all the commotion. 'You two, give us a hand, and fetch some decent hay and feed for the big 'uns.'

I checked each sheep over thoroughly for any signs of illness or weakness, but they were a healthy bunch. And thankfully we didn't need any extra milk because the lambs were suckling from their mothers brilliantly.

Coco had lambed two healthy **gimmers** – females – and Chanel had had two good-size **tups** – males. With the initial panic over, and after convincing the girls they didn't need to put coats on the lambs, I asked them, 'Go on, then, what are you going to name them?'

I thought they might choose some festive names like Holly or Snowy, but no, Clem named her gimmers Spotty and Dotty, and Annas continued the rhyming theme with Rambo and Lambo for her tups.

Despite the odds being stacked against Coco and Chanel, in reality everything went right – it was just the wrong time of year! And our weird little flock of mismatched sheep had three new additions. We kept the two gimmers and one of the tups; the other was sold at **auction**, although Annas claims she's still waiting for the money from Clive for that.

Talk about a Christmas gift that keeps on giving.

Our Winter Olympics

It was the first week of the new year, and at that moment it felt like any last bit of Christmas spirit had long gone as Miles and I battled our way to the moor tops.

The latest winter storm had well and truly arrived.

We had seen it on the TV weather report the day before and had prepared for it as best we could. Now all the newsreaders were talking about it, and the official advice was to stay indoors.

'Never! We can't do that!' Clive uttered. 'The worse the weather, the more the animals need us.'

Even without the forecast, we could see something was afoot because the sky took on a funny light in the mid-afternoon; it was almost a sandy-pink colour. Then the wind picked up and the snow began.

'Right, it's time for us to make a move,' I said, coming away from the window.

We have about 650 sheep on our farm, all spread out across different **heafs**. They were in lamb at this time of year, and needed to be sheltered from the storm so we could keep them well fed and safe.

It was time to divide and conquer.

Clive and Edith went off in one direction and Reuben and Sid in another, and Miles was joining me. I left Violet to stay with the little ones, pointlessly hoping they wouldn't get too soggy playing in the falling snow.

Bundled up in layer after layer, Miles and I headed round to the kennels to pick up my sheepdog Penny. She's a tri-coloured border collie with a black body, a white tummy and a distinctive white band around her neck, which almost, but doesn't quite, meet. Her face is flecked with brown, with expressive eyebrows above her hazel eyes.

The relationship between a shepherd and their sheepdog is something special. They're totally and utterly devoted to you. And for a shepherd, the dog goes beyond being your best friend – they're your partner. My ability to herd our sheep, and do it well, is completely dependent on my dog.

Penny's help in a storm like this was going to be very important.

Miles and I hopped on the quad bike, and Penny jumped on the back, balancing with the skill of a tightrope walker. I drove out of the yard to the back of the house and started heading straight up the bank to find our flock.

The weather was so bad the bike soon got stuck and we had to abandon it. The snow was getting heavier and heavier and this was fast turning into a '**white out**', meaning we had near zero visibility. On foot, Miles, Penny and I kept heading upwards, trying not to lose our bearings completely. It's scary how the places that you're so familiar with, that you pass through every single day, quickly become unrecognizable in heavy snow. I couldn't look up because the snow was coming right at me, blurring my vision. I couldn't even see the dog. I could only just make out Miles next to me.

We eventually reached the first hill where we'd usually find the sheep. Not a sign of anything. I pulled down my scarf and started whistling into the white flakes swirling around me. I wasn't whistling to Penny; I was trying to call up my sheep. Being nervy animals, they'd usually run away from me, but at this cold and hungry time of year I would whistle to tempt them to come to the feed.

I couldn't see hide nor hair of them, and I got cross with myself, thinking we should have set off sooner. Then I spotted a different shade of white, but it was *moving*. 'They're over there!' I shouted to Miles, pointing up into the eye of storm. I whistled to the sheep again, and we tried our best to round them up.

Their wool had already started to freeze, clumps of snow piling up on their backs like they'd been in a snowball fight. There was no let up, and in fact the wind was picking up and snow was swirling around us. We could only hope we had them all: it was impossible to do a head count.

It was time to set off home.

With a gesture of my hand, I sent Penny to the back of the flock. I knew she was there, somewhere, but I still couldn't see her. I just had to trust that she'd got behind every single sheep. I couldn't even tell her what to do with whistles or voice commands in this weather, because the sound was getting lost in the wind.

We neared the farm at last and drove the sheep into an old stone **fold**. There was no roof and the walls weren't high, but it would protect the sheep from the worst of the weather.

We counted the sheep as fast as our frozen brains would allow and realized with relief that they were all there.

'She's done good!' Miles said, trying to give Penny a pat on the head as she shook the encrusted snow from her coat, all while her tail was wagging.

Back at the farm, Penny went to the kennels as Miles and I headed to the house to thaw out, exhausted but glad we'd got the sheep to safety. But, as I climbed into bed that night, the storm still raged outside the window, and I wondered what would await us in the morning.

The storm moved over us in the early hours and we woke up to a complete white out. I tentatively opened the front door for a better look and was met with a wall of snow where it had drifted up against the house. It quickly became clear that the children were going nowhere. We could barely make it out of the house, never mind travel on the roads to school.

Once I got back inside after feeding and watering the animals closest to the farmhouse, the winter sun had finally come up. The children, true to form, were itching to go outside.

'Can we go and play in the snow?' they asked.

'Yeah, course you can,' I replied.

The house quickly became abuzz with activity as layers of clothing were pulled on yet again, and within minutes the last balaclava was tugged down over someone's chin. They piled out of the back door only to be stopped in their tracks.

In front of us lay an endless sea of glistening snow, twinkling under a bright blue sky. It felt like the world had been muffled by a huge soft duvet. It was just so quiet. Every wall, boundary and field lay buried under pillowy white snow. There were icicles as tall as the children, and packed snow hung over the banks of the frozen river.

It looked amazing.

It is only through living and working in such a remote, high place that we get to experience sights like this. While the day before had been difficult, the upside was this magical view and the opportunity to have some fun in the snow. Here was our calm after the storm.

Clemmy broke the trance, shouting, 'Winter Olympics!' and with that the day's activities were decided.

We'd held many 'Winter Olympics' during our years at Ravenseat, and ice-skating, curling, sledging and even snowboarding were all on the agenda – farm style, of course.

All in agreement with Clem, the children headed to the barn and the loft, looking for where they'd dumped their skis, snowboards and sledges after the last snowfall. They appeared with a collection of ramshackle equipment under their arms: an odd number of ski poles, mismatched skis that you can clip on to wellies, a wooden 1950s-looking water-skiing board that Reuben had got at a car-boot sale, and a second-hand snowboard Miles had found on eBay.

'You got enough stuff there?' I asked, chuckling at the sight of them.

'This'll do for a start,' replied Edith, clutching the one 'good' snowboard.

'Can we take the dogs?' asked Sid.

'Hmm, I don't know whether they'll want to go,' I said, thinking about how exhausted poor Penny would still be from the day before. But, when Sid opened the kennel doors, there wasn't a moment of hesitation as Penny, Midge and Nelly came bounding out.

'How can you have this much energy?' I exclaimed, looking at Penny. But the dogs were always ready to work. They weren't very good at switching off (a bit like me!) but, whenever there was snow on the ground, they loved to play.

So off we went. But before anyone could start heading downhill, they'd got to get uphill first, and being a 'hill farm', we had a lot of those. What we didn't have was a ski lift!

It's hot, sweaty work hauling your gear through thigh-deep snow when you're all wrapped up, from your boots to your balaclava. After the second or third time traipsing up the slope, the layers were inevitably flung off, dumped and then snowed upon, only to be rediscovered weeks or even months later.

Skiing and snowboarding were first up, and, selecting from the array of old kit, there was an unspoken, agreed rotation: one or two of the children would try to ski or snowboard down the hill, chased by the dogs in play mode. Whoever came up last would cool off from the sweaty climb, while the rest of them made a pile of snowballs. Considering none of them had ever had a skiing or snowboarding lesson in their lives, I was always impressed at how upright the children would stay. And it was made all the more challenging by the snowballs they'd throw at whoever was heading down the slope next!

After a couple of practice goes, it was Edith's turn to show us how it's done as she took on Ravenseat's black run, the steepest hill on the farm. To climb up this, it was a case of crawling on your hands and knees – the incline was that sheer.

With snowballs forgotten and people, dogs and sheep all watching, we cheered her on with shouts of, 'Come on, Edie!' as she psyched herself up and then dropped over the edge, gliding to the bottom like a pro. No arguments: Edith took the gold medal in snowboarding that year.

It was not always such smooth riding though, and we have had to ban events in the past. Sledging was OK, but sledge *racing* could no longer be part of the Winter Olympics at Ravenseat. The last time we tried it was total chaos. Obviously, this being farm-style Olympics, we didn't use actual sledges – we improvised with something we have in plentiful supply: feed bags.

The idea was to fill them up with something, so there was a bit of padding between your bum and the frozen molehills as you came down the slope. But rather than going and getting anything comfortable, like a cushion, the children would just pile snow into the bags and tie them off – with baler twine, of course.

Clemmy and Nancy lined up to race and set off down the hill. They were absolutely flying! But what we hadn't realized was that as they'd been shaking the feed bags about, the rustling had caught the attention of the sheep at the bottom of the field, who clearly thought it was dinner time.

Clem and Nancy were neck-and-neck and approaching the end of the race when I suddenly realized they were heading straight for the flock, who had started running towards the girls. There was a horrible moment when Clem nearly took out an old ewe who was in the way.

'Look out!' I screamed from the top of the hill, like she hadn't noticed the great big woolly thing right in front of her.

This set the dogs off, who stopped playfully bounding after the sledges and got in among the sheep and children, not knowing whether they were on or off duty. It was total and utter carnage, and sledge racing was then banned.

After heading back to the house to fuel up, warm up and switch equipment, it was time to embark on the afternoon's schedule, featuring a firm favourite: ice-skating. No Winter Olympics was complete without trudging through the snow to the tarn, the small lake up on top of one of the moors. We lugged several pairs of skates and a flask of tea each to keep warm. It was a bit of a trek – in fact it'd be a lot easier just to stay indoors – but the experience was worth the effort.

Reuben had previously been on a trip to Sweden, which can be a very cold country with lots of snow and ice – perfect for skating. There he'd learned from a trained expert the special way to test the ice's thickness for safety, so it wouldn't crack when skated on. It was something we did each and every time we wanted to ice skate, and if the ice wasn't thick enough, we could not go skating – it was as simple as that.

We had a mixture of old-fashioned ice-skates, but also some double-bladed skates, easier for the smaller

children to keep their balance and gain their confidence. Even better, they could be worn with wellies!

Nancy might have been the youngest, but she definitely didn't need help with her balance. Her grace as a ballet dancer became clear as she pulled on her skates and just glided across the ice. And it was all the more impressive because this natural lake was nothing like a smooth and uniform ice-skating rink. A breeze must have been blowing at one end of the tarn as ripples of water had frozen on to the surface, but at the other side the ice was smooth (with a few rocks jutting out for added peril!).

Not seeming to feel the cold, the children happily spent hours up there until we all became mesmerised by the pink and orange clouds that reflected on the ice. The sun was setting, which meant a walk home in the dark. But it also meant we got to do a spot of stargazing en route. On those crisp, cold, clear nights, the white snow almost glowed and the inky black sky filled with a never-ending number of stars – the longer you looked, the more appeared, and the sight of a shooting star made the numb fingers, toes and snotty nose all worth it.

We've also tried our hand at some of the lesser-known Olympic games over the years. ***Skijoring*** is a little-known winter sport. I'd seen videos of it online, and the idea is that a person is pulled along on skis by a horse and rider. Thinking that my horse, Meg, was probably a little too spirited for this event, we rolled out Tony the Pony. And rolled is the word. The horses always loved to have a tumble in the snow, leaving a great big, dirty patch behind, making you realize how much of a groom they needed.

We hooked a pair of skis to our feet and held on tight to Tony the Pony's reins, but it never worked very well because he kept going where he wanted to go, and usually that was over various molehills. They have bumpy mounds of snow called *moguls* on the ski runs in Switzerland, but here, at Ravenseat, we had the equivalent - frozen *molehills*!

Skijoring was eventually retired after too many liftoffs that resulted in faceplants.

The next day, the children had decided they wanted to add a new sport to the itinerary: curling.

Curling normally involves one person sliding a rounded stone down the ice, similar to bowling, while two other people sweep the ice in front of it with special brooms to steer it in the direction of the target.

But who needs a curling stone when you've got a willing little sister?

The yard was raided for all the brooms and brushes they could find, and the children took them down to the river. There's a stretch of water, just before you get to the ford, where it curves around the corner, and there the ice was perfectly smooth and thick.

Clueless as to what was about to happen, I enquired, 'What exactly are we doing now?'

'Just wait and see, Mum,' Miles chuckled, as the children descended on to the ice.

Nancy stood there in her big, thick coat with its fluffy hood. After whispered instruction from the other children, she tucked herself into a tight ball like a hedgehog. Before I realized what was happening, Miles had launched her across the ice with a great big shove. She sped along, squealing with laughter, while Violet and Sidney started madly sweeping their brooms back and forth ahead of her to make her go faster. The children took it in turns to be sweeper, but Nance was always the curling stone.

And that's how we spent our morning . . . Until, of course, someone got a wet bum. We worked hard and played hard; that's what memories are made of.

So what's all this got to do with Christmas? Well, if you asked the children what presents they got for Christmas that year, I bet you they can't even remember – I know I can't. Because it really isn't about the gifts. Aye, you might want a new toy, new shoes, new whatevers. But how about making memories as well?

These are the Christmases I remember – not what we got, but what we did. Together.

Guess Hoo?

'Oh my goodness, look at that,' I breathed, signalling to the top of the frost-covered hill we were midway through climbing.

We all stopped to admire a tawny owl soaring in the fading midwinter light. The children whispered '*Shhh*' to each other while excitedly pointing towards the gliding silhouette on the skyline.

No matter how many times I see one, there is something very special about catching a glimpse of an owl. It's a sight that stops you in your tracks. We've always had them on our farm, but I'm rather proud to say that we currently have more owls than ever before, and it largely comes down to one simple reason: the way we farm our land.

Some farms grow cereals that you might have for your breakfast. Others grow fruit and vegetables. But all we grow here at Ravenseat Farm are fields of grass.

But it's more than just grass. It's actually made up of very special plants, herbs and wildflowers that are not only good for our animals to eat, but also good for nature as a whole.

When lambing time is done, we move the sheep out of the fields up to the higher ground on the heathery moors to let the grass grow. And at the height of summer, the fields become a sea of colours and smells, alive with the buzz of insects.

As we walk the ewes and lambs through the grass, closely followed by the sheepdog, the disturbance caused by their footsteps makes the flies and midges take to the air, creating a cloud of insects for the swallows to eat. They swoop and dive, making the most of this free meal.

And as the grass and flowers grow, the fields provide a perfect habitat for all kinds of birds to nest and lay their eggs. They feed a population of other tiny mammals too – shrews, voles and field mice. And, in turn, these feed the owls.

It's a prime example of striking the perfect balance between looking after animals, people and nature.

Done right, year after year, everything, and everyone, can prosper.

Once upon a time I would say to Clive, 'I saw a barn owl today,' and he'd say, 'Nivver, it's too hard a spot for 'em.' But he was wrong; they are making a comeback in Swaledale and are making good use of our many barns on the farm. And as the owl numbers have grown, so we all have come to learn more and more about them.

When Miles, Sid, Violet and I first discovered a clutch of round owl eggs in the loft of one of our stone barns, it was the start of a real learning curve. We read up on them in the *Big Book of British Birds,* learning about the different breeds, lifecycles and more. We were already trapping the mice that invaded our dairy (eating our cornflakes!), but now we could put them to good use by giving them to the owls to eat.

The children's excitement matched my own, and we've since become fully fledged owl enthusiasts. Annas in particular is the knowledgeable one when it comes to these birds; she will tell you anything and everything there is to know about them.

It makes me so happy to have barn owls permanently living in two of our barns. We've always had tawny owls that can be found nesting among the wooden beams, and little owls that have huge, round eyes set against tiny bodies. We even have bog owls that, despite their swampy-sounding name, have sunny yellow eyes and two endearing ear tufts. We sometimes happen upon their beautiful nests woven among the rushes while gathering our sheep from the moor.

With so many different kinds of these incredible, **endangered** birds living around us, I decided Christmas that year would be owl-themed. I bought the littlest ones – Annas, Clemmy and Nancy – everything owl-related I could get my hands on.

Come Christmas morning, my little gang of **ornithologists** unwrapped cuddly owl toys; an owl cushion; an identification chart to tell the difference between owl species, eggs, nests and pellets; a pack of Top Trumps cards of British birds; and a new book on small mammals so they could recognize the variety of things that owls eat – voles, mice, shrews (or 'sha-roos' as my children say) – that we have scurrying about the farm.

After the daily chores were done (because even at Christmas the animals still need their fodder) and while Raven and I put the finishing touches to the turkey in the kitchen, I could hear shouts from the fireside. Nancy had won another round of Top Trumps, her golden eagle beating the wingspan of Sid's last card, the tiny robin. I considered the gifts a complete success when I poked my head in on the young ones at bedtime and spotted the wing of an owl teddy squished in the middle of the double bed they always end up sharing.

On Boxing Day, once the sun had lazily risen several hours after the rest of us, we wrapped up and headed outside. We don't like being cooped up indoors no matter the weather, and the children had a mission lined up for that day: seeing how many different kinds of owl we could spot on the farm.

We started by collecting **owl pellets**. These are the parts of an owl's meal that they can't digest, like fur and bones, which they then throw up in one go.

Nancy, Clem, Annas, Sid and Miles headed to the barns, torches in hand, and were soon crawling along the floors and peering behind hay bales, looking for evidence. Seeing them emerge victorious while holding these dry, brown, stringy lumps, I found it quite funny how pleased they were to find something that was, for want of a better word, foul!

Next they found an old jam jar in the tool shed and filled it with water and the pellets. After giving it a good shake, the pellets soon dissolved and the solid parts sunk to the bottom of the jar. Crowding round, we all peered inside. There were tiny skulls, teeth – all sorts, and the chart helped us first identify which animal the bones and fur had come from and then which kind of owl had eaten it.

'It's a Tony owl,' said Clem confidently, more commonly known as a *tawny* owl.

We soon developed a bond of sorts with what we came to think of as 'our' owls. Maybe they were starting to accept our presence because we left food out for them and would then leave the barn without disturbing them. In no way were we trying to tame them; we simply wanted to see them thrive. They are still very much wild birds, as they reminded us in no uncertain terms one night.

With a freshly caught mouse in hand, Annas, Sid and Nancy headed towards the barn where the owls live. But as they reached the door and swung it open, an owl swooped down from the beams and brushed against their hair before flying off into the night.

This encounter only made the children's love of owls grow, and it became a source of pride that they had decided to make their homes on our farm.

So after the excitement of our owl-themed Christmas and watching the birds hunt through such harsh winter conditions, it was a relief when spring came round again. The land warmed through at last and everything burst into life. There were scuttling mice to be avoided with every footstep that you took; a nest of voles or shrews hidden under almost every stone that tumbled from the top of the drystone walls. There was owl-food everywhere, providing rich pickings for the sharp-eyed hunters, who no longer needed our help in order to get a full belly.

Soon there were more owls than ever, and they were no longer an unusual sight. One afternoon, during lambing time, Sid and Raven came to find me. Raven said, 'Did you know that there's an owl sat among the cows?'

'Really?' I replied and quickly followed them to see for myself.

There we found a tawny **owlet**, sat squarely in the middle of the cow shed – a ridiculous place to be, as it was certainly in harm's way and could easily have been squashed by a hoof. The owlet was **branching**, which is when the young owls first leave the nest but still need their parents to hunt for their food. Clearly it didn't fully understand the dangers of the world just yet.

Raven pulled on a pair of thick gloves and offered to move it. 'Where shall I put it?' she asked.

'You want to put it up high, out of harm's way,' I said, 'but not too far away, so its mother can still find it.'

So Raven carefully picked up the owlet, holding it at arm's length, and gently placed it on top of the straw bales. When you pick them up, you realize just how fragile these magnificent birds actually are. They can weigh only a couple of grams; their size is all feather and down.

Keen not to disturb it further, I headed back to the lambing shed and Raven went into the house. But it wasn't long before Reuben strode around the corner.

'There's an owl in my workshop,' he said.

'Really . . .?' I asked, feeling a bit confused.

'Yeah. It's just sitting there next to my vice, and I'm worried it's gonna fall in one of the oil containers.'

'OK,' I sighed. 'Don't worry about it. I'll get Raven to come and shift it.'

Off I went to find Raven and inform her that she clearly didn't do a very good job of moving that owlet to safety.

'Please can you try a bit harder this time? Thank you,' I asked crossly.

'Yeah, sorry,' she said, and disappeared to move it to a new spot.

Back to the lambs I went, when, only an hour later, Clive came in, really unimpressed. What do you think was on the seat of the machine he needed to use? An owlet, of course!

'It's just sat there, looking at me,' he grumbled.

It was now Raven's turn to be annoyed. 'It must be really desperate to stretch its wings. I thought owls were supposed to be wise?' she said flatly.

'Just go and sort it,' I said firmly. 'We don't want anything happening to the daft thing.' So off she went to move it yet again.

And so the day carried on. I was busy lambing, and the little ones were helping me muck out the pens, chucking away dirty straw and replacing it with clean, then filling up the hay racks for the sheep to eat.

As we made our way to the back of the barn, we suddenly heard a strange *click clack* sound.

'What's that noise?' Clem asked.

'Not sure,' I admitted.

We listened carefully and realized that it was coming from somewhere on ground level. 'It can only be that owlet again!' I realized. 'It's among the straw somewhere.'

This owlet was really getting on my nerves by this point. It was becoming beyond a joke. The last thing I wanted was for any harm to come to it, but this one seemed to enjoy living dangerously.

So I sent Clemmy off to get the thick gloves, knowing how sharp an owl's talons are, and passed her my phone to use as a torch. 'Have a poke about under the bales, there.'

Stepping carefully among the straw, it wasn't long before she found it.

'It's an owl!' Clem said excitedly.

'Yes, Clem, it's an owl.' I said tiredly. 'Get it out.'

After a moment or two she reappeared, holding the owlet aloft.

It was clearly all right as it was completely calm in Clemmy's hand, its expression perfectly blank. It must have just scrambled into the nearest, darkest place it could find.

'Right,' I said to Clem, 'we need to deal with this once and for all.' So I set her off to the back of the farm buildings to find a better place to put it, well out of the way of humans.

Not long after Clem had gone, Annas announced that she could hear a strange clicking sound . . .

'Oh for goodness' sake, there must be another one!' I exclaimed. 'Right, Annas, your turn.' But this time we didn't have any gloves, so she used her hat. Into the bales she went, crawling around, before reappearing with a second owlet wearing an equally casual expression on its face. I sent her round the back to find Clem, so we could reunite the pair.

Off Annas went, but can you guess what happened next?

The clicking noise returned!

'Nance! There must be another one,' I said, shaking my head. Nancy always wears a coat with a fluffy hood and she's absolutely fearless, so she whipped it off and disappeared into the bales, emerging shortly after with another owlet wrapped in her hood.

Three owlets – it was unheard of!

All this time Raven thought she was moving the same one! We never suspected there to be more of them, because usually only one or two chicks from a **brood** make it to this age.

Nancy and I headed off to find Clem and Annas, and as we chatted about the best place for these young birds, Reuben appeared from the house.

'Have you moved the owl from my workshop?' he asked.

'Aye, we have,' I replied.

'Well then, why did you put it int'porch?' he laughed.

And, lo and behold, we had a *fourth* baby owl, the same size as the other three. I couldn't believe it. Never mind twit-twoo or twit-three – this was twit-four!

Now Clem, Annas, Nancy and I were all holding an owlet each. 'This is incredible,' I said, with a sense of pride. Somehow, among our busy farmyard, these four owlets had been hatched and were clearly doing well.

Determined to keep them all safe, we gently placed them on a high wall, and let them be. They'd had enough handling for one day, and it was time we got on with our jobs.

While finishing my final rounds for the evening, I heard that *click-clack* noise again. I looked up and saw the baby owls had returned. They were now sitting in a line on a beam above the cows, in the shed where Sid had found the first one.

I hurried back to the house and ushered everyone quietly outside. Taking them to the shed, I pointed upwards. 'Look at them,' I whispered, and that's when we spotted one of their parents nearby. We all stood there silently, amazed.

For the next couple of weeks we watched the owls coming and going, toing and froing. We never stopped worrying about them, and if we could only spot three, we'd panic.

'Where's the other one?' we'd ask ourselves.

'Oh, it's there,' we'd realize, calmness restored.

We had felt such a personal connection to these owls throughout the year. What a hoot it had been to watch them grow from chicks to fully fledged owls.

But as winter drew near once again it was time to bid them goodbye, as the grown owls spread their wings to well and truly fly the nest at last.

A Snowy Game of Hide and Sheep

As the year comes to an end, nature slows down and the land falls asleep, so we farmers must look ahead. A shepherd's year begins now, at **tupping** time, which is the very start of the sheep-breeding season.

We bring our flock into the fields for mating and it's a restless time for them, as they only feel truly at home when grazing on the mountain tops. But as the cold creeps in and the sheep's natural food – the grasses and mosses of the moors – becomes buried under frost and snow, so we, their shepherds, have to fodder, or feed, them.

This is where we found ourselves in the run-up to Christmas. The whole family had plenty to keep them busy before and after school: feeding the chickens, watering the horses, checking on the sheepdogs, milking our house cow, Buttercup, and mucking out the pens.

On top of all that hard work a snowstorm was forecast. The children were extremely excited about it because they predicted they would get a day or two off school. I didn't want to dampen their spirits, but I thought the storm would mostly bring fast winds and heavy rain. But still, it was important that the cows and horses were tucked up safe in their barns and stables.

Sheep generally hate the indoors, preferring to hunker down in a muddy hollow or at the back of a drystone wall. So long as they stayed in the more sheltered fields in the lower lying land, all should be well. Our Swaledale sheep are a **hardy** breed, as wild and rugged as the moors they come from.

We studied the weather updates constantly, and it certainly seemed that we were in for a battering, but I could never have imagined that such a ferocious storm was brewing . . .

The next day was no different from any other. The children were at school, and Clive and I were busying around the farm. With the storm due overnight, we agreed it would be sensible to fodder the sheep before we went to bed. We would open all of the doors to the barns in the fields and fill the hay racks too, giving the sheep a place to shelter should they so choose.

By the time the primary-school children had got home the wind was whipping up. Clem, Annas, Nancy and Sid closed the henhouse and top stable doors, threw extra straw into the kennel boxes and retreated indoors. Later, as the older children – Miles, Edith and Violet – came hurrying over the packhorse bridge towards the house, they had to run bent over, heads down, clutching their coat hoods tightly, as the first specks of powdery snow swirled into the floodlit farmyard.

'Inside, inside!' Breathlessly I ushered them in, slamming the door shut and kicking the draught excluder into place.

'Aye, it's a nasty night out there,' said Clive. 'But we've got everything we need, and everyone's safe.'

'No school tomorrow!' chorused the little ones.

'Perhaps,' I replied.

The best thing about a stormy night is that the whistling wind that comes barrelling down our old chimney causes the fire in the hearth to burn extra hot. With rolled-up towels wedged beneath the windowsills and the curtains pulled shut to muffle the rattling panes, we were well prepared to weather the storm.

Chalky and Sprout, our terriers, lay by the fireside as the embers in the grate glowed. Every now and then one of us would traipse to the porch and peep out of the tiny window. But there was little to see in the darkness – we would have to wait until the morning to assess the situation.

After tea we settled down for a while.

'Are we not going to school tomorrow?' Clem asked hopefully.

Before I could reply, the lights plunged us into darkness as all power was lost. We sat waiting, hoping that it may just be a temporary outage. Upstairs our oldest son, Reuben, let out a shout as his hot shower was rudely interrupted. The only light we had was in the living room, where the fire cast dancing shadows across the children's nervous but excited faces.

'Can't have a shower, so can't go to school,' decided Annas.

'Early night for us all,' said Clive.

It wasn't unusual to be without electricity when we lived in such a remote place, so we had plenty of candles and torches to keep us going in the short-term. And for a little while it could be quite wonderful to be out of touch with the busy outside world. So we went to bed, fully expecting a difficult day ahead of us, but not feeling too worried about it.

We all woke up much earlier than usual. The children were excited for a day off school, while the rest of us wondered what awaited us outside. I peeked between the bedroom curtains and needed a moment to take in the breathtaking scene.

A thick blanket of snow covered absolutely everything, as far as my eyes could see. The wind had driven it into every crack, burrow and hollow. It was a white out, and it was still snowing – not gently but angrily!

I took a deep breath. It was time to rally the troops.

We suffered our first setback within about ten seconds when we discovered that we still had no electricity. The chances of a cup of tea were looking rather bleak, but not to be disheartened, I started rattling up the embers in the hearth to get the fire going.

The smaller children didn't seem worried. They were far too busy rootling through the cupboards for their gloves and hats. The older children were rather less enthusiastic. They knew the reality of thawing drinking troughs for the horses with hot water from the kettle and carrying full buckets up from the river that hadn't yet frozen over.

Everyone had tasks to do, so we set to work.

The priority was to check that the farmyard animals were all well and then take hay to feed the sheep in the fields.

Outside, the children jumped and rolled in the fresh snow. Only Nancy, the littlest, stood still, gazing upwards, flakes landing on her cherub-like pink cheeks and tongue that was stuck right out.

'Look how deep it is!' Miles said. 'This is great!'

It was difficult to say exactly how much snow had fallen overnight. Soft and powdery, the wind had blown it around, so the front door to the house was out of sight. I'm about six feet tall and the snow was up to my waist in places, but only ankle-deep in others. It was too soft for snowballs (thankfully), but brilliant for making snow angels.

Many hands make light work, so the saying goes, and the whole family pitched in to help with the day's tasks. We carried armfuls of hay to the stables, fetched buckets up from the river, and in no time at all we had the animals snug in the buildings with food to munch and water to slurp.

I took a moment to rest, sitting on the bales in the barn. Steam rose from the cattle in the crisp air as they pulled at the hay, throwing particles of dust up into the cool light.

'Right, we need to start the next part of the plan,' I said to the assembled children. 'Little ones, you need to go inside, warm up a little. Have some breakfast.' I smiled fondly as Nancy, Clem, Annas, Sid and Violet stomped off towards the farmhouse.

'Big ones, could you dig out the front door and stock up on wood for the fire?' I watched on, a proud mum, as Edith, Miles, Reuben and Raven got to work.

'And we need to feed the moorland sheep,' Clive said. 'I'm going to bring Bill.'

Bill was a great big black-and-white sheepdog. He was loyal and smart, but not above enjoying a silly game or two. He loved to run out in an arc before lolloping back towards the other sheepdogs and bowling headlong into them, knocking them over. They fell for it every time. We called it dog skittles.

On a normal day, we'd travel to the sheep in the fields on a quad bike with a trailer attached, loaded up with hay and a sheepdog. The hungry sheep hear the quad bike roar and come running to us. But the snow had drifted across the tracks, road and even the walls. It was nearly impossible to see where we were going, and it wasn't long before the quad bike's wheels began to spin and we could go no further on it.

We whistled for the sheep and carried the hay bales between us instead, while Bill loped along behind. The sheep sent clouds of snow into the air as they hurtled towards us. Each sheep followed in the footsteps of the previous one, the greediest going at the very front.

We spread the hay out in a line and did a quick headcount while they began hungrily eating it.

'All present and correct,' said Clive.

We did this for the other four lots of sheep that were nearest to the farm. Because of the deep snow it took far longer than usual, but we were happy to know that they were all safe.

We had one flock of sheep left that needed to be fed. They stayed the furthest away from Ravenseat and would be the hardest to reach. This time we were going to have to wade through some impressively deep snow drifts.

Reuben stayed at home. His job was to start the rusty old snowmobile that we kept for emergencies. He was also keen to take part in winter sports with his siblings. Plans were now afoot to both build an igloo, and to find a sledge and a snowboard.

Clive and I set off, heads down, each of us with a bale of hay on our back. It was my faithful sheepdog Kate who came along this time. She was clever and hardworking and, although old age was catching up with her, you'd never know it as she bounded ahead of us.

The walk was hard but we ploughed on uphill and to the cattle grid. At the halfway point we turned to survey the scene below us, now the weather had cleared and the wind had dropped. The snow glistened beneath a bright blue sky. In the distance, smoke curled upwards from the farmhouse chimney. It was the picture of wintry peacefulness.

We carried on, stumbling and slipping, sometimes stopping to catch our breath. We didn't speak; it took all our energy to move, and we were red-cheeked and snotty-nosed by the time we got to the field gate.

The sheep were certainly pleased to see us, welcoming our arrival with a chorus of bleats.

'There are hoofprints by the door. These ones have been in the barn,' I said. 'Clever sheep.'

'Aye! We'll put their hay in the racks inside,' said Clive, throwing his bale into the field. Kate scrambled and squeezed through the bars of the gate as I got my bale over it.

'There's some snow here,' I said. 'Look at those drifts!'

'Well, let's have a count-up,' said Clive. 'There should be fifty in this lot.'

I counted the sheep silently in my head. Clive muttered to himself. I got to forty-five and then started again.

'Forty-five,' Clive said at last, his number agreeing with mine. 'We're five short.'

I was worried for the lost sheep, but we still needed to feed the ones we could find. So I went into the barn and started filling the racks with hay, while Clive whistled loudly and looked around the field for any signs of them.

'They must be buried under it,' he said, shaking his head. 'The snow is so deep I can only just see the top stones of the wall. We need to go home and get something to dig them out with.'

As we walked back, we could hear the sound of an engine. Nearing the farm, we spied the children playing in the fields on a sledge and Reuben going round in circles on the snowmobile. He'd fixed it!

'Brilliant!' I called. 'Now we can move around much easier. Come on, Reubs, let's go and find our lost sheep.'

Clive and I grabbed a couple of shovels and a stick each. Kate, now worn out from our icy expedition, had made her way indoors to snooze by the fire.

'She can stay here,' I said. 'I don't see any need for her to come with us again.'

Back at the gate, we could finally get to the bottom of the field on the snowmobile. The once grassy, gently sloping pasture now resembled the sea, with waves of glistening snow that had been sculpted by the wind.

But there wasn't a hoofprint in sight.

'Where do we even begin to look?' Reuben asked.

'Beside the walls,' Clive said.

The driving snow would have soon covered the sheep. That in itself was not dangerous. They could survive beneath a wintery blanket for a few days, as the warmth of their bodies melted the snow immediately around them. The real problem is when a thaw comes. The snow above them would become heavy and the buried sheep would sadly die. We had to find them, and soon.

We began high-stepping silently through the snow. We listened hard for any faint sounds from beneath the surface, regularly stopping and poking our sticks into the drifts that lay beside the boundary walls. Panting, and getting colder by the minute, Clive and I waded up the hill. We decided to focus on a few snow-filled dips in the ground, where the sheep might lie hidden, as Reuben took the snowmobile back up to the gate.

Should we keep going? I wondered. *Will the next poke of the stick find them?* Chances were that they had bunched together for warmth, but the snow was white and the sheep were too, so it was like looking for a needle in a haystack!

After one full circuit of the field, we decided to call it a day and return to the farmhouse. Our hands were raw and our feet numb from the biting cold. It was the right thing to do, but it was also hard not to feel like our search and rescue attempt had ended in failure.

'Come on,' said Reuben. 'We need to head home and sort out how we are going to stay warm and feed ourselves with no electricity.'

We were just getting back on to the snowmobile when my sheepdog Kate appeared.

'Goodness me, I left her sleeping by the fire at home!' I said. 'I didn't want to tire the old girl out.'

Kate knew that I was talking about her and looked up at me, wagging her tail enthusiastically.

'Aye, my Bill has more sense,' Clive joked as Kate strode towards the field gate.

'There's nothing to do now, you daft old dog,' I said.

The sheep took a pause from their hay nibbling and peeped nervously out of the barn door towards Kate. She stood still, statue-like, ears stiffened, nose upwards and with a front paw raised as though pointing to something.

'Come on, Kate. Time to go home now,' I said.

But she didn't move a muscle.

Clive and Reuben were ready to go, but Kate, who was usually the most well-behaved dog, glanced backwards over her shoulder towards me and then boldly set off in the opposite direction.

'Sorry, sorry, sorry, I don't know what's got into her today!' I cried apologetically as I followed in Kate's paw prints. 'Wait for me,' I begged. 'I'll go and get her – she's not gone far.'

I could hear her barking now.

I went around to the back of the barn, where during the summertime a bed of stinging nettles grew among the rock-strewn remains of an old quarry. Kate was there and still barking. I wasn't pleased that she was dawdling around when there was so much farm work still to do.

'That'll *do*, Kate!' I shouted.

This time she didn't even glance at me; she just stared down towards a particularly smooth patch of snow. I walked over, curious as to what was holding her attention. There really was nothing to see – the snow was unmarked and perfect – but Kate was not moving, and her barking had now been replaced with whining.

'What are you doing?' asked Reuben, who stomped around the side of the barn, closely followed by Clive.

'Something is really bothering her,' I replied.

Clive strode towards Kate, who had woken from her trance and was now pawing at the ground. He poked into the snow in front of her with his stick. It was far deeper than it looked!

Kate was pawing frantically now and, as Clive prodded once more, a small crust of snow collapsed inwards revealing an air pocket beneath. Kate sprang forward, thrusting her nose into the hole, and in a frenzy began biting at the snow around the edges.

Reuben ran for the shovels. Clive and I, both kneeling now, dug with our hands, pulling back the snow as it caved inwards. It wasn't long before a pair of eyes peered up at us.

We'd found the sheep at last!

There was no hiding Kate's joy for this snowy version of hide and seek. She bounced, dug, barked and worked tirelessly alongside us while we unearthed the five missing members of the flock.

We stood for a minute to catch our breath. Reuben leaned on a shovel. Clive wiped sweat from his brow with his hat. I wiped my nose with mine. The sheep, now free from their icy jail, blinked in the bright daylight. Thankfully they were none the worse for their experience.

'I have to say,' said Clive, 'your dog's done well!'

I ruffled Kate's fur, and I was sure that I saw her smile.

Her doggy presence wasn't welcomed by our five ungrateful sheep though. After a few trembling steps, they shook the remaining snow from their fleeces and sprang off to join their woolly friends inside the barn.

Kate casually squeezed back through the gate, homeward bound. It was all in a day's work for her.

Back at the farmhouse, the entire family retreated indoors to the fireside. Kate resumed her position by the hearth, basking in the warmth of the flames and the glory of being top dog, counting sheep in her sleep.

An Owen-Family Christmas

Christmas at Ravenseat isn't perfect. There's no fine china, neat decorations or getting dressed-up for dinner here. And, believe it or not, it's not always a white Christmas either.

As with everything in life, we approach the day in our own way, and we make it about family, friends, farming and festivities. That's why it's perfectly suited to us.

So I'd like to invite you to join us for a *very* Owen-family Christmas!

There were a few days left before Christmas Day, and I was standing in the supermarket looking at rows of nuts, chocolates, crisps and crackers. As shoppers hurtled around buying things, I was reminded how much I dislike this time of year. Not Christmas itself, but the stress and the expectation that surround it.

It's not that I'm a Scrooge or that my children go without. If they need something, I'll of course buy it (within reason!). But when it comes to Christmas presents, I'd rather get them something practical and useful, rather than throwaway.

Sometimes, on Christmas Eve, when I'm looking at the small pile of presents that will fit neatly into one Bag for Life, I wonder if the children will think it's not enough for all nine of them. *Will they be disappointed?* I ask myself.

But I know for a fact that the most memorable Christmases for the children are likely to be the chaotic or lively (or dramatic!) ones. They'll say, 'Do you remember when a mouse ate all the chocolates out of the advent calendar?' or 'Maybe we'll see Chloe the reindeer on the moors again!' Those are the kinds of silly Christmas memories we treasure.

As I thought about this while wandering aimlessly down the aisles of the supermarket, suddenly I decided to abandon the trolley and head out of there – empty handed.

Needing both an escape from the crowds and to find inspiration for some thoughtful Christmas gifts, I headed over the road to the **cobblers**.

Christmas Tales from the Farm

I love this place. It's a really traditional, proper shoe menders, with old-fashioned machines, new leather soles, zips, sewing needles and polish. And there are rows and rows of wooden shelves, packed with shoes and other bits and bobs.

'Your shelves are brimming with stuff! Some of it looks quite old. Does it belong to your customers?' I asked the cobbler.

'Aye, quite a bit of it is footwear that folk never came back for,' he replied.

Looking at all the different shoes I suddenly spied some **clogs**; the traditional type, with **corkers** – metal horse-shoe shapes on the toe and heel.

A few weeks before, we had been scrubbing the flagstones in the living room, getting our home ready for Christmas. And I'd been explaining to the children while we cleaned that the reason the floor was so uneven was due to hundreds of years of clogged feet, belonging to all the people who'd lived in the farmhouse before us, wearing a tread, or a path, into the stone.

An idea started to form in my mind . . .

'You've got a real collection there,' I commented as he plucked a pair of clogs from the shelves and set them down on the counter. Now, these weren't your modern clogs, like the ones with rubber soles that are in fashion. These were more practical, made for working in. They were an unusual gift that I hoped would *spark* the children's curiosity.

'Don't suppose you have another eight pairs, do you?' I asked. 'And a discount for bulk buying!' I added.

And with that, I had found this year's Christmas presents.

That night, when the children were in bed, I set about cleaning and polishing the clogs, trying to restore the dry leather. There were no sizes in them, seeing as they were so old, but with a bit of guesswork I reckoned there was a pair to fit each child.

Pleased with my purchase, I felt that everything was shaping up perfectly . . . until I thought back to my shopping list, which hadn't included clogs but did include a turkey!

While the children would hopefully appreciate their unusual gifts, I figured they might be less understanding about their Christmas dinner. But rather than shoving my way back into the supermarket I decided to try something different that year, and bravely wait until Christmas Eve to get the turkey . . .

On Christmas Eve, I shepherded the middle three – Edith, Violet and Sidney – into the pick-up truck and we soon set off.

'Where are we going?' asked Edith.

'We are on a mission, and it's an important one. But it'll be fun,' I promised.

Half an hour later, we pulled up at the auction mart and headed inside. I was instantly at home here, as it's where we sell our sheep and cows throughout the year. I knew the people, I knew the venue, and the festive atmosphere hit me instantly, with Christmas music playing, mulled wine on offer and a few Santa hats to boot.

Up for sale were oven-ready turkeys, geese, ducks, pheasants and chickens – ones that hadn't been sold in the run-up to Christmas. And they wouldn't be expensive either, because any organized person would have already bought their turkey by now, rather than leaving it worryingly late . . .

While the children wandered, I talked to the farmers and butchers who had cared for the birds and prepared them for the table. They could tell me all about the breeding, what they fed them, and which were boys and which were girls. I liked that this information created a connection in my mind to the meat that we'd be eating; as a farmer myself, knowing that the animals had been well looked after was important to me.

As I walked around the auction, eyeing up the different birds, I remembered Clive's only request: 'Just get a big 'un.' There would be many people round our table on Christmas Day, so I was looking for a super-sized bird to feed them.

Suddenly the children came running down the aisle. They had found it – the monster turkey that looked like it had eaten all the others! Other people were laughing at it in astonishment, wondering who was going to buy it and who was going to attempt to roast it. But I hoped there was only one person for the job – me! It would be perfect for feeding us all.

I was writing down the number of my potential purchase when I spotted Sidney sitting at the ringside as the **auctioneer** began their sale. A bell rang, summoning people to take a seat, but it looked like Sidney was already bidding for a six-kilo goose. He was waving his arms to get *my* attention, but the auctioneer was taking his arm waving as bids! If he wasn't careful, I was soon going to be buying a very expensive goose.

Sid soon stopped accidentally bidding once he saw the look on my face . . .

'I nearly won a pheasant!' Edith excitedly declared, as we all joined Sid ringside. It was time for me to give the children a pep talk, explaining that they had to sit on their hands for now, or this would become a very expensive day (and they'd be eating turkey, pheasant and goose all year!).

'Listen. You can bid for the giant turkey when it comes into the ring,' I told Sid. 'You'll know which one it is, because they'll need to use a wheelbarrow to bring it in!'

As predicted, the enormous turkey was cheap. And with birds going for such reasonable prices, I tasked Edith and Violet with buying three smaller turkeys to put in the freezer.

'You're gonna struggle to get all that int'oven!' muttered the woman at the front desk, a touch sarcastically.

Homeward bound, I was in good spirits, until I had a sudden thought. *The big day is tomorrow. But this turkey is going to take about thirteen hours to cook . . .*

I had somehow saddled myself with a load more work on Christmas Eve!

As soon as we were through the door, I had to spring into action and get the turkey roasting. There was no point trying to do anything fancy with it, so I just shoved a few herbs and lemon halves inside. Then it was all about practicality – could I even fit it into the oven?!

As it happened, I didn't have to worry about any of this, as I quickly realized that the kettle on top of the oven – which was usually always simmering – was cold. A quick wave of my hand over the hot plate told me that we had a *big* problem – the oven had run out of fuel, on Christmas Eve! There was no possibility that I was going to be able to get it going again.

For a while I stood in silence, weighing up my options. But Christmas dinner wasn't optional – it had to happen and there was no point *getting in a flap* about it – I just had to be smart.

As you've maybe gathered from the clog-buying episode, I'm a collector of weird and wonderful objects that I think are interesting – **bygones** I call them, or junk, as Clive would say. So I knew that in the woodshed, beside the logs, there stood an old, clockwork spit roaster – though goodness knows when it had last been used!

All I had to do now was pretend that this was entirely planned and part of the Christmas fun. So I sent Reuben to the workshop for some chains to suspend the bird from the hook on the top of the roaster. Once the turkey was in place, hanging upside-down in front of the open fire, all we needed to do was take it in turns to wind the brass key that spun the meat and – in theory – cooked it evenly. And the final task was to keep the fire in the grate burning. Surely, between eleven of us, it couldn't be that difficult?

As it happened, this 'plan' caused more trouble than I'd first imagined, as the children then began to worry that Santa wouldn't be able to get down the chimney during the night! I assured them that it wouldn't be a problem: Santa can always find a way.

Generally speaking, roasting the turkey isn't something that everyone usually gets involved in. But that year, it almost became the main event of Christmas! It was a challenge that everyone enjoyed (including the terriers, who were *very* interested in the now easy-to-reach dogs' dinner!). And once the turkey started cooking, it made everyone very hungry – the smell was absolutely mouth-watering.

Christmas dinner was now rescued from near disaster, but there was no time to sit back and congratulate myself as we heard a sudden hammering at the door . . .

. . . and in came a whole brass band!

This was not a total surprise, as it was an annual event and a joyful one at that. But I have to say that between the turkey, the children, the terriers and the band members holding everything from trombones to trumpets to euphoniums, it was snug in there! Not many people's living rooms would look this chaotic on Christmas Eve.

The tradition was that the local brass band would make their way down the dale on Christmas Eve, stopping off here and there playing carols, eating mince pies and enjoying a tipple or two.

I always considered us to be the lucky ones as we were the first house that they visited. By the time they'd got to the bottom of the dale – more than twenty miles away – I reckoned that they'd be pretty out of tune!

After a few classics, including 'In the Bleak Midwinter' and 'Oh Come All Ye Faithful', it was time for requests. We'd had enough of the traditional Christmas tunes and fancied something a bit more upbeat.

'Anything by Elvis, please,' came a polite ask from Violet.

'Lady Gaga?' said Annas.

'I think they mean something more festive!' I laughed.

'What about "The Twelve Days of Christmas"?' asked Raven, and what followed was a spirited argument about whether it was eleven or nine ladies dancing and how many lords were leaping. No one could agree, but the shouts of 'Five gold rings!' brought such joy that it was an excellent request.

Before the band left, they had a request for us. Would it be possible for Miles and Reuben to join in, as the youngest members of the band? Miles had been learning to play the trumpet, and Reubs the flugel horn (another cheap, random purchase).

The grand finale was a very slow version of 'Away in a Manger', and then it was time for them to go. It wasn't just the band that was marching on – time was ticking, and the children had their letters to post to Santa.

Each year the children write or draw the gifts they're hoping to receive and post their letters up the chimney. The flames from the grate carry their messages up the flue, across the skies and to the North Pole.

After side stepping the turkey, the notes were sent on their merry way. If the mince pies and glass of sherry we left out for Santa weren't enough to tempt him to Ravenseat, maybe the smell of the roasting turkey would do it!

It was Christmas Day at last.

We're always up early – no change there. The children love to delve into their stockings to find that Santa has visited and left a few chocolates and a token gift – a little model farm animal or piece of toy machinery.

While the children were chattering, I tested the turkey to see how it was coming along. Things were looking good, and all was going to plan. The children were soon amusing themselves with their new toys and already dealing with the realities of farm animals and equipment.

'The wheel has come off my digger,' exclaimed Sidney.

'My cow's got a droopy lug!' Clemmy informed me.

'Never mind,' I said. 'Let's go and see if Santa has visited the stables and kennels.'

Working on Christmas morning might not seem very festive, but actually this is part of the daily routine and life we all love and enjoy, and Christmas Day was no different. If anything, we take a bit more time and effort with it, and all our jobs are done while wearing Santa hats. Only when the work is done is it time for presents and dinner.

Miles went to see the sheepdogs, and shouted to the younger ones, 'Santa's been!'

There were dog treats for Penny, Midge and Nelly. Well-deserved too.

Nobody had been forgotten: there were treacle licks for the horses and sheep, and rock salt licks for the cows. Even the chickens had got a tin of **poultry spice**. It smelled of cinnamon and they *loved* it. It was a sight that sparked such joy.

But that was just the start of the sparks that would fly today, as finally it was time for the children to open their gifts.

It really was lovely to be back in the warmth of the living room, which was filled with the smell of slow-roasted turkey. The children, still dressed in their everyday raggle-taggle farm clothes with straw and hay in their hair, were strewn about the room, some parked on the **fender**, others sprawled on the sofa and on the windowsill. I reached under the tree, and handed each of them their gifts, all wrapped in brown parcel paper, which made brilliant fire kindling afterwards.

They unwrapped their new footwear and immediately began chattering excitedly about them.

'Look at this,' said Reuben, tracing the shape of the metal corkers on the soles of his clogs. 'I was once told how to make sparks fly with these.'

'How's that?' asked Miles.

I explained that with a bit of practice you could, right here in the living room, strike the heel on the flagstones, and see a quick flash of fire.

'Ah, well I know a better way,' announced Reuben. 'Dick from road end used to say that, when he was a young lad, he used to ride a motorbike wearing his clogs and would drag his heels on the road leaving a trail of sparks behind him!'

'Cool!' came the cries from the others.

'No, hot!' Reuben laughed, as he swung his foot backwards and forwards to show them how it was done.

The thick curtains were pulled shut, and the lights from the fireplace and the Christmas tree cast a beautiful glow around us all.

It wasn't long before the children had become very good tap dancers! And useful ones at that, with their newfound ability to light up the room with their sparks.

It reminded me of how, in times past, the flagged floors of the farmhouse were cleaned by scattering a generous amount of sand on them. Children were encouraged to grind it in by walking on it, polishing up the floor ready for the sweeping brush afterwards.

While my children played, chatted and opened a few more little gifts from friends and family, I prepared the rest of the dinner. It felt normal to me to be cooking for so many people, and I do like to be left to do it alone. Every now and again someone would appear around the kitchen door and ask, 'How long 'til dinner?' and I would give them my usual reply: 'When it's done!'

The door suddenly swung open and in walked our old friend Alec. He was a sheepdog trainer, and for many years he had helped us to gather the sheep in from the moors.

'Are you stoppin'?' I asked him.

Never mind that it was Christmas Day – everyone was welcome; it wasn't like there wasn't enough food to go around. In fact over the years many people had dropped by for their second Christmas dinners, knowing full well that we wouldn't eat until it got dark.

Alec nodded in thanks, and went through to the living room to sit with Clive by the fire. Clive finally began to carve the turkey – it had taken a huge effort not to allow him to make a start on it before dinner!

There were no fancy place settings, nothing matched, and there wasn't even enough room for everyone to sit around the table. The whole meal was spread between three rooms and light-hearted arguments ensued:

'Where's the gravy boat?'

'Who's had all the pigs in blankets?'

'Pass the roast potatoes!'

Sid was perched on an upturned washing basket, Alec used a milk churn and I sat on the arm of the sofa. It wasn't fancy, but it was homely and welcoming, just how we liked it.

After dinner, there was an enthusiastic attempt to use the clog sparks to light the brandy on the Christmas pudding. And it has to be said that the sight of a good-sized Christmas pudding, sat on the floor like a football, with the children looking like they were about to take a penalty, made me nervous as to where the pudding was going to end up!

It was late by the time all was finished. Some of the children went to bed and some went outside to feed the dogs and other animals, while Clive and Alec chatted into the night.

It was the perfect end to another imperfect Owen-family Christmas.

Merry Christmas, everyone!

Glossary

Appleby Horse Fair
A yearly fair attended by people from the Gypsy and Traveller communities where horses are shown and sold.

auction
A place where things are sold to the person who offers or 'bids' the most money.

auctioneer
A person who runs an auction, selling items to the highest bidder.

bale
A bundle of hay or straw, either rectangular or round in shape.

bantam
A small kind of chicken.

beck
A stream or small river.

bog
Soft, wet ground.

bracken
A kind of large green fern plant. When it dies in winter, it turns the moors an orangey-brown colour.

branching
The time when young owls first leave the nest but still need their parents to hunt for their food.

bridle
A headpiece for a horse to which reins are attached.

a brew
A cup of tea.

brood
A group of chickens.

browband
A leather strap that sits across a horse's forehead and keeps the bridle in place.

bygone
A historical object.

cattle grid
A metal grid with shallow holes in it that stops cows, sheep and other animals from passing along the road.

clogs
A type of leather shoe with wooden soles.

clutch
A group of eggs.

cobblers
A shoe repair shop.

colostrum
First highly nutritious milk needed by a newborn mammal.

corkers
Metal pieces nailed to the toe and heel of clogs, used to stop the wooden sole from wearing down.

drystone wall
A traditional kind of wall made by interlocking stones rather than using cement to stick them together.

eartag
A numbered plastic tag that is attached to the ear and identifies each individual animal.

endangered
A word that means that not many of that plant or animal are left in the world.

ewe
A female sheep, sometimes pronounced 'yow' or 'you'.

fell
Another word for moorland, big areas of high ground.

fender
A fire guard that can also be sat upon.

fodder
To feed the animals.

fold
A large, drystone-walled pen used to hold sheep and also as shelter from the weather.

foot-rot
An unpleasant condition that sheep get in their feet.

forelock
Part of the horse's mane that falls over the front of its face, like a fringe.

gimmer
A young female sheep.

habitat
The natural home of an animal or plant.

halter
A simple headpiece worn by a horse and used to attach a lead.

hardy
Able to survive tough conditions like very bad weather.

heaf
An area of land that has no wall or fence but the sheep always remain there.

kids
Young goats.

lug
  Another word for ear.

manger
  A low wooden, stone or metal trough that is filled with hay to feed the animals.

menagerie
  A collection of different animals.

moors/moorland
  A large area of open land.

muzzle
  A horse's mouth, chin and nose.

ornithologist
  A person who knows everything there is to know about birds.

owl pellets
  The parts of an owl's meal that they can't digest, like fur and bones, which they then throw up in one lump or pellet.

owlet
  A young owl.

peat hagg
Raised lumps of rich soil that often have overhanging edges. Found on wet, cold boggy moorland.

piebald
A horse whose coat has a pattern of black and white patches.

poultry spice
Food for chickens, geese and duck that contains wheat, minerals and spices that are good for them.

quad bike
Like a motorbike, but with four wheels instead of two.

reins
Straps that attach to a horse's bridle that the rider uses to direct where the horse goes.

sheep nuts
Food for sheep that come in the form of pellets.

Shetland pony
The smallest kind of pony.

skewbald

A horse whose coat has a pattern of white patches and any other colour than black, for example brown.

skijoring

A winter sport played in Norway, where a person holds onto a horse's reins as they're pulled along on skis.

tack

All the equipment used to ride a horse, from the bridle to the saddle, reins and more.

tarn

A small mountain lake.

t'owd

Another way to say 'the old' – for example 't'owd bridge' would mean, 'the old bridge'.

treacle/salt lick

Like a yummy lollipop for horses. It might contain sugar, salt and other things they like to eat.

trough

A large container used to feed animals or give them a drink.

tupping
    The very start of the sheep-breeding season.

tup
    Male sheep.

twine
    String used to hold bales of hay together, among other things.

white out
    What happens when snow covers everything, so the entire landscape looks white.

Acknowledgements

There are so many people who have made this book possible.

My family, of course, are the inspiration, and without them I certainly wouldn't have the material in the first place.

Also Jo Cantello, who has steered me throughout the whole process, and the creative team at Puffin. Thanks to Fenella, Meg, Corinne and Becca, and particularly Katie Sinfield, who has displayed a saintly patience during our numerous video calls that have been interrupted by enthusiastic children and inquisitive animals.

And thanks to you, dear reader. I hope you enjoyed reading these stories as much as I enjoyed writing them.

Turn the page for more festive farmyard fun!

Can you remember the names of these animals from the book?

1.

.... and .... the sheep

2.

.... the terrier

3.

........., ... and .... the pygmy goats

4.

Little ....

5.

.... the reindeer

See how much you remember from the stories by having a go at these questions!

1. Raven did some reindeer research and found out their top speed is . . .
   a)   10 mph
   b)   20 mph
   c)   40 mph

2. What kind of machines did the older boys use to search for Chloe the reindeer?
   a)   A tractor
   b)   Motorbikes
   c)   Quad bikes

3. Which chicken was the champion at the local village show?
   a)   The Silver Spangled Hamburg
   b)   Linda, the oldest hen
   c)   The Golden Sebright cockerel

4. What is the name for a small mountain lake?
   a) A tarn
   b) A lakelet
   c) A trough

5. The two Jack Russell terriers were named Chalky and . . .
   a) Tess
   b) Pippen
   c) Snowy

6. Where was Chalky found?
   a) In a pub twenty miles away
   b) Under a tractor
   c) In the school playground

7. What did the pygmy goats get for Christmas?
   a) Woolen scarves
   b) Fluorescent jackets
   c) Corks for their horns

8. Which item of clothing did the pygmy goats chew?
   a) Clive's hat
   b) Reuben's pyjamas
   c) A guest's Jimmy Choo wellies

9. Where are horses and ponies traditionally sheltered?
   a) A sty
   b) A stable
   c) A barn

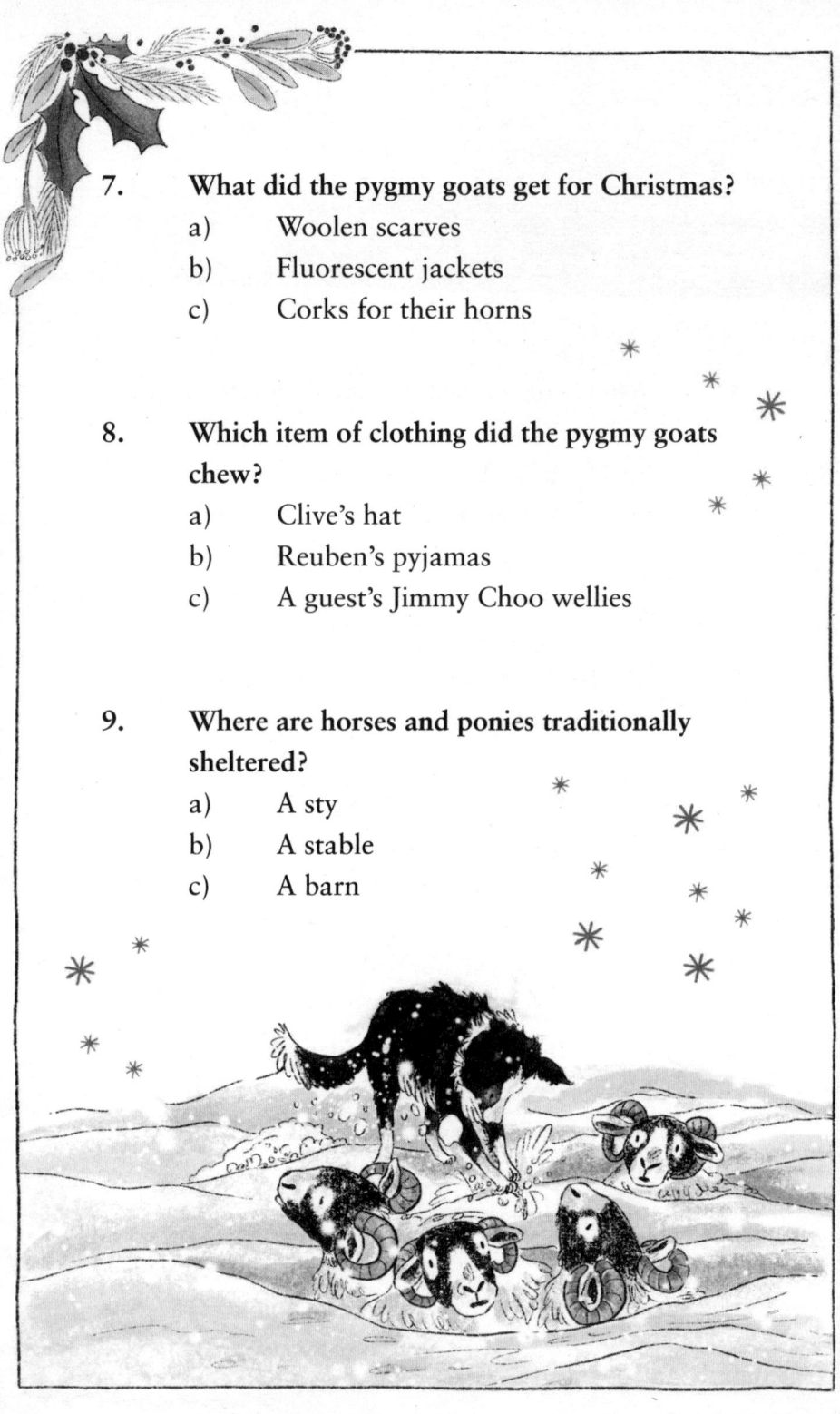

10. What colour was Little Joe's browband?
    a) Red and gold
    b) Blue and silver
    c) Green and bronze

11. What did Coco and Chanel knock over?
    a) The Christmas tree
    b) A feed bucket
    c) A snowman

12. When were Coco and Chanel's new lambs born?
    a) 1 December
    b) Christmas Day
    c) 1 January

13. Which of the below activities was not included in the Ravenseat Winter Olympics?
    a) Curling
    b) Snowboarding
    c) Ice hockey

14. What is skijoring?
    a) A game where you throw snowballs at a target
    b) A sport where a horse and rider pull a person on skis
    c) A breed of cow from Norway

15. What did Clem call the tawny owl?
    a) The Tommy owl
    b) The Tony owl
    c) The Tina owl

16. What's the name for the owl species that has bright yellow eyes and two ear tufts?
    a) The bog owl
    b) The swamp owl
    c) The field owl

17. What was the name of Clive's sheepdog?
    a) Bobby
    b) Benny
    c) Bill

18. Where were the missing sheep found?
    a) Behind the barn
    b) In a hole in the ground covered by snow
    c) On the other side of the icy lake

19. What kind of bird did Sidney almost buy at the Christmas Eve auction?
    a) A pheasant
    b) A goose
    c) A duck

20. How did the family cook their Christmas turkey?
    a) On a barbecue outside
    b) Using a spit roaster over an open fire
    c) By borrowing the neighbour's oven

Answers:

1 – Coco and Chanel
2 – Chalky
3 – Rocky, Billy and Sonny
4 – Little Joe
5 – Chloe

1 – a. 10 mph
2 – b. Quad bikes
3 – c. The Golden Sebright cockerel
4 – a. A tarn
5 – b. Pippen
6 – a. In a pub twenty miles away
7 – b. Flourescent jackets
8 – c. A guest's Jimmy Choo wellies
9 – b. A stable
10 – a. Red and gold
11 – a. The Christmas tree
12 – c. 1 January
13 – c. Ice hockey
14 – b. A sport where a horse and rider pull a person on skis
15 – b. The Tony owl
16 – a. The bog owl
17 – c. Bill
18 – b. In a hole in the ground covered by snow
19 – b. A goose
20 – b. Using a spit roaster over an open fire

Photo © Lorna Roach

Amanda Owen

is a shepherdess, mother of nine children,
TV star and bestselling author. Born in Huddersfield,
Amanda is a first-generation farmer who escaped
the city for the rugged landscapes of Ravenseat,
a 2,000-acre hill farm in North Yorkshire.
Amanda and the Owen family have starred in several
tv series, including *Our Yorkshire Farm*, *Amanda
Owen's Farming Lives* and their latest TV adventure,
Our Farm Next Door: Amanda, Clive and Kids.
Amanda has penned five *Sunday Times* bestselling
books and is a hugely popular public speaker.
Christmas Tales from the Farm is
her first book for children.

Photo © Ben Battell

Becca Hall

is a full-time freelance illustrator who grew up in
the beautiful Lake District. After 28 years among
the lakes and hills, she followed her dream of living by
the sea. These days, she lives on the Cornish coast with
her husband and their two cheeky border terriers, Pippa
and Evie. Alongside illustrating numerous children's books,
Becca illustrates maps and giftware, including designing
a commemorative Harrods bag for the King's
coronation, and shares monthly illustration tutorials
on her Patreon, inspiring people of all ages
to enjoy drawing and helping aspiring
illustrators grow their skills.